# BLOOD WARNING

I opened my eyes and looked at my hand, now wet with blood. I felt my ankles stinging against the wet concrete. Twisting my right leg, I saw the lines.

The cuts had been made with an artist's fine touch, the lines straight and true. Like the hard-scored marks of tailor's chalk, a map to show the planned alterations: two parallel lines bisected my hamstring, two parallel lines crossed my Achilles tendon. I checked my left leg; the same two sets of parallel lines.

I'd been drawn a thoughtful, detailed guide to what I could anticipate if I continued following the trail of Alicia's death, the knife left in front of my face so it would be the first thing I'd see when I opened my eyes.

Next time, the cuts would be deep enough to cripple and disfigure me.

# DETECTING LIES

**JANICE KIECOLT-GLASER**

AVON BOOKS ◆ NEW YORK

AVON BOOKS
A division of
The Hearst Corporation
1350 Avenue of the Americas
New York, New York 10019

Copyright © 1997 by Janice Kiecolt-Glaser
Published by arrangement with the author
Visit our website at **http://AvonBooks.com**
Library of Congress Catalog Card Number: 96-96930
ISBN: 0-380-78991-4

First Avon Books Printing: March 1997

AVON TRADEMARK REG. U.S. PAT. OFF. AND IN OTHER COUNTRIES, MARCA REGISTRADA, HECHO EN U.S.A.

Printed in the U.S.A.

RA   10  9  8  7  6  5  4  3  2  1

# Prologue

"**I**'m Dr. McAlistar. I study lies."

That's the opening I always use for the first of my annual lectures to medical students.

I wait for my opening salvo to register on the students who fill the lecture hall. After the babel has muted to a few whispers, I continue: "People show they're lying in an enormous number of ways: slips of the tongue, fleeting facial expressions, changes in vocal inflections like a tightening in the voice or a change in pitch, obvious swallowing, body movements, the kinds of gestures they use."

I push the buttons on the podium to dim the lights and turn on the slide projector. My first slide shows the Mona Lisa. "More than fifty different smiles can be distinguished, based on the muscle groups involved. False smiles are often used to conceal other emotions. Smiles of genuine enjoyment produce bags under the eyes and crow's feet wrinkles, and the eyebrows move down, very slightly."

I always wear my white lab coat with HALEY MCALISTAR PHD stenciled on the pocket when I lecture—a flag of authority, an important accoutrement for female faculty. Underneath my lab coat I'll often wear a silk dress, a vivid blue or green; I like the cool softness next to my skin—and bright colors in nature function to warn predators that potential prey is poisonous or otherwise dangerous.

At this point in my talk I'll pull my laser pointer out of my pocket and trace the crow's feet wrinkles around the Mona Lisa's eyes. "Leonardo da Vinci captured the flirtatious smile, a genuine smile made while her body was facing away and she was looking away; the quick, stolen sideways glance is characteristic, just long enough to be noticed."

When I was fifteen and returning to school after a long illness, I had to give a talk in front of the class. I wanted so badly to do well, to be cool; I threw up as I started to speak. My stomach still churns fiercely each time I begin a lecture, one of the reasons I overprepare.

I've delivered variants of this talk to first-year medical students a dozen times in as many years as part of their series on communicating with patients; I repackaged a straight lecture on nonverbal communication as lie detection to make it more appealing. I've worked hard to make this lecture interesting and memorable.

I'll change my lecture notes next year—because of Alicia Erle. She took it as a challenge, a dare. I don't want someone else to try to prove to me that they're better at detecting lies.

# Chapter 1

I drove into the parking lot beside Rugton Hall, the Psychiatry Department building, at six in the morning on Wednesday, September 9.

I stretched and regretted it immediately as the small of my back spasmed. I'd upped my mileage, running six miles a day for the last two days, twice my normal daily quota. Too large an increase, especially for a woman of forty. But the more I exhausted myself, the better my chances for untroubled sleep, I'd told myself. Only it hadn't worked that way last night.

At one in the morning, unable to fall asleep, I'd finally arranged two pillows lengthwise, molding myself around them the way I used to fall asleep, cupping Ian's back. Looking for warmth and comfort, wanting to hold and be held, willing myself to settle for the lie. Then, all too soon, I woke sweaty and breathless from a recurrent nightmare: paralyzed, unable to scream for help, defenseless against the stranger hovering over me, overwhelmed by a feeling of impending doom. At four in the morning, with everything bleak and barren, the world was Noah's ark, and unpaired people would be swept away by the approaching flood.

After we'd been together eight years, Ian died when his Porsche skidded off the road in the rain. Now, eleven months later, I still haven't learned to think of myself as a widow; I still feel as isolated and out of place as a cellist in a marching band.

Ian, a journalist, had been tall with a thinness approaching gauntness, blue-green eyes, and fiercely wavy black hair. When he'd felt good, he strutted like a blue jay, his jaunty presence filling the room, as inconspicuous as an elephant strolling through the petunias.

I've been shut up like a pocketknife since Ian's death.

After concluding that sleep was a lost cause this morning, I got up and made coffee. I read the *Houston Chronicle* from front to back before coming to the office.

I pulled into one of the closer spaces, piqued by the car in the middle of the center row parked over the line so it took two spaces. A vintage Cadillac Coupe de Ville, probably a '59, two-door, yellow.

I got out of my car and walked over for a closer look at the Cadillac. My face felt flushed and damp. Houston's September weather alternates between frying and steaming, frequent thunderstorms dumping enough water to keep the air saturated and tempers simmering. This year we had near-record highs in the first eight days of the month. Last night I watched the Channel 51 meteorologist struggle to maintain an obviously false smile as she explained why the coming week would be as bad or worse.

I touched my hair, still damp from the shower. My mother's hair had been a subdued auburn; my own, short and thick, shouted red. My Scottish ancestors had passed along fair skin and blue eyes as part of the package; I look washed out if I don't spend time with mascara and lipstick. This morning I'd gone to extra trouble, trying to cover the dark circles under my eyes, but it felt like the heat and humidity were already eroding my efforts.

Closer up the Caddy still looked good, no visible rust spots, the chrome well polished. Dew dripped down the Caddy's mammoth trademark fins.

I was wondering who owned it when I looked inside. I wished I hadn't looked. I had an urge to run, to jog for miles, to keep moving down country lanes that stretched into forever. As long as I didn't have to deal with what was inside the car.

I forced myself to look again. Alicia Erle, one of my patients, lay in the back seat. She was on her back, arms by her sides, knees slightly bent, eyes closed. Her face looked pale, innocent of any makeup. She was dressed in a faded pink T-shirt that proclaimed LIFE'S A BEACH, pink-and-blue plaid shorts, and pink sandals. Her only jewelry was an oversized watch with a black plastic band and a silver face. So carefully dressed each time I'd seen her before, Alicia now looked defenseless. Her purse lay in the middle of a front seat as big as a park bench.

I waited for her head to move, expecting Sleeping Beauty to awake. "Alicia?" I knocked on the window as I called out her name, hoping that any second I'd see her head jerk up; hoping for an angry, indignant look; wanting to hear the contemptuous retort Alicia would use to cover her embarrassment.

No movement.

I dropped my purse and my briefcase and pounded on the window, as if disregarding the pain in my fists might make the things I saw magically disappear: the empty prescription pill bottle beside her on the floor, the cap at its side, an empty fifth of José Cuervo tequila beside it.

Maybe I was wrong, maybe the woman in the car only looked a lot like Alicia. It wasn't the gray Ford Escort I'd seen her driving. *Not suicide. Not Alicia. Don't let her be dead.*

The air, moist and heavy, full of the smells that collect and linger in the dark, hung about me like a wool cloak, making it hard to move and breath. I looked at Alicia, saw a shininess above her upper lip. Sweat, I tried to hope. Sleeping. Hot. *Not dead.*

I tried to open the driver's door. Locked. I stumbled around the car and found the passenger door locked. My legs felt shaky and unreliable, as if I'd been bedridden for some time.

I ran inside the building, feeling like I was moving in slow motion, running in soft sand. I grabbed the phone at the unattended reception desk. "This is Dr. Haley McAlistar," I told the sleepy-sounding operator. "Call a Code Blue for the Rugton Hall parking lot." A second later the paging system started bleating the call for emergency assistance. The message would be broadcast in the main hospital as well, where the physicians on call would hear and rush over.

A custodian shuffled into the lobby, weighted down with the vacuum cleaner he carried. "Don't leave this lobby until someone gets here to answer the Code Blue!" I yelled.

I looked around the lobby for something to use as a tool, something to smash the car windows. I grabbed a lamp that had a wooden stem and a shiny gold-metal base, lifting it up and pulling the plug in one movement.

The custodian watched me, his mouth open as if to protest. "When they get here, tell them to go to the yellow Caddy in the parking lot." I heard the fear in my voice.

I didn't wait for an answer, pushing the door open with my shoulder. The lamp held in front of me, I ran awkwardly, feeling heavy and clumsy and sluggish, as if running with concrete weights wired to my wrists and ankles.

*Let her be sleeping off too much booze. Please let her wake up.*

I used the metal base of the lamp to smash the driver's side window, trying not to smack it so fiercely that the breaking glass would ricochet and hit Alicia. The window finally shattered in the center with my third blow, breaking into small cubes. I struck the window twice more, until enough of the glass had splintered in little pieces around the doorframe, enough fragments had fallen on the seat, to reach inside and grope for the lock.

I smelled Alicia's gardenia perfume and tequila; then a sour, musty smell, dark and fetid.

"Alicia! Alicia Erle!" I kept waiting for her to move, willing her to respond. I caught my arm on a fragment of glass still embedded in the doorframe as I fumbled for the lock in the door frame. Blood ran down my arm as I searched. Finally I found the button and yanked it up. I opened the door and pushed the front seat forward so I could climb into the back seat with Alicia, reaching across to touch her.

Trying to remember the steps for CPR, I put my fingers on her neck, looking for the pulse in her carotid artery. I flinched when I felt Alicia's neck: Her skin was cool and firm, too firm to yield softly to pressure. I think I moaned something then, still expecting her to bellow back at me. Still hoping. Still not believing.

It took effort to hold my fingers on Alicia's throat, to search for a pulse. I wanted badly to pull back my hand from the clamminess of her body, but I kept it there by force of will. My own heart thudded so strongly, it seemed a very long time until I felt confident that there was no answering rhythm, until I could let go of the breath I'd been holding.

Alicia's expression was blank. No passion, no anger, no spite. Wiped clean by death.

I looked up and saw two white-coated figures running out of Rugton toward the parking lot. I reached across Alicia's body and unlocked the other door. Getting out, I called to them, waving both arms to flag them down.

As if they could really do something to help.

As I watched them checking Alicia's vital signs, I remembered when I had seen her for the first time, three weeks earlier.

She had come, uninvited, to my lie detection lecture on August 18.

I was walking the class through four slides illustrating asymmetrical facial expressions, one of the best clues to lying, when a young woman in the front row caught my eye. She leaned forward, nodding her head every so often, listening with an avidity that bespoke a strong personal interest. A small woman, she sat alone, empty seats on either side of her. Her streaked hair, pulled back in a stylish bun, emphasized the sharpness in her face that made her attractive, rather than beautiful. Our eyes met, and she gave me a judgmental, appraising look. Then she nodded once, deliberately, in the expressionless, perfunctory manner of old adversaries meeting on the street.

Turning off the slides, I gestured toward the video monitors. "Next I'll show you an interview where the patient was trying to get a verdict of not guilty by reason of insanity. She'll illustrate much of what I've been saying," I said, as the tape started.

"You'll notice how carefully she's choosing her words; that's a good clue. It's a lot easier to control your words than your face, your voice, and your body." I cleared my throat, wishing I had a glass of water.

"As you'll see, her story is well rehearsed. Most liars get caught because they're not adequately prepared, or because their emotions are so strong that they interfere: The greater the stakes, the more people leak clues to their real feelings through other channels, like body movements.

"Pay particular attention to her indignation, her attack on her interviewer. The best mask for a liar is a false emotion that camouflages real feelings while it deceives the viewer."

I'd been looking forward to this part of my lecture, a time when I could relinquish center stage and fold myself back into the woodwork. Feeling like I was in a sauna, I took my white coat off, uncovering my blue silk dress underneath.

I smoothed my hair, trying to remember if I'd combed it before class. My lips felt dry; I pressed them together, wondering if all my lipstick had worn off. I caught the track my thoughts were taking: Why the sudden self-consciousness?

I looked up and saw the woman in the front row with her eyes fixed on me, ignoring the video, as if I were the material for the lesson—as if the darkness provided no veil, the moving screen no distraction.

When I'd been ill as a child, my father had read history and nature books to me. I remembered one story about the utility of silk as battle armor: *Mongols wore silk undershirts in battle because arrows wouldn't penetrate silk. If they got wounded, they'd tug on the silk, and the arrows would come out; their flesh wouldn't get ripped further by struggling to extract the arrow.*

Wondering why I'd dredged up that particular story now, I saw the woman in the front row, her head turned sideways as she adjusted the two black lacquered chopsticks tipped with gold triangles that speared her bun, like arrows in a quiver.

When the videotape ended, I stepped up to the podium, cloaked again in my white coat. "I need two volunteers, two potential suspects, for a murder inquiry; the rest of the class will serve as the jury." Two hands shot up immediately: the woman in the front row and a man sitting on the aisle a few rows back. Taking them outside the lecture room, I let them choose between two sealed, unmarked manila envelopes. I asked them to read the contents and imagine themselves in the role of the person described.

I returned to the class and continued lecturing for five minutes before I told the students that one of the two envelopes contained a murder scenario and a picture of the supposed victim, the other an article about a researcher responsible for recent advances in the treatment of depression.

"The killer poisoned the victim with arsenic, then buried her body in the forest. You'll use the suspects' behavior to help you identify the murderer." I explained that I would read a list of words, some obviously relevant, some unrelated. The two "suspects" would be asked to give their first association to each word.

When I looked around outside the lecture hall, I spotted the man first. He told me his name was Frank as we walked to the front of the class. He stood slouched beside me, a sheepish grin on his face, as I made sure he understood the exercise.

"Arsenic," I said.

"Poison." His voice squeaked and he cleared his throat. The class murmured, then quieted.

"Forest."

"Trees." His Adam's apple bobbed up and down as he swallowed.

"Grave."

He hesitated a fractional second before speaking. "Stone."

"Depression."

"Gloom." He rubbed his forehead, then thrust his hands into the pockets of his wrinkled too-long chinos, the cuffs sweeping the floor.

"Helplessness."

"Learned." His voice more confident now.

"Research."

"St-st-study."

"Bury."

He bit his lip. "Bones."

"Poison."

"Deadly." He blinked several times.

I saw several students nod and smile when we finished, as if already sure of the verdict.

As I started toward the back of the room to bring in the second "suspect," I saw one of the doors to the lecture hall close, softly, as if someone had been watching and listening through a crack. Outside the lecture hall, I found the woman from the front row sitting on a bench opposite the door. No one else was in the corridor.

Going back inside, I asked her name as we walked toward the lectern. "Alicia Erle," she said, enunciating carefully. She paused, her eyes scanning my face. "My name doesn't ring any bells for you?"

She was short, five feet tall at most, her body shapely. Close to average from shoulder to hip, her legs and arms seemed almost stunted, as if the plans for her trunk and limbs hadn't been drawn on the same scale. Not someone I'd have forgotten if we'd met.

I shook my head no and watched her lips narrow in response.

"I'm not a medical student," Alicia said, as we neared the front of the class. "I just wanted to sit in on your lecture." Her expression was hard with hope; she acted as if she'd given me all the answers I needed to questions I hadn't asked.

"Arsenic," I started with the first word on my list again, wondering why she'd come to my lecture, why she'd been so eager to volunteer. The lecture schedule was posted outside the room and students from other fields often sat in, but it was customary to seek the professor's permission in advance.

"Old lace."

The class tittered.

Dressed with the care of a Barbie doll, Alicia looked overdone compared to the casually clad student crowd. Her short denim jacket, trimmed in gold braid, had a red-satin heart appliqued on the left breast pocket; beneath a second red heart on her left shoulder, the words ON MY SLEEVE were stitched in gold. A denim miniskirt and red heels completed the outfit.

"Forest."

"Trees." She smiled and shrugged.

"Grave."

"Matters." Her prompt response came in a matter-of-fact voice.

"Depression."

"Treatment." She spoke quickly, almost before I'd finished. As if she'd known exactly what was coming next.

I'd used this classroom exercise ten times, successfully. Before now.

I felt my stomach churning and I swallowed. I took a deep breath and let it out slowly.

"Helplessness."

A small hesitation before she answered. "Not."

"Research."

"Evidence."

"Bury."

"Dirt." Alicia had pudgy, pale fingers. She made a quick movement with her hands, ruffling her stumpy fingers. I pictured white grubs, struggling to hide after an overturned rock exposed them to the light.

I read the last word from my list. "Poison."

"Men." She smiled broadly as the class roared.

Alicia had assumed a model's stance when we started, one foot in front of the other, her head carried high, one hand on her hip. Now she broke the pose, turning from the class to me. As if she thought we were finished.

I looked down at my list. "Spy."

Her eyebrows rose, and she started to speak, but she took several beats longer than any previous response before she answered in a mild voice: "Bond. James Bond."

I told the class to cast their votes as jury members, keeping in mind that being suspected of lying can make an innocent person act guilty, for fear of being disbelieved. Most importantly, they probably lacked the single most important key: knowing a person's normal behavior, since the best guesses are based on comparisons with everyday behavior.

I called Frank back to the front of the class. I asked for a show of hands from the class for Frank, then for Alicia. Only a handful voted for Alicia as the murderer.

"Open your envelopes and show the contents to the class."

Favoring me with a mocking smile, Alicia pulled out the picture of the murder victim and waved it over her head like a banner.

# Chapter 2

**O**nce the on-call physicians had confirmed that Alicia Erle was dead, the police were summoned. After the police finally finished with me, I went looking for Glee Dennison and told her about finding Alicia's body. Glee, my best friend and another psychologist in my department, poured me a cup of coffee that I gulped down. Then two more, saturated with sugar, swallowing them as rapidly as possible. As if I could drown my feelings of guilt and failure.

"Did she intend, perhaps, a suicide gesture? Maybe you were just supposed to find her unconscious," Glee suggested, her voice gentle.

I would have liked to believe that Alicia had underestimated the extent that alcohol would magnify the effects of the sleeping pills. But it was absurd to think that a woman with graduate training in pharmacology wouldn't know the most common drug interactions.

I shook my head. "No way."

Glee (short for Glenda), half Japanese, exuded a sense of quiet confidence. Her hands, always in motion when she talked, reminded me of the grace of a sea anemone, swaying in a gentle current: small hands, perfectly shaped nails, her only jewelry a large pearl ring set in filigreed gold. Her glossy black hair, cut short with bangs, framed a face that didn't seem to age; forty-five, five years older than I—usually I would have said she looked younger. Now worry lines creased her forehead.

"Maybe too drunk to monitor the number of pills she'd taken?"

With the greatest stretch of wistfulness, I'd already tried on that rationalization. But I'd stared long enough at the empty amber pill bottle to memorize the label while the white-coated physicians had checked Alicia's vital signs. Dated September 8, the previous day. Doriden, potent sleeping pills, prescribed by Dr. Oliver Tate, Alicia's boss—which made no sense. Was there more to their relationship than she'd bothered to mention? The bottle had held fifty tablets, 500 milligrams each. Half the dose would have been enough to kill Alicia when taken with alcohol. More than enough.

"No note, I take it?"

I shook my head no. Had Alicia really planned it carefully, fully aware that a suicide in the parking lot of a psychiatric hospital would draw maximal attention, maximal guilt, from everyone connected with her? Or was it an impulsive act, piqued by anger? Either way, it was a master stroke—the final coup of a woman who wasn't comfortable if she couldn't even up the score.

Planned or not, she would have left a note. Almost certainly, she should have left a note. I wanted so badly to believe that there would be a note from Alicia, maybe in the mail or in her apartment—something that would tell me what I'd overlooked or underinterpreted. No matter how caustic or venomous, I needed to understand.

The phone rang, and Glee spoke briefly with the caller, then said to me, "Kurt heard about your patient and he's looking for you." Kurt von Reichenau was our boss—the chair of the Psychiatry Department. As I got up, Glee said, "Maybe, if all three of his neurons fire at the same time, he'll be able to listen intelligently."

Kurt wasn't known for his sensitivity or collegiality. When he joined the psychiatry department four years earlier as its new chair, he'd made a number of changes, including eliminating the departmental coffeepot that had held center stage in the library, ignoring faculty protests. I left him a paper from *Physiological Psychology:* Rats caged in groups who shared a common drinking bottle behaved less aggressively than those given individual bottles. The next time I was in the library I found a single drinking bottle in the nook where the coffeepot used to sit.

"I'm free later this morning, if you want to talk more," Glee said.

As I walked out of her office, a janitor was mopping the floor. The hospital smell of his cleaning solution transported me back to the time when I was thirteen, newly diagnosed with leukemia, a year after my mother had died giving birth to my brother. Hospitalized, surrounded by strangers, I'd worked on masking my feelings, making myself a blank screen—retreating into my own world, barring the door and slamming the shutters, as if keeping my pain hidden from others would keep it from myself.

I'd tried never to ask for help. Like a fur coat with the fur turned inside, softness and warmth hidden away. Feelings of weakness or pain were camouflaged by blandness. Anger escalating to scalding hostility warded people off when I needed solitude.

Ian had seen the softness beneath my armor and helped me turn it out. If he had been alive, I'd have called him and told him my troubles. He'd have understood how I felt, understood the text between the lines, the intimate shorthand of longtime lovers.

One time I came home after a particularly bad day at work and heard scuffling and cursing in the kitchen. I found Ian crouched on top of the kitchen counter, his long legs folded awkwardly beneath him. He was wearing jeans and a raggedy black T-shirt, a pair of plastic vampire fangs sticking out of his mouth.

"What're you supposed to be?" I'd managed to ask, between bursts of laughter.

Struggling to look injured, he'd said, "A vampire bat, of course. Hanging around, waiting for you."

Another time I found Ian sitting on the kitchen floor, calmly wrapping double-sided tape around himself, a magazine article on NASA's Venus probe in his lap.

I'd fished a green glass pitcher out of the cabinet and sat down beside him, kissing him hard, getting my arm stuck on the tape in the process. "If you're a Venus fly trap, then I've got to be a pitcher plant," I'd said. "Symmetrical, you know."

I hadn't felt very playful since Ian's death.

When Kurt von Reichenau wanted to be more collegial in his dealings with department faculty, he would come from behind his oversized walnut desk and gesture at the conference table in the corner with an air of noblesse oblige. This morning he didn't rise and move toward the conference table when I entered.

"I understand one of your patients killed herself in the Rugton parking lot, and you found her body?" He made it sound as if I'd committed a social solecism, like demonstrating card tricks in the middle of a funeral.

I bit back an angry response as I sat in one of the two armchairs with high straight backs that stood at attention in front of his desk. Not the time to battle with Kurt.

"How long had you been seeing her?" A large, burly man, Kurt had thick lips, an oversized nose—prominently veined—and bulbous eyes. He started cleaning his pipe with a silver letter opener. As he looked down, I could see his bald spot, the pale circle catching the light despite the gray strands combed over it for camouflage.

"I saw her for two sessions. I supervised an intake interview conducted by a graduate student. She came once to my outpatient group." And one final phone call.

He had paused in his cleaning as I spoke. Now he

began again, his gaze on his pipe. "Remarkably strong negative transference—and you only saw her twice?"

One way of telling me that if she had been that angry with me, I had bungled the case, botched it in the worst possible way.

If only I could disagree. I thought of touching Alicia's cold body and shivered.

"Why did she kill herself in our parking lot?"

"I don't know," I said, not liking the defensive note in my voice. "She got pretty angry with me, but nothing that made me think she'd kill herself—"

"So you have no idea why she committed suicide, let alone why she did it *here.*" He made a show of surprised disbelief, raising his eyebrows and opening his eyes wide.

His office smelled of pipe smoke, layers of apple or cherry blend laid down daily, tainted with the reek of the cheap cigars he smoked when alone. The bulky walnut furniture diminished the office, giving the graciously proportioned room the ambiance of a crowded secondhand store. The windows were hidden behind floor-length green-silk drapes that looked as though they might have enjoyed an earlier, better life in a formal dining room.

"The graduate student who saw her, he was working under your supervision?" Kurt asked.

I nodded.

"You're liable for his work under your license, of course."

"I'm well aware," I said, making an effort to keep my voice level.

"As Chief of Service for this department, I'm ultimately responsible for all clinical activities—and clinical problems. I wish you'd shown better judgment; I don't deserve this."

*Neither did Alicia.*

"We can expect the newspapers to pick up the story," he said. "A patient who kills herself in front of the psychiatric hospital where she's being treated makes juicy copy. Not the kind of advertising we need—not when we already have problems with our inpatient census. You saw the numbers."

Dean Verbrugge had met with the department the previous week to broadcast his displeasure about declining inpatient admissions and the consequent drop in revenues. At the beginning of the meeting Kurt had served the Dean coffee, not in the usual styrofoam throwaway, but in a china cup that tinkled against the saucer in time with his hand tremor as he passed it over. He'd kept his hands clasped together in his lap thereafter.

Kurt's expression when he spoke of the dean's visit reminded me of an evening when I'd gone into a Thai restaurant on Montrose and found myself the lone diner. The owner, a small, stooped man with graying hair and a thick accent, served as cook and waiter; he was too solicitous, too obsequious, too eager to please his solitary customer. More water? More noodles? More tea? Was the restaurant too hot, too cold, too drafty? And then, when the tardy waitress had finally appeared, a tirade was delivered at full volume in his native tongue.

Now Kurt played with his letter opener, grasping it in his right fist and pressing its point against the palm of his left hand. "Why didn't you consider hospitalization when you last saw her? Surely that would have saved us all this trouble."

"She explicitly denied any suicidal intent. She isn't—wasn't—clinically depressed. No indications for hospitalization."

I watched his eyes touch on my green dress, narrow, then dart away. I presumed I'd violated his beliefs about proper dress for a faculty member: too bright, too bold. But then that was his usual assessment of me.

"Obviously it hurts when you find you've misread a patient so badly. Certainly you must have had—still have—some countertransference problems that prevented you from hearing the seriousness of her condition. Or perhaps a more general problem with clinical judgment recently. Like your difficulties interpreting the Petersons' MMPIs for my custody case."

His triumphant look told me he'd been waiting for just the right moment to use the line. Last Wednesday morning Kurt von Reichenau had stopped me in the hallway as I was about to go up the stairs to my second-floor office. He'd patted my shoulder as if I were a horse he owned, a salesman's smile on his coarse-featured, florid face.

"I'm testifying in a custody case, the Petersons," he'd said. "Your psychometrists tested the husband and his new wife, whom I represent, and his ex-wife. The only interpretation you wrote for the ex-wife was something about being 'within normal limits,' but you wrote at least half a page about his new wife, and it wasn't very helpful. Not at all. You need to give me a better interpretation for the ex-wife. In writing."

The modern version of the gun-for-hire in forensic psychiatry. I was in charge of the Psychometric Laboratory that administered psychological tests for the department; this wasn't the first time I'd clashed with Kurt over test interpretations. The test the Petersons had taken, the Minnesota Multiphasic Personality Inventory, uses patients' true or false answers to 566 statements to produce a graph of personality scales that get interpreted like actuarial tables; more deviance from the MMPI's population-based norms hints at more troublesome traits in real life.

"I remember their data," I'd said. "There's no extended interpretation for the ex-wife because there's nothing distinctive to say about someone's personality or behavior who doesn't differ from eighty-five percent of the population on any of the clinical scales. That's the meaning of the phrase 'within normal limits.'"

I'd been well aware that I wasn't behaving in the way he expected his departmental faculty to act, a blend of gratuitous deference and hale-fellow-well-met; our department faculty included six psychologists and twenty-four psychiatrists, eight women and twenty-two men. I guessed that most behaved more congenially toward Kurt than I.

"I need something useful, in writing, for this custody case. You didn't interpret her test—"

His belt, buckled at the last notch, had been straining under his large belly. Positioned as it was, it must have functioned exactly like the underwire in a bra: uplifting, outlining, enhancing size—all the better to present and display.

Kurt had intercepted my look at his belly, and I could almost see him thinking of somewhere else—in his odd bookkeeping system—where I'd gone wrong.

"Just because the test results don't match what you want doesn't mean they're changeable." I'd turned my back on him and started up the stairs.

"Just a minute." His tone harsh, he'd put his hand on my shoulder.

I'd pulled away from him, backing up against the wall. "You wanted something else?" I'd tried breathing through my mouth to avoid the miasma of cigar smoke stirred up by his movements.

"You look tired." From someone else, it might have implied concern. From Kurt, it meant he'd found a reason for my poor judgment.

"Maybe you need to rethink the way you're making some of your choices. Perhaps you need some time away—a leave of absence—at the least."

So he could put someone else in charge of the Psychometric Lab, someone who might be more "helpful" with cases like the Petersons. "That's certainly one alternative," I'd said, as I turned my back on him.

Now I felt my nails digging into my fists. I swallowed hard, trying to frame a reasonably civil answer, trying to maintain my composure. I was distracted by the picture that intruded on my concentration: Alicia's body, lying in the back seat of her car.

The place where I'd cut my right hand when I smashed Alicia's window started to throb. I looked down and saw my hand was bleeding again. I cradled my right hand in my left, trying to hold it naturally while keeping the blood from getting on my skirt.

"A patient who chooses to kill herself in a place where she'll have the maximum impact on her therapist hardly suggests that treatment was beneficial."

A lecture about therapy from a man who'd never learned to connect the dots.

His Boy Scout approach to psychotherapy seemed to have only two components, from all accounts: exhorting patients to try harder, then blaming them for not trying hard enough if they didn't improve. He assured himself of regular successes by excruciatingly careful patient selection, taking only those candidates likely to progress even in the absence of any treatment: young, attractive, intelligent, and successful. Since these were the very kind of patients who were least likely to complain openly when the outcome was poor, his public image as a therapist outside the department remained strong.

Kurt's voice intruded on my thoughts. "You told the police she wasn't suicidal. They said you invoked confidentiality and wouldn't tell them anything besides her name and the fact that she was your patient, except to say she wasn't suicidal."

"Confidentiality survives death." As Chief of Service, Kurt was entitled to information, but not someone outside Rugton.

"Of course you wouldn't want to see it as a suicide. After all, it tarnishes your professional image—not to mention your feelings about yourself. But it's hardly helpful for you to tell the police that you had no information about a patient's intentions before the fact. Even if it's true. Especially if it's true."

So the two officers who'd come to investigate Alicia's death had spoken to Kurt as well. I shouldn't have been surprised, since they'd made no secret of their dissatisfaction with me.

Nor I of my displeasure with them.

"More flakes than Kellogg's," the taller of the two had said to his partner, gesturing toward Rugton Hall, loudly enough so I wouldn't miss it. His darting sideways glance at me made it clear he didn't just mean the patients.

"Pretty obvious suicide," the shorter one with pimples on his chin had told me after looking over Alicia's body in her car. "She was seeing a shrink—that's not something most people do on impulse, right? But the medical examiner needs to certify any unnatural death. A note would've helped. Also your evidence that she was suicidal. You're making the medical examiner do more work after the autopsy, talking to family and friends. Big waste of his time—like studying the contents of your garbage disposal."

Now Kurt said, "The police told me that you kept insisting it wasn't your patient's car. But they checked the registration, and it's hers, all right. Doesn't do much for your credibility."

So I'd given the police and my boss yet another reason to doubt my judgment. *But why would Alicia buy another car if she was planning to kill herself?*

Kurt had a collection of fossils on one wall, and I stared at one in the corner of the display, something long and slithery, maybe a snake or an eel. It reminded me of another of the stories my father had told me, how Henry I of England had died from eating stewed eels. Hardly the kind of information to pacify Kurt at the moment. As if anything would.

Kurt took his time lighting his pipe, looking at me as if waiting for me to speak. Then, after taking several puffs and watching the smoke, he asked, "Were you negligent in charting your sessions with this patient?"

"I countersigned Perry's two-page intake note the day after the session. Since the record room's locked by the time we finish group, I write each of the group therapy notes on a new blank chart page with the patient's name at the top and then leave them for Thelma Lou to file in their charts."

"And you just, shall we say, 'forgot' to leave your patient's chart back in the record room with the intake note?"

"What do you mean?"

"When I heard about your patient's suicide, I asked Thelma Lou for the chart, so we could give the police the names of next of kin. It's not filed, and there's no file marker with a sign out."

"But it's got to be there somewhere. Probably misfiled. You know Thelma Lou—"

"Of course," he said, his tone skeptical. "But if it's not found, it'll raise more unpleasant questions about your judgment. Her family will certainly want some good answers about why she chose to kill herself here, of all places, and this mystified response from you isn't likely to assuage them. A well-documented assessment is no protection against a wrongful death suit that names you, and most likely the department, as well, but it would certainly help. Hardly an appealing prospect for any of us—a trial without the chart."

Like crossing the ocean without a compass.

I felt my heart accelerate. The word of a student like Perry would hardly count for much. "It's got to be in the record room. I'll help Thelma Lou go through all the charts—"

"You'd be better advised not to get directly involved with the search for the chart. Under ordinary circumstances, a patient's suicide doesn't automatically make family members embrace the idea of a malpractice suit. But when she kills herself on your doorstep . . . liability judgments against therapists whose patients kill themselves can be very costly—financially and professionally."

He avoided my eyes as he stood up to signal the end of the meeting. "I've already called the medical school's lawyer to set a time to discuss the department's . . . stance on the issue. I'd suggest you consult a lawyer, for your own protection."

Looking at him, I knew that Kurt von Reichenau

would have enjoyed throwing me to the wolves if the department's reputation wouldn't be stained in the process. My stomach was tight with anger as I walked out of his office.

# Chapter 3

I'd been taught that a patient's first few sentences in the initial interview, the "presenting complaint," could foreshadow the essence of the therapeutic work ahead. I remembered a training seminar sixteen years ago where we'd spent an hour discussing a college freshman's response to the standard what-brings-you-here question: "I can't whiz in public." Granted that difficulties urinating when not alone made public restrooms problematic. But why seek therapy? And the answer—the sexual feelings for men he couldn't yet face—had been forecast (conjured, I would have said, back then) by the psychologist who led the seminar, based on that one sentence and the uneven tone that accompanied it—her accuracy confirmed months later.

Two days after I'd met her in my lie detection lecture, Alicia Erle had sat across from me for her initial interview in the Rugton outpatient clinic. "I've got problems with a whole gang of piranhas, sharks, and buzzards—that's what drove me to see a psychologist," she'd announced.

I couldn't begin to guess what she meant.

Perry Urbay, a second-year graduate student I'd begun supervising in early August, was responsible for directing the interview. Alicia sat in the chair beside Perry's desk.

I knew from Alicia's answers to the clinic's phone screening interview that she had a master's degree in pharmacology, she'd been employed as a research assistant in the Department of Pharmacology for the last year, and she'd not sought mental health treatment previously. She'd specifically asked for group therapy—not a common request, especially from someone who'd never seen a therapist previously. I ran the only therapy group at Rugton.

Alicia looked me up and down as she sat opposite me, not bothering to disguise her appraising look, not offering the usual token smile to soften the challenge.

I looked over at Perry, waiting for him to take the lead. Broad shoulders, curly black hair, tortoise-shell glasses that magnified blue eyes, even a cleft in his chin, Perry looked like the archetypal young professional featured in whiskey ads. If he stood perfectly still in the men's section of a department store, he'd blend in well with the manikins. All too well.

"A bit warm in here," Alicia said, her voice implying blame. She set her styrofoam coffee cup on his desk and pulled off her silk jacket, a pink so bright it probably glowed in the dark. Her movements fanned the scent of her gardenia perfume, the smell moving from suggestive to assaultive in Perry's small, poorly ventilated office.

Perry had his pencil poised over a legal pad. He frowned as he looked at Alicia's coffee cup encroaching on his desk blotter; he moved his chair a couple of inches back and drew himself up even straighter. As he opened his mouth to speak, Alicia preempted him.

"The receptionist said something about why I was getting two for the price of one," Alicia was looking from Perry to me, "but I was in too much of a rush to ask questions since I was running a little behind . . ."

"As she probably told you, this is a training clinic. I'm Perry Urbay, a clinical psychology graduate student. Dr. McAlistar supervises my psychotherapy cases, and she sits in on all my intakes—my initial interviews."

"So she tells you what you should have said." A flashbulb smile popped so quickly that it never made it all the way to her eyes. "And you're how far along in your training?"

"Uh, this is my . . . second year of graduate school." He tugged at his earlobe, smoothed his hair, then pulled his hand away too quickly and rested it on the arm of his chair. "Does that address—do you have any other questions?"

"I'm sure I probably will—later." Her cotton turtleneck, a shade darker than her rosy lipstick, stretched snugly across her breasts. She crossed her legs and her skirt crept up her thighs.

"When you sat down, you said, 'problems with a whole gang of piranhas, sharks, and buzzards . . .'" Perry's voice trailed off.

"Too cryptic for you? Trouble with men—it's always trouble with men. I'm going on a men diet." She ran her fingers through her shoulder-length streaked hair, exposing dark roots. The gesture was too smooth, almost like she was patting herself in an approving fashion for her difficulties.

"I was seeing this man—we'd been together about six months—when I found out he was sleeping with his secretary, this mousey nineteen-year-old—and he's my age, twenty-six. Here's something that will tell you everything you need to know about her: You know those cutesy-pootsie stuffed animals with the suction cup feet that people put on their car windows? She had four of them in her car"—her silver charm bracelet jangled as she waved four fingers for emphasis—"one on each of the side windows in the back seat, two on the back window.

"So here she is, so wet behind the ears that she still plays with toys, and she's after my boyfriend. . . ." Her voice quivered and she looked away.

"I knew something was wrong when I went to his apartment after work and saw these long black hairs in his comb in the bathroom. So . . . when I spent the night with him a few days later, I made sure he knew I'd be tied up all day the next day. I parked outside his apartment just before twelve o'clock, his usual lunch hour."

She spoke in a rush. "I saw them go inside together. I left him a message on his answering machine at work suggesting he'd left one cheek hanging out when he tried to cover his ass—he always hated it when I talked like that."

One of the florescent ceiling lights dimmed, the tube buzzing like an angry wasp, flickering before it went out.

"I decided to make him more *memorable* to his clients, something they'd think about whenever they considered doing business with him. He always traveled during the first week of the month; the next time he went out of town, I had everything all set. I still had keys to his apartment and his car, so it was easy. I draped the interior of his Volkswagon with a few layers of plastic sheeting to waterproof it, filled the bottom with sand, then stuck in some plants, rocks, a big piece of driftwood, and four dead catfish. I sealed all the doors and all but the very top of one window with caulking. I stuck a hose in the top of the window, and turned it on full blast. Then I called a couple of local television stations to tell them about this great mobile aquarium he'd set up to help raise money for his favorite charity, the animal shelter," she snickered. "Actually, he'd always said that spending money on mistreated pets was a waste."

She laughed harshly. "I watched from a distance—a great scene even without dialogue, these guys filming his car. Absolutely hilarious."

Alicia picked up her styrofoam coffee cup from Perry's desk, its rim branded with her lipstick. She stroked a long pink fingernail down its side, shivering at the grating sound. She took a small sip and twisted her mouth in a grimace. "Bitter." She set the cup down on the floor. "And cold."

I heard the faint note in her voice, the first hint of honest pain in the session. When Alicia looked at me, I raised my eyebrows. She opened her mouth, then hesitated, a bleak expression on her face. I nodded once, encouragingly.

Perry had been writing notes, not looking up. Now he asked, "Did you ever talk with him about it?"

Alicia shuttered her face and folded her arms over her chest. "You think I should do cartwheels to keep the peace? Talking with him wouldn't have changed anything—no way I was going to take him back, no matter what he said."

Which meant he'd never called again.

"What about other relationships with men?" Perry asked. "How have they gone?"

"Men aren't everything in the universe, you know. You could ask me about my work, for example."

"Well, earlier, you said, 'Trouble with men—it's always trouble with men.'" He read the phrase from his legal pad, his second bass voice giving it the air of a proclamation.

She spoke slowly, deliberately. "Oh—a comma and period man?"

Perry moved back in his chair. "Tell me . . . about your work."

It was like watching someone trying to measure height with a thermometer. I started to speak, but changed my mind as soon as I saw Alicia looking at me challengingly—as if she wanted an excuse to do battle with me. Or an excuse to push me away?

"I work in the Pharmacology Department, in Oliver Tate's lab. I recruit subjects for drug trials. I help collect information on side effects when they're staying on the research unit, then I enter the data from the trials in the computer, run simple analyses. Some graphite studies." As if searching for a clue to my response, Alicia looked closely at me.

Perry continued writing and turned the page in his notebook without looking up.

"You know, I'm taking this one course to get through

the rest of my requirements. Sometimes I get so busy taking notes that I miss important things in the lecture. I'm trying to see if I can just listen, not try to write everything down, so I can really hear things."

Perry stopped writing and looked at her.

"I—I was a graduate student in pharmacology, until about a year ago." She played with her charm bracelet, stroking a miniature silver lobster. "I got my master's degree . . . then I . . . decided to take some time off before taking my qualifying exams."

Alicia wrapped her arms around herself, holding herself tightly, her face pained. "I was having a lot of trouble concentrating, and I didn't want to do badly on my qualifying exams." Her voice wavered and she closed her eyes.

Perry held out the Kleenex box from his desk. Alicia opened her eyes and saw his gesture but pointedly ignored it, digging in her purse until she finally found a tattered tissue. She busied herself blotting her eyes.

Perry looked from Alicia to his watch and then down at his legal pad, his expression midway between a scowl and a sulk. She opened her eyes, intercepting his expression, looking away before he looked back at her.

"Speaking of detecting lies"—she nodded at me— "during your lecture I thought about something that influenced me: My dad taught me to play poker when I was a kid. I thought it was so nice that he wanted to spend all that time with me. That wasn't the real reason, of course; once I learned the basics, whenever he had poker parties in our house, my job was to act like I was just playing with my dolls in the room. I'd try to peek at the other players' cards, signal him if their hands beat his. If I picked up Barbie, it meant he should hold; Ken meant he should fold. I was such a good little actress, even then. No one ever suspected."

I felt as if I was straining to listen to a song on a radio station full of static, never sure if I'd caught the words and melody between off-putting bursts of empty noise. I had the sense that it was deliberate.

"I matured early, had a body by the time I was

twelve. I started getting too much attention from the guys my dad was trying to sucker; this one guy made a pass at me and I just froze. My dad found us and he got nasty, like it was my fault, somehow. When I wasn't useful anymore, well, I was consigned to the outer limits."

Perry's wooden swivel chair groaned as he shifted his weight. Alicia looked over quickly, as if resentful of the intrusion.

"Then he got the idea that maybe he could use me to distract the other players. Told me to wear something low-cut and put me at the table when I was fifteen. I cleaned out everybody at the table three times, including him. By the third time he was absolutely livid, like I wasn't supposed to have the brains to win, just to be a shill." Alicia looked down and toyed with the row of buttons on the left side of her skirt that ran from the waist to the hem, unbuttoning one, then rebuttoning it, unbuttoning the next, rebuttoning it. "He humiliated me that night, taunted me until I left the table in tears. Getting even, that's one of his main missions in life."

Like father, like daughter.

"Now and then I still play. It's not like you're just poker-faced, not if you're really good. What's important is covering any real emotion. You keep yourself in motion all the time, so no one catches on when you really have something to hide. You put everything that matters out front; then you wait to see if anyone's smart enough to catch on. Almost no one is."

Just like now. I held my breath. In the silence I heard a siren approaching the hospital, the wail growing, intensifying, the closer it came.

Perry cleared his throat. "Where was your mother during all this? I haven't heard anything about her."

Alicia stopped playing with her skirt buttons and flashed another Instamatic smile. "No, I guess I . . . left her out. Her name's Shelly; once I started high school, she didn't want me calling her Mom any more. Vain. Never opens the front door without checking herself in the mirror first. You know how people talk about comfort food, the kind they grew up with? I think of home cooking and I remember salad, no dressing, a single chicken breast, no skin.

"Shelly's thin, very thin; used to tell me I needed to lose weight, no matter what I weighed." She put her hands on her hips and looked haughtily left and right like a model on a runway, then looked ruefully down at her curves. "Besides, enough men seem to like me the way I am." She raised her eyebrows and stared at Perry.

Perry fumbled with his pencil, then dropped it. As he bent to pick it up, I saw Alicia look pleased; her expression was neutral when he looked back at her.

Alicia looked over at the small window on her left. "It's really stuffy in here. I'd like to open a window"— she glanced at her watch—"but I can probably survive another few minutes."

I wondered if Perry had caught the implication and hoped he'd ask her to talk about stuffiness or surviving. He turned the next page of his legal pad without looking up.

"You know, my father has this—this delusion that he's such an understanding person, but if I don't behave the way he thinks I should, well, he just blows up. You know what I'd like? To see him humbled for a change; let him see what it's like."

*Oh, yes, you've been acting out that scenario for some time now.* I looked at Perry, but he was busily writing notes, his face impassive.

Alicia mimicked the piercing voice of her mother— "Don't you ever come home again with a grade like that!"—and her father's sarcastic, disparaging responses—"Surely, you can control yourself better." Her voice was strident and pleading when she imitated herself trying to make peace with her parents. She gave Perry a quick sideways smile. "Whatever can you do with someone like me?"

Hardly an idle question.

Perry's cheeks turned red. "I—I need to get more information before I can outline a treatment plan." He started asking the standard mental status questions next, making sure Alicia didn't hear voices or see things that other people couldn't hear or see, have periods of excessive energy or lethargy, or experience memory problems. "Any thoughts or phrases or songs that keep running through your mind, seeming like they're beyond your control?"

Alicia picked up her jacket. "Bit cooler in here now." She busied herself putting on her jacket. "I'm probably too compulsive about tidiness sometimes, if that's what you mean. Kate Wheelon, my old roommate, said I drove her crazy when we lived together, wanting everything exactly in its place."

I wondered what she'd decided not to say.

"When I met you at my lecture on Tuesday, you asked if your name rang any bells," I said. "What was that about?"

Alicia's gaze lingered on a spot on the wall where the pale-green paint had peeled, exposing a darker shade of green underneath. Her right foot tapped a silent syncopated rhythm. "I'd already set this appointment when I saw your name on the lecture schedule. I thought you might recognize my name from the clinic calendar."

"Why'd you ask for group therapy?"

"To work on my relationships with men. Problems with men, like I said at first. I'm sure *you* remember," she said, looking at Perry.

On the surface it was an obvious, reasonable treatment choice. But there was more to it, something she wasn't saying.

The first interview with a new patient is supposed to be like the unfolding of a mystery story: a time to search for the evidence needed to yield solutions to the riddles of diagnosis and treatment; a time to probe for clues, decode symptoms, decipher behavior, and interpret motivation; a time to gather sufficient data to put a name on the problem.

With Alicia, I felt as if I was trying to read a letter through a sealed envelope.

"Why did you decide to call for a clinic appointment when you did—not two weeks earlier, not a month from now?" I asked.

She shook her head and her earrings caught the light, strands of silver teardrops that reached halfway to her shoulders. When she spoke again, her voice was strained. "I read this newspaper story about Albert Schweitzer. There was a phrase, they quoted him, it rang—it hit me, somehow. I don't know. He talked about 'the fellowship of those who bear the mark of pain.'" Her voice caught on the last word. "I feel so mixed up, just so mixed up. I feel so upset. So trapped."

The static vanished completely for the first time since we'd started. I leaned forward in my chair.

"Things haven't gone completely smoothly for me in the last couple of years." She met my gaze. "That's like saying the *Titanic* wasn't completely watertight."

I didn't return her sarcastic half smile.

Alicia chewed on one of her long nails. "I've felt pretty rotten for some time. I—I know I've been behaving destructively, especially when I feel rejected; it doesn't take much to set me off." Her eyes flicked briefly to Perry and away.

"Just before I scheduled this appointment, I woke up in the middle of the night; I was in my kitchen, holding a burning match. I must've gotten out of bed, taken a matchbook out of the drawer, and lit one, all in my sleep. It really scared me."

Perry leaned forward, his voice hesitant. "Have you ever thought about suicide?" He made the question sound off-color.

Alicia shifted in her chair, moving as far away from him as possible within the confines of the chair's arms, her body and feet angled toward the door. "No. Of course not. No."

Protesting that much meant yes—but Perry had asked the wrong question. Most everyone has had the thought that death could offer an escape. But Alicia didn't feel like an imminent risk, and I worried that she wouldn't return if we pushed too hard now.

"Have you ever done anything like this before in your sleep," Perry asked, "or done anything else that might be dangerous?"

"Never." Alicia spoke with a firmness that reassured me.

The phone rang. Alicia started at the sound.

Perry picked it up, listened. "I'll tell her." He hung up and looked at me. "Your four o'clock appointment is here."

I turned to Alicia. "Are you still interested in joining my therapy group?"

"Of course. That's why I'm here."

"Something's bothering you. Something matters a great deal. Something you haven't felt ready to talk about." I looked hard at Alicia, holding her gaze, trying to break through.

She started to nod, then caught herself and gave me a defiant look instead, leaning back away from me in her chair.

"If you change your mind or want to talk further before group, call me."

A curt nod.

"I have to go now." I stood up. "Perry needs to get some more background information from you."

"Thank you," Alicia said, "you've been remarkably . . . helpful." Her tone suggested the opposite.

# Chapter 4

I tried to call Oliver Tate, Alicia's former boss, after I got back from my meeting with Kurt von Reichenau. I wanted to talk with someone else who'd known Alicia—and to find out why he'd prescribed sleeping pills for an employee. "I'll let him know you called when he's free," his secretary said, as soon as I'd told her I was calling about Alicia. She dropped her voice. "He's with the police now."

Ten minutes later I heard a knock on my office door.

"Oliver Tate," the man at the door said, holding out his hand.

I wasn't pleased to see him appear abruptly at my door. I'd wanted to talk with him in his own office where I might get a better sense of him—and where he might be less guarded.

Oliver Tate stood with his shoulders back and his chin up, as if deliberately selecting the best possible way to display himself to advantage. He looked mid to late forties, tall and muscular with a well-tanned face, his thick gray hair cut fashionably short.

He gave me ample opportunity to observe him at close range as he continued to grip my hand after shaking it, standing too near, looking at me too long.

Alicia's former boss—acting as if we already shared

some understanding. Or some intimacy. I pulled my hand away.

"It seems we have a common problem," he said. "The late Alicia Erle."

*A common problem,* he'd said. Not mentioning any sense of regret or loss. I motioned him to one of the chairs grouped by the door. He moved toward it with the grace of an athlete.

His glance around my office was openly appraising. Not interested in the institutionally approved menu of paint colors, I'd spent the better part of a Saturday painting three of the walls a light shade of turquoise. For the wall around the window I'd used a darker shade, with stronger notes of blue. I'd taken down the ancient plastic-lined beige curtains with red triangles that came with the office, hanging in their place sheers that didn't block the sun. I'd covered the brown linoleum with an area rug, swirls of blues and greens. A dish of potpourri sat on the windowsill, the sun's heat intensifying the smell of roses and cinnamon. He nodded approvingly.

I sat in the chair opposite him, already feeling two strikes down.

"Her suicide's really shaken me up—not to mention the people who worked with her on the unit." He ran his hand through his short hair.

"I just got back in town this morning. I was sifting through a week's worth of mail and messages when the police showed up on my doorstep. I'd gone away for a few days of vacation, then had a meeting in Austin over the Labor Day weekend—Eichon, this pharmaceutical company I consult with; they got us to do business on the holiday by combining it with a golf tournament. One cop told me about Alicia's suicide and asked me about her Doriden prescription; they thought I was her physician." His eyebrows, heavy and black, lifted with remembered irritation—maybe some surprise mixed in. "They wanted to know how she seemed yesterday. It took them a long time to understand that I didn't write the prescription."

"Then who did?"

"Alicia, almost certainly. I keep my prescription pads on my desk, and my DEA number is printed on them. She could've gotten a pad and forged my signature. Not hard at all when she'd been working on my unit for a year. Not difficult."

He rubbed his chin the way a man with a beard would have stroked it. "In retrospect, her death—her suicide—wasn't unexpected, after the problems she'd been having recently. But you know all about that." His last sentence came out in a hurry, faster than the rest.

My phone rang and I got up to answer it, glad for the diversion, wondering what I was supposed to know. My desk was on the wall opposite the door, positioned so that I could look out my window when I sat at it.

I had a picture of Ian on my desk in a silver art deco frame. I watched Oliver's reflection in the frame's protective glass as Esther Fernandez asked me to come to Washington the following week to be part of a grant review panel for the National Institutes of Health.

Oliver stood up and turned to look at my bookshelves. As he surveyed the contents, he looked relaxed.

It would have been more polite not to take the call, but I wasn't feeling polite toward Oliver Tate. Esther's voice sounded harassed as she apologized for the short notice, explaining that the assigned reviewer had just had a heart attack. "I know it's rotten timing, but I'd love to see you. We'll go to dinner and gossip like fiends."

I continued to watch Oliver's reflection as he looked over a bowl of seashells on my shelf, picked up an angel wing, and ran his finger down the edge as he looked at me. His eyes traveled down my body, but no muscles in his face moved, as if divorced from all emotion. Like a lizard sitting motionless on a fence, waiting for a fly to come within range.

He put the angel wing back in the bowl and picked up a book I'd written about my research, leafing through it.

I agreed to come to Washington and said good-bye.

Reshelving the book, Oliver asked, "Why did you decide to study deception?"

I felt as if he was asking me to talk about whether I favored lacy bras or the plain, utilitarian variety.

"You said Alicia had been having difficulties at work in the past few weeks." I said as I sat down. "What kind?"

Oliver remained standing. "Very moody. Preoccupied. Angry at the world. I wondered if it was related to her therapy. Not that it was bad for her, just that . . ."

He sat again. "Alicia made a big deal of the fact that she was seeing you. She tried to find out as much as possible about you." His glance was a dare and an invitation.

A door slammed somewhere down the hallway, leaving a hollow echo in the silence, like a starting pistol.

"The police asked me about you, too," he said. "But then, they didn't seem too sure how to deal with either of us. They said you told them she wasn't suicidal—then I told them I didn't write a prescription that had my signature on it."

I wondered what else he'd told the police, but I wasn't going to question him when he seemed to be so clearly marking the path he wanted me to follow—the grown-up version of you show me yours and I'll show you mine. "What was Alicia like at work?"

"She was the senior research associate for my pharmacology research unit, in charge of all the ongoing studies on a daily basis. Her job was a mixture: screening subjects, monitoring the trials, recording data. Lots of record keeping." He touched one of the three gold buttons that marched down each wrist of his well-cut brown jacket; each was engraved with his initials, like discrete advertisements for his influence.

"I travel a great deal. She used to call me Dr. Stealth—joked about how I was in and out again before she knew it. She resented my absences."

He smiled, a charming, boyish smile, the kind that made me wonder if Alicia had been ensnared, become more than an employee. Or if she'd wanted to be more than an employee and been angry when she wasn't.

"Alicia resented more than my absences. She wanted to be my equal, to make executive decisions on protocols. She didn't have the background or the knowledge."

He stood up again, put his hands in his pockets, paced up to my desk, then back to his chair. "Sorry," he said, catching my eye. "Restless. I shouldn't be surprised, really, that she burned me, in the end. She'd become . . . increasingly disgruntled. I expected her to resign and leave me stranded when she knew it would do the greatest damage."

*Sowing trails of revenge behind her.*

"Alicia messed up data from one study—badly; I only caught it by accident, just before I left town. After seeing the problems in this case, I'm frankly concerned about whether we've got problems with data from other studies." He stood looking down at me. "I can't help but wonder if the errors were deliberate. Sabotage." He moved close to my chair. "I was hoping you could give me some feel for whether she systematically altered data, or if this was only an isolated problem." After a minute he put his hand on my shoulder.

I wished I'd worn different clothes, something thicker, impenetrable, maybe a suit with heavy shoulder pads—almost anything besides the green challis dress that lay close against my skin, leaving me unprotected, the heat of his hand traveling through the thin fabric like an electric current through copper wire.

"Not a good strategy," I said, my voice cold as I stared at his hand. He moved it away. I thought of a buck in the forest, rubbing against a tree, marking it with his scent. I worked to control the impulse to lift my hand to my shoulder and brush away the lingering feeling of contact.

When he was seated opposite me again, I said, "Alicia's right to confidentiality isn't changed by her death."

He leaned forward, his hands on his knees. "If she

messed up data, innocent people could be hurt. In the case I found, the changes made a painkiller look more effective than it was; patients looked like they were reporting a lot less pain. Those data could have been the basis for FDA approval." He held my glance a beat too long.

I dropped my eyes first. "I can't help you." I couldn't believe Alicia would have sabotaged his drug trials. But I'd learned not to trust my judgment where Alicia was concerned.

"You don't have to say anything directly—just act like you've got an ice cube in your right hand, a Bic lighter in your left." His smile was sardonic. "Wave the lighter each time I get closer to the truth, the ice cube when I'm getting colder."

Again I shook my head no.

He studied my face, then slid his eyes down my body, a passing glance designed to be obvious but not overtly offensive. "I've been trying to figure out why you look familiar. I think I know. I've watched you swimming at the health club. From the restaurant above the pool. Your suit's a navy one-piece."

I didn't think he'd just figured it out. I'd bet he recognized me when he first saw me, but held back, waiting for the moment to show the next card in his hand.

"I play racquetball there twice a week," he said. "Plus whenever they have a tournament, of course."

Of course.

He shifted in his chair, and I gave myself half a point.

"Alicia was a remarkably histrionic woman, I'm sure you'll agree," he said. "When I interviewed her for the job, she acted like someone auditioning for a game show, trying to impress with enthusiasm and knowledge. If I had it to do over again, I wouldn't have hired her—look at the flack I got."

I noticed that he hadn't said he wouldn't do it over again because his original judgment had been flawed. Or because he had any regrets about her death.

He looked at his watch and stood up, thanking me

for my time, saying he hoped he'd see me around. The expression on his face as he left stayed in my mind.

It was the look of a man anticipating victory.

# Chapter 5

After finding Alicia's body on Wednesday, I'd canceled all my appointments except for my supervisory hour with Perry Urbay and my five o'clock therapy group. Alicia had only attended group one time, but she'd stirred up strong feelings. I didn't want group members to read about her death in the papers, then wait a week to talk about it.

I hadn't been able to reach Perry Urbay to tell him about Alicia until our supervisory hour before group. He looked shocked. "Something I did?"

"Nothing you did." We spent the hour talking about her. Twice more Perry asked whether he was at fault, and I tried to reassure him; too timid about pressing Alicia, hearing few of her nuances, he'd hardly done sterling work—but he hadn't done anything toxic.

"Time to get going." We arranged four chairs in the center of the room, and I opened the door to the group room.

Gerald Yablonski came in first and sat in his usual seat—the one nearest the door—wearing the same navy windbreaker he always wore, no matter what the weather; he never removed the windbreaker during group, and he was always the first person out the door as soon as group ended.

When I first discussed group therapy with Gerald,

he'd said, "The Chinese had this health campaign. They tried to switch people from chopsticks to forks. Always dipping back into a shared dish, you get problems with diseases like hepatitis." Normally impassive and distant, tonight he kept shifting back and forth in his chair, biting his lip.

Jane Friblee, a realtor in her midforties, walked in next. She'd cut her wilting pageboy short and frosted her hair, and she wore a burgundy dress that flattered her instead of her usual pastel blouse and flowered skirt. I wondered if her clash with Alicia two weeks ago had provoked the changes.

"We're meeting this week without a quorum?" Jane asked, looking around the small circle as she sat down. I'd cancelled group last week when we hadn't had our four-member quorum.

I started by reminding them that Norman Zuckerman was out of the country for a month. Then I relayed the long message Carlyle Stocklin had left with our receptionist. He'd been at a meeting in Austin and had a bad asthma attack Tuesday night, bad enough to send him to the emergency room. He'd had too little sleep and still wasn't feeling well enough to come to group tonight—so sorry to have missed three in a row.

"Where's Alicia?" Gerald broke in.

I told them how I'd found Alicia's body in front of Rugton that morning, the empty sleeping pill container beside her.

Gerald looked at me with disbelief when I finished. "Can't be true." His voice boomed, then trailed off. "She didn't kill herself—doesn't make sense."

An accountant, Gerald had sought therapy after he turned forty and found himself without any close male friends, his longest relationship with a woman having ended after two years. Group members had started to target his stinginess in ordinary conversations; Jane had pointed out that he used as few words as possible. He'd been a stutterer when he was young; his mother died when he was nineteen, and he stopped stuttering within the month. He'd been arrested twice as an adolescent for peeping into neighbors' windows.

"Maybe . . . I could've helped—" Gerald breathed heavily, his red face looked close to tears. It was the first time I'd seen Gerald show any real emotion since he entered the group.

"No—if it was anyone, it wasn't you, it was me . . . I mean, it was I," Jane said.

Themes of loss and guilt dominated the rest of the session, liberally laced with anger: some toward Alicia for killing herself in front of Rugton, with the implicit message it sent to the group; plenty left over for me for not seeing the danger and keeping Alicia alive; and several very long silences that I spent remembering the last group session when Alicia had been present, two weeks ago.

When we opened the door to the group room two weeks ago, Alicia, Gerald, and Jane had been waiting outside. I checked the hallway for Carlyle Stocklin before I shut the door and sat down. "Carlyle's supposed to be coming tonight, but he must have gotten delayed." His wife had left a message for him, asking him to call home before he left Rugton. "Norman's out of town for four weeks. We have two new additions. This is Perry Urbay, a student therapist who'll be coleading the group with me for the next six months." I gestured at Perry; he inclined his head, his eyes sweeping around the circle. "And this is Alicia, a new group member."

The fluorescent fixture that lit the room flickered uncertainly. The room had started its life as the departmental library, and shelves of books and journals, none more recent than 1970, covered the wall to the left of the door, their musty smell heavy in the air. The mirror in the wall opposite the door was usually used for videotaping the group, but the woman who handled the taping was out on maternity leave. I'd used the tapes in training seminars and in group, giving members a different perspective on how they interacted.

"Alicia Erle." She said her name distinctly, pushing her sleeves up over her biceps as she looked around the circle, then at me. She was wearing a long-sleeved purple cotton T-shirt with oversized shoulder pads, a purple scarf around her neck. On first glance her mascara, smudged under her right eye, looked like a bruise.

"Gerald here." He stared at Alicia's breasts as he spoke, until she folded her arms over her chest.

"I'm Jane Friblee . . . if we've finished the introductions, I've had the worst week at work, and I'd like to talk about it." She looked around the circle, daring anyone to object. "There's this new receptionist, she's a real witch, spelled with a capital B." Jane spoke in a mincing manner, carefully pronouncing each word. "I tried to show her how to do the expense forms, and I would have thought she'd be grateful for the help I gave her, but she just acted like she wanted me out of the way."

At the very end of the last session, when there was absolutely no time for any response, Jane had given gifts to each of the other group members. She'd given a newspaper article on men's fashion to Gerald as she stared at his navy windbreaker and an article on psychosomatic illnesses to Carlyle. I was expecting fallout from her "generosity" tonight, some of it probably directed at me for not letting the group go overtime.

"Helpfulness, speaking of—" Gerald said, looking pointedly at Jane. He gave Alicia a cautious glance after he spoke, as if balancing his anger against his interest in creating a good impression.

Jane acted as if he hadn't spoken. She told a detailed story about her difficulties with the new secretary, then complained about her boss's lack of support when she'd discussed her concerns. She spoke rapidly while staring at the wall, ending with, "I work with a bunch of donkeys."

"Asses," Alicia said. "You mean you work with a bunch of asses." She ignored Jane's angry look. "You can say the word, it won't hurt you."

Gerald gave Alicia an approving wink. Revenge by proxy.

Jane's mouth tightened as she watched the interplay between Gerald and Alicia. She sat up straighter in her chair and folded her hands in her lap. She crossed her legs at the ankles, tucking them under her chair. Looking at Perry, she said, "We're usually a little better at taking turns, giving people feedback only when they've had a chance to finish speaking, not interrupting them quite so . . . abruptly." She turned to Alicia. "What brought you here to the group?" Her tone suggested that she expected to hear something distasteful.

Alicia stared at the empty chair in the circle. "Trouble with men." She recited the story about her unfaithful lover that Perry and I had heard before.

This time I was struck by the flatness in Alicia's recital—as if she wasn't in the room but maybe twenty or thirty feet down the hallway, pacing up and down, trying to decide how much to trust. "Anything else bothering you right now?" I asked.

Alicia gave me an irritated look, shook her head no. She half stifled a yawn and arched her back, then swung her shoulders back and forth, stretching, broadcasting a sleepy sensuality. Jane looked envious, then disgusted. Gerald followed her movements with obvious interest. Perry was making a show of cleaning his glasses.

Remembering Alicia's story about her skills at poker, I wondered what she wasn't saying. "Any newer business on your mind?"

"Animals don't bare their throats casually," Alicia said. "Don't rush me." She looked at me defiantly, then checked herself in the mirror over my shoulder. She wiped away the smudged makeup underneath her eye.

"You always get even with ex-boyfriends?" Gerald asked.

Alicia chewed on her lip as she considered the question. "I don't take it kindly when someone dumps me. Most people don't, right? One other time I was so angry, I got really . . . I was dating this lawyer, fresh out of law school, and he told me about how he was so terribly concerned about the impression he made on the senior partners in his firm—straight arrow, ultra-conservative types. When he broke off with me, I decided to help him out at work. I gave him a gift I knew he'd enjoy: a subscription to *Hustler.* Since he had to spend so many hours at work, I had it delivered there. I made sure his name appeared on a few other relevant mailing lists, just to be sure." Her face looked content, full of remembered pleasure. The lipstick smudged across the bottom of her front teeth made them look small and sharp.

Perry spoke for the first time: "I'm pleased you've trusted us enough to share how vindictive you can be, when you feel hurt."

I winced. *Don't use a hammer if you're a glassblower.*

Perry glanced at me. I saw anxiety and fear, and, unfortunately, pride in his efforts.

"How do you feel about what Alicia's told you so far?" I asked the group. Jane folded her arms protectively across her chest. Gerald, slumped in his chair, sat staring at the floor, a crease between his eyes. Perry shifted restlessly back and forth. Everyone except Alicia avoided my gaze, like people lying flat in a field in a thunderstorm, afraid of becoming living lightning rods.

"How did you feel when you were telling the group about yourself?" Perry asked Alicia.

Alicia shrugged, but her rigid posture belied her nonchalance. She kept her gaze fixed on the faded curtains that framed the one-way mirror. A fox-hunting scene was repeated half a dozen times down the length of the drape. In each frozen vignette a fox ran just out of the reach of the hounds, followed by a group of hunters. A single hunter brought up the rear.

Jane wasn't wearing her wedding ring tonight, the first night she'd come without it. She kept touching the spot where it had been, gently, like an animal worrying a wound. Alicia was watching her.

"Are you married?" she asked, looking at Jane.

"Uh . . . we separated. We'll probably get back together soon, I hope, but it's still too early to tell." She looked around eagerly, with the air of someone hoping to hear that others were even more optimistic.

Gerald made a show of staring at the bookshelves. Alicia raised her eyebrows and looked skeptical. Only Perry looked encouraging.

Jane's voice got louder, more insistent. "Lots of couples separate sometime during their marriage; when they get back together, they realize how much they missed each other. Separations can help a couple appreciate each other, like the saying: 'Absence makes the heart grow fonder.'" Her voice cracked on the last word. She bunched her skirt in her fists.

"'Absence makes the heart go wander' was the way I heard it," Alicia said. "That's the way it happens. You need to get some good legal help as soon as possible, protect yourself financially," she continued in a matter-of-fact tone. "If you're not careful, you'll get cooked like a steak."

Jane made a show of smoothing the wrinkles she'd left in the sides of her skirt, and then she looked fixedly at the wall, biting her lip, her eyes shiny. When her face was more composed, she asked Alicia, "Did you ever consider that we managed perfectly well here before your arrival?"

Alicia stood up. "I don't know about the rest of you, but I need a bathroom break. I gather there's no scheduled dispensation for small bladders, but I just can't wait."

I wanted to say that there wasn't much time left, couldn't she just hold it, and caught myself. More like a grade-school teacher than a therapist.

Gerald spoke to Jane as soon as Alicia was out of the room. "It sounds like a tough time." Perry added a sympathetic murmur. For the next ten minutes Jane talked about her separation, her loneliness, and her upcoming court date to formalize her separation, her voice unpolluted by its usual saccharin edge.

They stopped talking as soon as Alicia walked in the door, her face flushed, her rapid breathing audible. She stopped inside the door, looking around. "Such sudden silence. I must have provided lots of interesting material."

Jane covered her ringless left hand with her right. Gerald reached down to pull up his socks.

"We weren't talking about you," Perry said.

*"Of course* you weren't," Alicia said.

"How do you think the group sees you so far?" I asked, trying to reach her, trying to break through.

"Unwelcome trouble." Her voice wavered. "Seems to be my strong suit . . ."

"Who in here seems most like you?" Perry asked.

Alicia looked around the circle, then up at the curtains at the side of the mirror. "The fox on those curtains. Running as hard as he can to escape the hunters and hounds. Running for his life. And the rider who's trailing behind the pack, unable to keep pace or control it . . . that's you," she said to me. Her voice was coarse and loud.

"We're already over time," Gerald said, before I could respond.

"Sounds like we have some business for next week," I said to Alicia. Not the time to end, but I could hardly set one standard for the group and another for myself. And maybe it was for the best, I thought, feeling my stomach tight with frustration—and concern. Had I erred by allowing Alicia to join the group?

I turned to push my chair back. I thought I saw a flash of light through the one-way mirror, like someone had opened the door from the observation room to the hallway. By the time I got out the door, the hallway outside was empty; maybe I'd just imagined the light. I tried the door to the observation room. It should have been locked, but the handle turned easily.

The observation room was small, the furnishings sparse. The one-way glass started three feet up one wall, the other walls were bare. A shelf ran under the glass to serve as desk space, and three chairs were pulled up underneath the shelf where observers could sit. The unaired, closed-in smell gave me hope for a moment. Then I walked all the way inside, put my hand on the amplifier for the sound system. Still warm.

I left the observation room, closing the door with unnecessary force, double-checking to make sure the lock caught.

# Chapter 6

Ever since I found Alicia's body this morning, I wanted to get out of Rugton, to go home. Now, my long day over once my therapy group had ended, I headed to my home in Piney Point Village, a Houston suburb. Old oaks tower over my house, crepe myrtle crowds beneath them, the dense growth isolating me from my neighbors.

A snarling cast-iron wolf's head is the centerpiece for my front door. On the console table in the entry, a seventeenth-century swan greets callers; carved from pine, its raised wings and coiled neck make it look as if hissing and preparing to attack. Winged griffins support the table holding the swan.

Visitors who make it past my welcoming committee find an assortment of art deco furniture. On one of my living room walls I've mounted a dozen red oak boxes at two-foot intervals where I display teapots of every size and color and age. An ornate gilt Victorian mirror hangs over the fireplace. Resting against the wall beside the sofa, a plain cardboard box holds Ian's ashes.

Hard to believe that all the weight and force of someone you loved can get distilled into a few pounds of ashes—maybe half the size of the proverbial bread-box no one uses anymore—now inert and unresponsive.

I plan to scatter Ian's ashes in the ocean off Maine, where he grew up. I haven't felt ready to make that trip yet. I keep promising myself I'll do it soon.

I thought of Queen Victoria and the forty years she spent grieving for Prince Albert—his rooms kept as they were at his death, his clothes hung in his closet, changes laid out daily. Ian's clothes still hang neatly upstairs, his socks and underwear still fill drawers. I can empathize with Victoria all too well.

I made my way to the kitchen and punched the play button on my answering machine, inspecting the contents of my refrigerator as I listened to a message from a man who wanted to sell me insurance. I poured a glass of orange juice and stuck a frozen lasagna dinner in the microwave.

This morning, after finishing with the police, I'd tried to call my father, dialing his number without consciously thinking about what I was doing. As I'd listened to the phone ringing, I remembered he was out of the country on business.

I'd been surprised at my impulse to seek comfort from my father, and by my disappointment when I realized I couldn't reach him. Maybe hopes about a parent's ability to provide solace never catches up with reality, like the belief that an umbrella really keeps you from getting wet or wearing gloves means your hands wouldn't get cold.

My mother had died giving birth to my younger brother when I was twelve, leaving my father, already stretched thin by his fledgling import business, a widower with young children. And then I was diagnosed with leukemia a year later.

I remember how I'd read matchbook covers, cereal boxes, historical tomes, natural history, anything to find a common language, trying desperately to unearth something to share with my father that would spark a response—all-too-rare moments when I'd engaged his full attention.

One memory sticks in my mind. We'd gone for a consult with an oncologist. The white-haired doctor was sitting at his desk, talking about possible treatments, when he said "The corpus of literature on childhood leukemia—"

My father had jumped to his feet, leaned across the desk toward him, his fist raised. "Don't talk like that—not those words," he'd said, his voice fierce. Then he'd pulled back, dropping his fists, his tone again so carefully neutral that I almost believed I'd imagined the incident.

In his free time my father reads books on history, botany, geology, physiology—never novels, nothing that looked like pure entertainment. When someone says "Monroe," most people probably think of Marilyn. My father is the sort of person who would think of the Doctrine.

I'd assumed my father had always dressed himself in grays and browns and beiges—until I found a picture of him with my mother shortly before her death. Dressed in a red sweatshirt and red-and-blue plaid shorts, his arm tight around her, he was smiling widely. I'd had to look twice to be sure it was he. I've framed the picture, reassuring proof that my scattered memories of someone not colored gray weren't forged by wistfulness.

My father hadn't wanted me to become a psychologist. "Not a real science," he'd said. "Study something practical, like chemistry or engineering."

I didn't doubt his love, but my father was hardly the best person to comfort me now.

As I ate my lasagna, I watched a moth with tattered wings beating against my closed glass door in a half-hearted way, as though it had given up its illusion of a better world but still felt compelled to go through the motions of looking for paradise. I opened the door to release it, then watched it flutter every which way except toward freedom. Finally I herded it step by step toward the outdoors, using two newspaper sections as goad and barrier, until it finally saw the new vista and made good its escape.

I knew something about fortunate escapes. Married

once before when I was twenty-two, divorced within a year, I'd fed my wedding dress to a bonfire while swearing never again.

Then I met Ian, drawn to him like a dowser toward hidden springs of water. He gave me a sense of belonging. For once, I hadn't felt out of step. And then he was killed last October.

With Ian, the pleasure on his face had shone honest and clear when I walked in the house at the end of the day—a warmth so genuine and solid it made me overlook how very different we were.

Neither of us had been much good at compromising at first, and we'd had some interesting times rubbing up against each other, sparking like iron and flint. I didn't look forward to evenings with strangers; Ian had loved parties and late nights on the town. He'd been remarkably sociable; talkative and garrulous, he'd had no problem in his work as a journalist with calling strangers, asking questions. Not willing to take no for an answer, he'd turn on the charm and push all the harder.

We'd been together six months before I realized some of the reasons behind our differences. Out to dinner with a couple who were friends of his, I'd felt uncomfortable all evening in the face of their pervasive acrimony toward each other, their smile-and-slash repartee. I'd wished, not for the first time, that I could shut off my watchfulness, my scrutiny so I could miss behavior and focus only on words, ignoring the blaring message of the emotional subtext—like a violinist teaching beginning students who yearned for the talent to turn tone-deaf at will. I couldn't wait for the evening to end.

As we were driving home, I'd said, "Things are pretty rotten between them. Is the trouble recent, or have they always been like this?"

"They get along just fine," Ian had said, laughing. "They don't mean anything by the way they go at each other—just their way of playing."

He had enjoyed the evening immensely. I'd tried to explain to him how tense and strained the dinner had felt to me, but it was like trying to describe shades of blue and green to someone who was color-blind.

Ian had been absolutely astounded when they separated six months later.

I remembered a story Ian had told me once. "I went for a massage training session when I was in college. All the students worked on each other. You know one of the best things in the world? Having one person massaging each limb—four people working on you at once. Heaven, absolute heaven."

I'd shuddered at the image, flashing back to times when I'd been held down for spinal taps as an adolescent. Four strangers touching me at once sounded as much fun as being plastered face-to-face against a stranger on a crowded elevator.

Before he stormed out of the house the night he died, Ian had said to me, "You keep part of yourself at a distance, protected. When you're with me, you're not ever quite there, even in the really good times. Maybe as much as ninety percent, but never all the way, never fully trusting."

I couldn't imagine that I would ever be different. Could ever be different. Ian had seen it as a conscious choice I made, to hold back.

Ian had been going too fast when he misjudged a bend in the road, the police said, based on the skid marks. Maybe if we hadn't just had a fight, Ian would've been more careful. Maybe he'd still be alive.

After Ian's death I lost the ability to feel comfortable alone at home, unable to shut out all the odd bumps and creaks and groans. I finally got a security system for my house. Now, looking at the darkness outside the window, I realized I hadn't reset the alarm after I got home.

I opened a bottle of wine after I set the alarm, drinking it in large gulps, like bad-tasting medicine. I thought about the last time I'd talked with Alicia, a week before her death.

I called her late Tuesday afternoon because I'd gotten a message from Carlyle Stocklin; he was spiking a fever and didn't think he'd be well enough to come to group tomorrow. Norman Zuckerman was still out of town, so Carlyle's absence meant we wouldn't have the four members needed for a quorum for Wednesday night's group.

Alicia had answered on the third ring. She took the news about the group cancellation in silence, then said, "I was thinking of calling you. I know psychologists don't prescribe drugs, but can you hook me up with someone who'll give me a prescription for sleeping pills?"

"Sleeping pills?"

"I've been having the same nightmare—waking me up every few nights—for the last month; I can't fall back to sleep afterward. Now I've had it three nights running, and I'm dead on my feet."

"What's it about?"

"In my dream I'm lying in bed, watching my bedroom doorknob turning. It's turning really slowly, but I can see it moving. I know they're after me; they want me, me especially—there's a very personal sense about it. They've come for me, they've caught up with me. I'm stuck. Frozen. I want to scream, but I can't move, can't even whisper. Then the door starts to open.

"It's still in slow motion, like they know I'm set in concrete, and they're taking their time to make it even worse. It's dark beyond the door; that's all I can see for the longest time. Then, I see what it is. I've been expecting a man, and it isn't—it isn't a man at all. It would be a relief if it were." I'd heard her take a deep breath, let it out slowly.

"It's a skeleton. I can see the empty eye sockets in the skull, and they seem to be looking right at me. It starts walking toward me, a confident walk, not like a pile of bones, but like it knows just what it has in mind, and it's looking forward to it. Then it reaches out a bony finger, about to touch my shoulder. That's when I wake up screaming and shaking."

She cleared her throat. "Can you help me get a prescription?"

The dream's message bothered me. A warning to herself? An expression of grievance? I wondered, briefly, if it was simply another fancified story she'd embellished to get a prescription for an occasional restless night. It didn't feel that way. "Would you be willing to talk about your dream in group, next time we meet?"

"I—I'm not sure." Something in her voice made me pause. Maybe a feeling of vulnerability that I hadn't heard before. I remembered the way she'd jabbed me each time I'd seen her. Vulnerability ringed with barbed wire.

"The skeleton never touches you?" I'd asked. "You always wake up before then?"

"No, it doesn't." Alicia had sounded surprised. "It's never managed to touch me."

"That makes it easier. If it still troubles you in a few weeks, we can meet individually, maybe try some brief hypnotic work. But I think you'll find a way to stop your nightmares before then."

"How?"

I knew a lot about nightmares, about people's windows into darkness. I'd begun exploring the topic because of personal interest and had learned some useful clinical strategies along the way. I'd tensed at the obvious disbelief in her voice.

"Two things. First, think back to what was happening when you started having the nightmares, especially the feelings around that time. Second, think of associations to the parts of the dream, just like the class lie detection exercise. If you think about the skeleton, you may discover something surprising about it— something you never noticed before."

"You mean you won't help me get sleeping pills." I'd pictured Alicia holding the phone at an angle from her ear, looking at it in disgust.

I'd started to explain what I thought she already knew, that sleeping pills suppress one stage of sleep and nightmares get worse right after stopping the pills, but she interrupted me.

"Bet you've got one of those T-shirts that shows an empty couch with a printed message underneath: 'Thanks for not telling me your troubles.' I guess I'll see you next Wednesday—if you can get a quorum together." The line went dead.

I'd thought about her request for sleeping pills. Aside from the obvious, it could have been her way of trying to get assurance that she was special and I'd take care of her. Or it could have been another way of telling me that I wasn't helpful, as she'd done twice before. If I'd had a better sense of who she was and what she wanted from therapy, I could have made a better guess.

I'd felt like the visually impaired, leading the blind.

Now I drank wine and asked myself the questions I'd been avoiding all day: Was my judgment so impaired that I'd missed all the signs with Alicia? Had I been so obsessed with my grief that I'd missed her messages, her warnings? If I'd been more attentive, would she be alive now?

If only I could have had Ian beside me now, his arms around me, holding me tight. He would have soothed me, helped me believe that things could work out.

I went upstairs and got ready for bed. I was a little drunk and very tired, but sleep eluded me for most of the night.

# Chapter 7

On Thursday morning, the day after Alicia's death, Roy Hilderbrand belched as he lay on the hospital bed in front of me. Not the mouth-covered, restrained murmur of a housebroken adult, but a deliberately amplified sound, like a seven-year-old trying to outshine his best friend. Loud and long, smelling of sour milk and garlic. He stared at me throughout his production.

I stared back, not blinking. I thought about how satisfying it would be to turn my back and walk out of his room without speaking—or, better yet, to reply in kind. But even if I could find some way to justify a return of his courtesies, I'd have been hard pressed to match his volume and timbre.

The consult form I'd received described Roy as a "22-year-old unemployed married man with self-inflicted burns," followed by a request to evaluate suicidal potential. An ordinary, routine clinical evaluation that felt like a perverse challenge the morning after finding Alicia's body.

I worked to keep my voice neutral as I looked at Roy now. "Tell me about your accident."

Roy had been at least a week without a shave, judging by the clumps of stubble on his chin and cheeks. His black hair, a damp and tangled thicket, probably hadn't seen a comb for at least as long. A blue snake tattooed on his right bicep crawled among the scabs that peppered his arm. His feet and ankles were much worse: puffy, blistered blotches of thick dark crusts, oozing shiny wet in spots.

"My father-in-law's responsible for my burns. Totally responsible."

The thin-faced man spoke with obvious effort, perhaps to accentuate his complaints about the soreness of his throat, still raw (he maintained) from smoke inhalation and the nasogastric tube used to extract pills and alcohol from his stomach. The nurses said the soreness from the NG tube should have been gone—long gone—soon after its removal. It was four days by now.

"How so?"

"He made me do it. Made me set myself on fire."

He looked down at his right shoulder and clenched his fist; the blue snake tatoo seemed to slither when his muscle rippled. He made a point of admiring his show, prolonging it when I didn't comment, stretching out the writhing movement.

*Scintillating social skills.*

Finally he looked back at me. "The bastard wouldn't help out anymore on our rent. He knew we needed money, needed it bad. He acted like losing my job was my fault."

Roy had a picture of himself on his bedside table, posing in a muscle shirt, his arms flexed as he lifted dumbbells, a pit bull by his side. A shadow in the background might have been his wife, but it was hard to see any details.

"How did he force you to set yourself on fire?" A man who kept his own picture beside him for comfort—hardly the best sign.

"Said he didn't care what happened to me. Or to Betty, if she's stupid enough to stay with me. He told me I could burn in hell before he'd lift a finger to help us again."

Without hearing anything else, I could guess what

else he'd say, directly or roundabout: He was the type who enjoyed lying, fooling people, making sure people knew he was in control of any relationship. He believed good guys lost, and he'd learned to look for the bad parts of people. I could see him gambling with strangers, buying them drinks, and then not understanding, somehow, when his new-found friends cheated him.

He was not at risk for another suicide gesture, I'd have bet without hesitation two days ago, before hearing any more. But that was two days ago. Before Alicia's death.

"He was supposed to stop me. If he'd acted right, I wouldn't be in this mess now."

Could Alicia have miscalculated, assumed she'd be found in time, before the pills and booze killed her? Not likely.

"You wouldn't have a cigarette on you, would you?" Roy winked, attempting what he probably thought passed as an ingratiating smile.

A predictable request from a man who'd spent the last four days in a hospital where smoking was absolutely forbidden. I shook my head no.

He looked peeved, as if I'd evaded my responsibilities. "I thought shrinks were supposed to be helpful."

This was part and parcel of the way he usually acted, the nurses said: moaning, demanding that more be done for him, intolerant of noise from other patients, manageable when he had a nurse constantly at his bedside, working himself up to screaming fits when left alone, at his worst whenever a new admission needed the nurses' full attention, shouting his resentment when the attending physician and his covey of residents, interns, and medical students visited other patients before him during their morning rounds: "Doesn't anyone care about me?"

His eyes had the beady look of a burrowing animal peering up to check for lurking predators. "You can sit on the bed with me while we talk." He ran his eyes down my body to emphasize the crudeness of his gesture.

"I'll stand." I was glad the yellow paper gown worn by visitors to the burn unit hid my body from him as I thought about the way he'd condensed an entire series of invitations to trouble into one. He'd been told about the dangers of contamination, why staff and visitors alike entered the unit masked and gowned, hands encased in plastic gloves, shoes shielded by disposable booties. Now he invited me to join him among the rule breakers. Bold enough; for an instant, I admired his nerve, if not his means.

"So, what good's a shrink to me? I'm not crazy. I've got nothing to talk about with you."

I looked at him and counted to ten, deliberately delaying my response, hoping he might have second thoughts in the silence. "Probably not crazy . . . but setting yourself on fire doesn't strike me as the best move you could've made."

A nurse poked her head inside the door. "Dr. McAlistar, please stop by the nursing station when you're done—someone else for you to see."

I kept looking at the nurse, as if making up my mind about leaving now. Immediately Roy began talking, filling the room with a gruff baritone, crowding his competition out of the room.

I heard his story of how he'd brooded, gotten drunk, swallowed pills, and swirled gasoline over himself as he stood in his father-in-law's front yard, waiting for someone to stop him. Then, when he couldn't hold out any longer, he'd struck a match. The story was told in a voice crosscut with resentment and a grudging sense of what the world owed him.

His drunken haste and a near-empty gas can had saved him, his admission chart note said. Which was bad luck for others, subsequent chart notes implied, detailing how he'd acted on the unit: A nurse had given Roy a bottle of mercurochrome, telling him to paint over the raw areas and scabs on his arms—part of his training in the self-care skills needed for discharge; she'd walked away while he insisted he couldn't manage without her help. Roy had poured the full bottle

over himself, his bed, the floor; when the nurse returned, he'd told her he just wasn't capable of control-
ling his shaking hands. It was unreasonable to expect
him to manage on his own, he'd said.

Now he coughed, cleared his throat, reached beside
him for a tissue, and spat into it. He glanced at the
wastebasket beside his bed. With an exaggerated trem-
or in his hand, he dropped the tissue on the floor a foot
away from the basket.

Phlegm, brown and viscous, flowed from the tissue
onto the linoleum. "Help me, would you?" He gestured
at the tissue.

I was hot under the paper gown, tired of standing.
"Classy behavior." I pitched my voice flat and low,
deliberate, hoping to sting.

"Huh?" Underneath his sullenness, there was a hint
of surprise. I hoped. "I don't need this shit from you,"
he finally said. "The nurses'll treat me better—they
know enough to see I need help."

I pointed at his picture on the bedside table. "After
all that time lifting weights—pity you're not strong
enough to lift a Kleenex, isn't it?"

Avoiding my eyes, he pulled himself out of bed,
picked up the tissue, and dropped it in the wastebasket.

When he looked up at me again, he had the cunning
look of a man standing on a balcony above a crowded
street, caring only if he'd get more attention by dropping a flower or a flowerpot. "If you knew what it's like
to hurt so bad, if you had any idea, you'd treat me
better."

Other burn patients had told me that the pain was
worse than anything you could imagine. Not so much
the burns themselves, but the treatments: cutting
off the dead skin, spreading antibacterial ointment
over the freshly opened wounds, removing undamaged
skin from buttocks or thighs and grafting it over the
burns—procedures that came with iron-clad guaran-
tees for misery.

When I didn't respond immediately, he looked as if

he'd just scored a coup. "I bet you've never even spent a night in a hospital," he crowed.

I couldn't begin to count the nights I'd spent in hospitals when I was growing up, after I was diagnosed with leukemia. The memories still made me stiffen reflexively: Needles, lying stiff and straight for X rays, the feeling of numbing medications traveling down my body . . .

I'd hardly been a model patient myself. By the third day of my first admission, I'd learned not to sleep too soundly. Better to sleep fitfully, attuned to the noises and smells and shadows moving through the night, than be jolted awake by the touch of a stranger's hands. Thereafter I refused or feigned swallowing sleeping pills, hiding them under my tongue until I was alone.

My time in hospitals had fed my interest in watching people, trying to fathom the reasons behind their behavior; I'd tried to make sense of small gestures, the words people chose, and made a game of guessing what they'd do next—anything to make the situation more predictable, more controllable. By concentrating on watching, on figuring out, I could travel outside myself—away from my own pain and isolation and uncertainty.

"Hard for you to believe that anyone hurts as much as you," I said to Roy now.

"Damn right." Roy picked up the picture from his bedside table and pointed at the dog. "That's my pit bull. Name's Bulldozer. A pit bull—get it?"

"Did you think about how family and friends might react to your death?" I asked Roy Hilderbrand. Suicidal people often have elaborate scenarios about the reactions of friends and family on hearing the news of their death; Roy didn't.

Dying in the Rugton parking lot didn't seem to fit with Alicia—unless I'd missed something very meaningful in her reactions to me.

I walked Roy through the standard questions about suicide risk indicators: Disposal of property, self-neglect, severe insomnia, radical shifts in behavior, no future plans, loss of an important relationship, "anniversary" reactions—the time of year when other losses had occurred, economic problems, alcohol and drug problems. None of them fit Roy except for the obvious ones, but I hadn't expected that they would.

I was checking off the list for Alicia at the same time, not seeing anything in her that should have set off alarms any more than in Roy—at least up to the last time I'd seen her. I still couldn't make sense of Alicia killing herself—let alone at Rugton.

I remembered Oliver Tate's broad hints about Alicia and her therapy; I cursed myself for not asking him what she'd said.

After I finished with Roy, I saw the other patient the nurse had mentioned. Then I wrote a note in Roy Hilderbrand's chart. He was behaving like an obnoxious brat—but he was among strangers, feeling out of control and afraid, in pain, lacking a sense of how to cope. I wrote that he was no longer an acute suicide risk, a judgment that would relieve the nurses and rapidly alter their tolerance for his behavior. I suggested that the nurses adopt a consistent, contractual approach: Tell him in advance when painful things would be happening, provide choices where possible, set clear limits.

As I left the burn unit, I found myself shaking my head as I thought about Alicia. I had enormous gaps in my understanding of her—but I couldn't believe she'd committed suicide in front of Rugton. It felt all wrong.

I stopped in the hallway, picturing her as I'd seen her yesterday, wearing only a faded T-shirt and shorts, no makeup, no jewelry. I knew what had been bothering me.

She wouldn't have killed herself without dressing for it—not Alicia Erle. For her last moment, she'd have done everything possible to make herself memorable. If she had taken the trouble to drive to Rugton, she would have dressed better for her last appearance.

I considered the only real alternative, the idea I'd

kept pushing out of my mind yesterday as too preposterous. Patients recreate the same kinds of troubled personal relationships in therapy that cause problems in daily life—or so the theory goes. If Alicia's impact on me and the group mirrored real life, she had a remarkable capacity for kindling powerful emotions. Powerful enough for someone in her "real life" to kill her?

# Chapter 8

Rugton Hall, the Psychiatry Department building, stands one hundred yards away from the rest of the hospital. Rugton staff refer to the remainder of the hospital as the "main house," as if our building were the servants' quarters.

Overhanging eaves cast Rugton's entrances into perpetual shadow. The hospital smell, not as strong as in the main house, remains a constant undertone; over there the antiseptic smell is adulterated with the scent of too much disposable plastic, fresh out of sterile packaging, and cafeteria food cooked beyond redemption. The dusty staleness of Rugton smelled of worry and doubt and remorse to me as I walked back to my office from the burn unit.

Built as a state-of-the-art psychiatric hospital in the 1950s, Rugton Hall has the air of a middle-aged man struggling to pretend he hasn't changed much at all, not really, since college. Stained linoleum tiles have been replaced in spots with newer, lighter tiles that stand out like gray hairs on a dark head. The paging system works intermittently, sometimes blasting visitors in the corridors with a request for Dr. Salzman, sometimes emitting a querulous static grumble. Peeling room numbers, once embossed in gold on the wooden doors, have been supplemented by black plastic nameplates beside the door with a slot for the newest occupant's tag. The bulletin board by the ground-floor departmental office is layered with announcements of professional meetings that convened two months ago and faculty positions available last year.

As I walked up the stairs to my office, I remembered a time two weeks ago when I'd been waiting for the light to change so I could get out of the medical center after work on Friday. I'd turned on the radio and heard the Beatles singing about a hard day's night. I started singing along, beating time on the steering wheel.

I'd glanced over at the car to my left, a gray Ford Escort, and saw Alicia Erle staring at me, a half smile on her face. I nodded at her and turned away. With great difficulty I'd resisted the impulse to gun the engine as soon as the light changed.

I'd hoped she was far enough away so she couldn't see my flushed face.

I don't do much individual therapy. More to the point, I actively avoid taking on patients beyond my group and a handful of individual sessions each week. I only follow those patients with whom I feel a connection, a sense that we speak enough of the same language to work well together; for those where it's missing, I make careful referrals. I haven't figured out the common denominator, if there is one.

I hadn't liked parts of Alicia, but I'd felt connected to her. Stronger than usual. That's why I didn't hesitate to have her join my group, despite our rocky beginning. Since then I've certainly had ample reason to question my judgment.

I went to two committee meetings after lunch, each lasting an hour and accomplishing little. One of the three psychometrists that I supervised reminded me that tomorrow would be her last day at work, offering me a discount if I used her new catering business.

I decided to take a break before starting on a stack of paperwork to get a Dr Pepper, hoping the caffeine, the twenty-three secret ingredients, or the walk would give me some energy. My shortcut to the cafeteria took me through the hallway outside the art therapy offices, where a dozen drawings were mounted between sheets of plexiglass. The display changed every week when the art therapy inpatient group took up a new theme. As I walked by the latest series, I counted two cats, one elephant, one giraffe, one leopard, one lion, one parrot, one bear, one fish, and two four-legged somethings where enthusiasm had outdistanced artistic skill.

I paused in front of the last frame, captured by the artist's skill. Strokes of green created a leafy jungle; a red hibiscus bloomed amid the lushness, and a chameleon climbed the hibiscus stalk. It was signed boldly at the bottom: VERMILION. As I stepped back to admire it, I saw Glee walking toward me.

"Thelma Lou told me she saw you heading this way when I stopped by your office. How're you doing today?" she asked, looking at me closely.

"More or less," I said, smiling and shrugging. I wasn't ready to talk about my suspicions about Alicia yet. "Thanks for the lawyer's name. I've got an appointment next week." Glee had recommended a woman who'd had lots of experience with malpractice cases.

"Let me know how it goes, or if there's anything I can do," Glee said—and meaning it, I knew. Glee had been a lifeline since I lost Ian, treating my feelings about his death very matter-of-factly. She was open to talking about him; she didn't push the topic, she didn't avoid it. She didn't wince or withdraw when I got weepy or angry. A good woman, a fine friend.

"Thanks. I appreciate it. You left a message for me late Tuesday about a lab problem. I never got back to you. What's up?"

"I wasn't going to bring it up again this week— figured you already had enough on your mind. There's a problem with one of your psychometrists."

I had a bad feeling about the likely source of the problem—not one I was eager to tackle.

She gestured at the frames on the wall. "Personally, I'd be an otter if I were choosing another form. Sliding around. Free-spirited. Mischievous. Spending all my time near the water, not just on weekends. You?"

Exactly right, I thought, looking at eyes that matched the green baize of a pool table.

"A pterodactyl," I said, without a pause. "Big teeth. Thick skin. A cold-blooded reptile, able to fly away at will." It wasn't the way I would have responded before Ian's death, I realized. I hadn't felt the need for thick skin with him.

"Certainly not just an ordinary bird." Glee raised her eyebrows. "Why don't you come with me on the boat this weekend—we'll go down Friday night and come back Sunday evening. Meet some men, if you're interested, eat good food, and have some fun."

Glee keeps her sailboat docked at Galveston and spends most weekends sailing in the Gulf, usually with a man on board. She normally juggles two or more relationships at once, calling it her spare-tire strategy.

Glee fixed me up with dates a couple of times since Ian died. I'd felt as awkward as a teenager, a home-grown tomato pretending to have the thicker skin of the store-bought variety.

"Thanks, but I've got plans already." Before she could ask me something that might expose my subterfuge, I asked her about the lab problem she'd mentioned as we headed toward the cafeteria.

"Stuart Crego."

I was sorry to find I'd guessed right. This wasn't the kind of problem I looked forward to trying to fix.

"Stuart tested a patient I'd referred," Glee said. "Civil case. Memory problems following an auto accident. The patient had already been tested once; the defense asked me for an independent determination."

I've done my share of forensic work and I consider myself good—but Glee is great. She brings a particular kind of strong, directed intelligence, a remarkable sincerity, and a staggering memory to the cases she deigns to champion as her "causes." I once watched Glee testify as an expert witness. The plaintiff's attorney, twenty years her senior, had persisted in treating her with the kind of flirtatious gallantry that spells condescension; then he made the mistake of asking her to cite all available data to back up one of her statements. He finally stopped her after she'd given him the full citation for the fifth article and showed no signs of stopping.

Glee reminds me of the German Raiders in the early years of World War II, ships whose powerful engines and artillery were camouflaged by false sides to make them look like slow freighters from a distance. Up close, they dropped the facade, exposing the deck guns so they could use them freely.

"Stuart got the patient confused with someone else, or so he says. He only administered half the test battery I requested. The part he did administer had three scoring errors."

When we reached the cafeteria, Glee broke off while she got iced tea and I got my Dr Pepper. After we paid for our drinks and started walking back, Glee continued: "Based on the data I saw, I think the woman's trying to exaggerate deficits to get a bigger settlement, but Stuart botched the testing, so I don't have the data to base a solid defense. The family's only obligated to go through one independent assessment for the defense, they're saying."

Bad news, indeed. I told Glee how I'd found errors on tests Stuart had administered and scored last week. Obvious carelessness. When I'd met with him, he sat stony faced as I listed his infractions, acting as if I were selling insurance and he was steeling himself to sit through the presentation out of politeness. I'd been concerned enough to write a memo to his file about the problem and his response.

"I'll talk with Stuart again. One more strike and he's out."

With one psychometrist leaving tomorrow, only one of the three would be left if I had to fire Stuart. I could imagine Kurt von Reichenau's reaction if reports of lab troubles reached his ears now.

When we reached Glee's office, she asked, "Got time to sit and chat?"

I shook my head. "I'll go talk to Stuart now and get it over with."

The sound of Stuart Crego's harsh, angry voice reached me when I was still ten feet away from his closed office door. I heard a shrill female voice respond. Then Stuart said, "You say these tests are worthless, but you aren't really trying very hard, are you? Wasting my time and yours with your bluster."

I knocked and Stuart opened the door. "I'm busy with a patient right now." He looked pointedly at the cardboard sign clipped to the door: TESTING IN PROGRESS. DO NOT DISTURB. He started to close the door.

In profile he displayed a sharply etched chin and high forehead. Head on, he looked decidedly less appealing: sloping shoulders, too-long arms, a damp sheen on his face. His balding head added years to his appearance, making him look closer to forty than thirty. His moralistic air aged him further, weighing him down with righteous anger that had etched wrinkles of displeasure around his mouth.

Stuart reminded me of a big bird of prey.

"I need to talk with you for a minute. Now." I walked a few feet down the hall and he followed me with obvious reluctance, his lips pursed.

I pitched my voice low. "I could hear your conversation out here, even with your door closed. You can't speak to patients like that. Tell the patient something's come up, and you need to end the session now; tell her someone else will call her to schedule a time for finishing."

"But it was so obvious she was malingering! The only way I was going to get valid data was to call her on it."

"No. Your job is to administer tests, by the book, so they're standardized—remaining courteous to patients as you test them. Come to my office as soon as you've made excuses to the patient."

Ten minutes later Stuart walked into my office without knocking and sat down. "Let me set the record straight. The girl I was testing wasn't even trying. She got belligerent when I told her she needed to try harder; then she started bad-mouthing the tests. I needed to handle her firmly, not soft-soap her. I've dealt with plenty of patients like this girl before. I know what to do."

"How old is this 'girl' you were testing?"

He grimaced. "Forty-four."

I let his answer hang in the air. "You were way out of line, and you know it."

Stuart Crego had been hired during my month-long leave of absence after Ian's death. I hadn't liked him from the beginning. The first time I saw him, he was sitting in his office with his door open, talking with a friend on the phone: "Before I came to this lab to offer enlightenment . . ." He'd pronounced his words too carefully, his voice pitched unnaturally low so that he sounded forced and artificial. Though he was ostensibly joking, I knew he wasn't speaking facetiously.

Now he looked at me with a faint smile. "If you don't like my work, you can have my resignation. I'll walk out of here right now."

I realized that he expected me to beg him to stay on since I was already short one psychometrist; more, he expected me to beg him to stay since he thought he was so good.

I didn't think it was reasonable to trade a chronic headache for a passing upset stomach. "Fine. I accept your resignation."

He sat looking at me. The veins in his forehead swelled. His face flushed. "You'll regret your . . . wretched judgment."

# Chapter 9

**J**ust before five on Thursday afternoon I went to talk with Thelma Lou, our clinic receptionist. "Has Alicia Erle's chart turned up?"

"Not yet. I'm really sorry, I can't think what could've happened." Thelma Lou was in her early fifties, short and wide, her forehead furrowed with worry. "I looked everywhere I could think of. No sign of it. But I'll keep looking."

Not good news at all. I'd been hoping Thelma Lou would have located Alicia's chart by now.

Thelma Lou made a show of straightening the Lucite frame that held the newest Polaroid snapshot of Greta, the cement goose who sat beside the doorstep of her house. Today Greta was dressed in a new outfit, a pink bonnet and pink-flowered cape, and Thelma Lou waited for me to comment.

"Cute. Very cute."

Greta's picture frame had a lightning bolt etched in the upper left-hand corner, Thelma Lou's trademark since she'd been struck by lightning four years ago. Phone messages taken by Thelma Lou might bear her own initials, a webbed foot, or LL, for Lightning Lady. Her LL signature meant she'd been having trouble with her memory that day, a side effect of her close encounter with lightning—invoked whenever she had trouble locating a chart among the packed metal shelves in the room behind her desk. The appearance of LL on Thelma Lou's messages at least once a week testified to the frequency of misfiled charts. Now I guessed she was trying to remind me of her memory problems, hoping for understanding.

"I'm missing another of your charts—I couldn't find Carlyle Stocklin's chart when I went to file your note from his session with his wife," Thelma Lou said, looking away. "Bad couple of weeks. I'm very sorry."

She almost always found charts eventually, I told myself; Alicia's chart would surely resurface soon.

Thelma Lou's comment reminded me that I needed to talk to Carlyle Stocklin. I wanted to ask if he'd recovered from the asthma attack that had kept him out of group Wednesday night—and to find out if he was really planning on returning after missing his third group in a row. I left a message on his home answering machine, skeptical about his latest in a series of elaborate excuses. He'd been less than truthful before.

When Carlyle called to apologize after missing group two weeks ago, he explained that an important meeting at Eichon, the pharmaceutical company where he worked, had run much later than expected—which was why he hadn't been able to call to let me know he wouldn't be at group. Then he asked if I'd see him together with his wife Bethany, right away. "She wants a joint session. She's—she's thinking about leaving me. Says I've lied to her long enough." I wasn't surprised. Carlyle, a forty-year-old British biochemist, was a handsome man who seemed all too interested in his impact on women during his six months in the group.

The following afternoon I entered the reception area where Carlyle and Bethany Stocklin sat waiting. The carpet deadened my steps, and I watched them, unobserved, as I approached. What I saw wasn't reassuring.

Bethany's glossy brown hair was drawn back in an immaculate, austere twist. In profile she had a classical look: high forehead, patrician nose, full lips. She held a manila folder in her lap, and an open briefcase half full of other folders rested at her feet, but her attention was fixed on Carlyle, sitting in the chair to her left. Bethany watched him without turning her head toward him, keeping her back straight and her head high, the vigilant alertness of a stalking cat.

Carlyle clutched an old *People* magazine, open to a picture of a woman in a bikini, but he was staring at the blank wall opposite him. His black hair, shot through with gray-white streaks, didn't move when he shook his head back and forth once, sharply, as if confirming his decision against something.

Carlyle put down the magazine and absently toyed with his wedding band, taking it off, putting it on again. Bethany blinked and swallowed as he removed his ring.

Not the kind of trouble I looked forward to meeting. I felt a sense of intrusion as I approached. "I'm Haley McAlistar." I held out my hand to Bethany. Standing, Carlyle smoothed his tie and smiled brightly. Bethany didn't look at me; in one smooth, sinuous motion she returned the folder to the briefcase on the floor, then stood. She ignored my outstretched hand, shifting her body at an angle to block Carlyle, who had taken a step forward with his hand out. Only when I started to drop my hand did Bethany finally acknowledge the gesture, returning my handshake with an uncomfortably tight grip, her face grim.

Most women would have walked gracelessly, precariously, in heels as high as hers, but Bethany strolled down the hall to my office as if she'd been wearing sneakers, looking around as though inspecting the premises, her expression suggesting the report would be unfavorable. When they reached my office, Bethany sat on the edge of a chair, her hands rolled into fists, her right fist covering her left. Carlyle sat down beside her.

He spoke first. "Shall I tell our story?" He glanced in Bethany's direction, but he didn't look up far enough to meet her eyes, and he didn't wait for her response.

Bethany jumped in with, "I don't think that . . ." even as Carlyle started to speak. They both talked simultaneously, escalating in volume and intensity.

I waited to see the outcome of the contest, then held up my hand like a traffic cop when it became clear that neither would voluntarily yield the floor. Neither looked pleased at my intervention.

"Each of you needs to get a chance to speak without interruption. Carlyle, you started first; what made you schedule this appointment?" Bethany had folded her arms across her chest; Carlyle gave her a self-satisfied look that made me regret my choice.

"As I told you the very first time I called you, Dr. Martinez referred me to you. He thought my stomach problems might be related to stress in my marriage, but Bethany refused to come with me to discuss things." Carlyle's British accent gave his words a sense of authority.

I ignored his implicit plea to blame Bethany, asking, "But what happened that you called yesterday?"

Carlyle took a deep breath and let it out slowly. He didn't look at me or Bethany. He tapped his left foot, then his right foot. On his thin, elegant feet—small for a man of his size—he wore black loafers made of such supple leather that I could see the muscles of his foot ripple when he tapped it. European shoes—probably Italian—the heels at least half an inch higher than the domestic varieties. I found it interesting that a man who stood over six feet wore shoes to make him look even taller.

Bethany watched him, her lip curled in disgust, before she spoke. "I left a message asking you to tell Carlyle to call me before he left for home after group. He never called, but he said he'd been at group."

A well-planned sting operation, and I'd been set up as part of it.

"Haley, *you* remember I was in group. You must have forgotten to give me the message." I saw Bethany's eyebrows lift when Carlyle called me by my first name, the only movement in the pool of stillness around her.

Outside my window someone tooted a horn—beep-beep-beep, waited for five seconds, then beeeep-beeeep-beeeep.

Carlyle fondled the lapels of his expensive gray suit; set off by a red paisley silk tie and matching pocket handkerchief, it would have done him justice at any board meeting, any dinner party short of black tie—or any funeral. I looked at Carlyle without saying a thing, knowing that the absence of a response rendered the verdict that Bethany was seeking.

"I knew he was lying, but he wouldn't admit it," she said to me. "I came because I need to know if you think he's capable of changing. I don't think he is, but if I'm all wet, I need you to tell me that, too. Or maybe I should just bail out now." She covered her mouth with her hand.

When she put her hand down, I could see a flourishing cold sore on her upper lip, now only partly hidden by makeup. Another symptom of the sense of struggle she wore like a cloak.

I remembered how Carlyle had confessed in group that he'd slept with a woman he met when he was out of town on business. But only that one time, he'd insisted. Only that one time. "Why don't you ask him?" I said to Bethany.

Avoiding my glance, Carlyle quickly cut in: "If you could believe I was faithful, would you want to try to work things out?"

From across the waiting room Bethany had looked no older than midtwenties, the illusion fed by the grace of her movements. Up closer, the fine tracery of wrinkles around her eyes and mouth that even artful makeup couldn't conceal proclaimed a woman in her early forties. Her expression aged her more, an aloofness, an air of condescension in the way her mouth turned up on one side as she spoke. "Maybe." Bethany's voice was low, a note of hesitancy in it that called for help.

"She spends all her time trying to trap me," Carlyle said.

Almost immediately she schooled her voice back into scorn. "After I married him, I found out that Carlyle had been kicked out of medical school for cheating on an exam. I only found out by accident. A whole part of his life I'd never known existed, something I swore would never happen to me after what I went through with my father and Noll. Of course I have trouble believing him——"

"It was an honor-code issue. Trivial. I couldn't bring myself to inform on a friend, so when they caught him, they booted me out, too." His voice got louder. "Bethany's a first-class businesswoman, senior vice president in charge of sales for Litvak, second biggest insurance company in the state. Behind her desk in her office, she's got this elegant little framed needlepoint motto that one of her staffers stitched because she'd heard her say it so often: 'Go for the jugular,' surrounded by rosebuds and ivy. Her motto at work and home."

Carlyle hadn't mentioned being expelled from medical school during his therapy. I asked Bethany, "Your father and Noll?"

"My devil-may-care father crashed his car when he was drunk. He ended up a vegetable. He'd been with another woman when it happened—not the first time—so my mother wasn't about to take care of him. She wanted to put him in a nursing home. I thought maybe he'd recover if I kept him home and took good enough care of him. He needed total care for a year before he finally died: feeding, diapering, wiping the snot from his nose. After he died, I found a letter he'd written to his mistress. He'd been planning to run away with her, start a new life under a new name.

"Then I caught Noll, my first husband, with his old girlfriend just six months after our wedding."

"That's a dreadful story," I said. "I can understand why you have trouble trusting Carlyle."

A beige leather skirt, shorter than fashion or good taste decreed, molded itself around Bethany's small waist, making her long legs an artistic statement. The embroidered tiger on her jade cotton sweater was frozen in an arching leap over the word MOZAMBIQUE. Hardly the daytime clothing I expected from a corporate executive; maybe she hadn't been at her office today, or had already been home and changed before the four o'clock appointment. Or maybe Bethany had chosen her clothes today for their provocative, nose-thumbing value.

"There's always a plausible story, always an explanation, always a reason to believe Carlyle. His stories wear thin—very thin—after a while. And you've just seen him demonstrate, again, that he's an ace at changing the subject." Bethany gave me a look—raised eyebrows and a shrug—as if she didn't know what to do with him, and no one else would either.

"He's just not there much for me. Not much at all. He withdraws into his work. And now he's seeing someone else." She looked at the floor as she spoke, her tone flat.

"That's not fair. She assumes because I have to work long hours that I'm with someone else. I'm still relatively new in the company. I have to play the game."

He turned to me. "Our CEO says our business is just like racing sports cars: 'If you're under control, you're not driving hard enough.' I have to work hard until I'm established, but I'm still pretty mild compared to most people in my company. Pharmaceutical development is a cutthroat, high pressure business."

Carlyle inclined his head toward Bethany. "I want to be a success for her. She doesn't have the slightest inkling of how hard I've tried. She wanted to marry a man who would be something. I'm so close, it's almost—When my new compound finishes the testing process, I'll be at the top, financially and professionally." His voice had a whining quality. "I'll be able to show her what I'm worth. If she stays with me that long."

Bethany had slipped off her heels and folded her legs up under her, her fists on her lap, her head high, her back straight. Her stillness compelled attention in a way that fidgeting or restlessness never would. She had a chilly, regal quality, like a queen listening to unwelcome petitioners.

Carlyle moistened his lips before he continued, his voice less sure. "She used to be so interested in sex. *She* seduced *me* the first time, not vice versa. She took me to an expensive restaurant on her expense account. Before we ate anything, we drank two bottles of wine. Then she pushed up this ultrashort skirt she was wearing; she'd written a sexy note in red ink on her thigh, saying how much she wanted me. We left right away, just as they were about to serve our dinners."

I saw her move her hand toward him, reaching out, uncurling her fingers, looking almost as if the gesture was unconscious, beyond her volition. Then she brought her hand sharply back into her lap, her fingers again tightly curled into fists.

"And now?" I asked Bethany, willing her to put her gesture into words.

"Fine," she said, too quickly. "Our sex life isn't really relevant to the things we came here to discuss."

"Right," Carlyle said, his tone sarcastic. "Aside from the fact that I'm impotent with her lately, it's fine, just fine. But clearly that doesn't bother her." He looked pointedly at her short skirt.

"Notice his choice of words," Bethany said, "'impotent with her.' But not with other women."

"That's her crazy jealousy again." He looked me in the eye, an unwavering glance. "She's convinced I have someone on the side. There's no way to convince her that she's wrong. I'd certainly be justified, the way she keeps rejecting me. But I don't."

"There's no magic litmus test that turns suitably pink to provide the proof, but I feel the difference between us," she said, her voice tight. "I think there's been more than one woman. When I get the evidence—and I will—that'll be the end of our marriage." She took a deep breath and paused, speaking more slowly, with satisfaction. "Our prenuptial agreement is void if I get the proof, that's one of the terms; he's not going to touch a penny of the money I've brought in—"

"She's paranoid about money; that's what drives her in all of this. She counts every penny I spend because I don't earn as much as she does. I didn't bring money into the marriage like she did—"

"Sometimes," Bethany said, "I feel our relationship is parasitic, and I'm the host."

Her statement conjured up an image of a trout with a lamprey glued to its side, the lamprey's ring of teeth rasped through the skin and into the muscle, sucking the blood in a leisurely way. Until, eventually, the trout dies. I wondered about Bethany's choice of words.

Carlyle blinked heavily, then closed his eyes for a moment. He looked exhausted.

"Let's go back to the beginning," I said. "What attracted you to each other? Why did you choose each other out of all the possible people in the world?" I was hoping to find a chink in the chain-mail suits they wore with each other.

"When I met Bethany, I thought she was the greatest thing I'd ever seen—sexy, bright, interested in everything. She spent a couple of years in a New York dance company before she went to college, then she put herself through school and got her MBA. She was so different—so exotic, that's the best way to put it. I'd been married before. It didn't work out, and I swore I'd never do it again, but I asked her to marry me a month after I met her. I couldn't imagine that I'd ever look at another woman again—"

"Just shows you how wrong you can be," Bethany said. "I gave up dancing because I don't like coming in second best. At anything."

She looked at me. "Carlyle's under considerable stress, no doubt. Stomach problems, migraines, allergies, asthma. If it's just job pressures, maybe you can help him deal with it. If it's another woman, then he needs to decide to fish or cut bait, or I'll leave him if—

*when*—I catch him. Either way, don't count me among your patients," Bethany said, her voice scornful as she looked at Carlyle. "I won't be coming back."

When Bethany stood, she unfurled her fists, and I saw her fingers clearly for the first time. Her nails had been chewed into rough stubs, several scabbed around the edge where the cuticle had been deeply gnawed. She followed my gaze to her hands and hid her nails by rolling her fingers into fists. Her expression had mixed defiance and shame and pain. And anger, most of all.

# Chapter 10

**F**riday morning Thelma Lou called to me from her desk in the reception area as I was walking toward my office. She wanted to make sure I'd gotten a message she'd left for me late yesterday about an early cancellation for today. Then she added, "I'm glad Stuart Crego's gone. He gave me the creeps."

Thelma Lou is perpetually good-humored, almost unnaturally so, so her statement took me aback. I've rarely heard her make negative comments about people. "What'd he do?"

"Back in May, Stuart went out with a friend of mine, Nancy—she's a secretary over in Radiology. Pretty woman, couple years older than Stuart. After they'd gone out a few times, she decided she didn't want to see him again.

"Things happened after that; they could've just been coincidences—but they didn't seem like it."

"Like what?"

"First Stuart started popping up at odd places, odd times. He wouldn't be doing much, just standing around."

I had an idea what she meant. When I'd first gotten back to work after Ian's death, I was talking with Thelma Lou; an uneasy feeling had made me turn, abruptly. Stuart had been staring at me. After a moment he'd smiled, an arrogant, condescending, supercilious smile that pretended warmth.

I'd stared him down, stone faced, until he turned away.

"Nancy likes to have everything in its place. She came back from lunch one day and things had been moved around in her office. Even her desk had been turned against the wall. Books were in all the wrong places in her bookcase. She had the hardest time being in her office for a few weeks—nothing was missing, nothing was damaged—but she kept feeling like she wanted to wash her hands, like he'd soiled everything he touched."

I watched as Thelma Lou toyed with a pen on her desk. I could see her lace bra clearly enough through her white polyester blouse to have counted the rosettes, had I been so inclined; the expanse, however, would have made it a formidable job.

"Something else about Stuart—he hoards grudges," Thelma Lou said, not looking at me, as if she was sorry to be the one to break the news. "Nancy said he recorded arguments on his calendar so he'd remember all the particulars if he wanted to resurrect the quarrel a month later."

Her latest picture of Greta showed the cement goose wearing a miniature Stetson, a red bandanna around her skinny neck. Thelma Lou fiddled with the picture frame then glanced up at me as if she was trying to decide about saying something.

"Yesterday, when he was giving me his paperwork for his termination, Stuart seemed pretty angry with you."

Thelma Lou reached over and patted my hand, like a nurse comforting a patient who'd just gotten word that her condition was critical.

"Is there something else about Stuart I should know?"

"Just that—well—he seemed a little too interested in things that didn't concern him."

"Oh?"

"When Alicia Erle came for her first appointment, Stuart spotted her talking to me," Thelma Lou said. "After Alicia went into Perry's office, Stuart tried to pump me about why she was coming here. He claimed Alicia was a friend of his and he just wanted to make sure nothing was wrong. Then he wanted to know what she'd been saying to me. I told him he could ask her himself."

*Stuart knew Alicia?* "Did he say anything else about her?"

She shook her head no.

I remembered how Alicia had gone out of her way to tell us she'd been running late and hadn't had time to ask Thelma Lou how the clinic worked. "What did Alicia say to you?"

"That's the funny thing. She was especially interested in who knows about who comes here. I mean, how safe are the notes you keep, your charts and where they're stored. And I still haven't been able to find her chart anywhere. . . ."

We looked at each other. I could easily picture Stuart Crego watching for a moment when Thelma Lou left her desk unattended, then slipping into the record room behind her desk. If that was what had happened, I'd never see Alicia's chart again.

"You're sure Alicia asked about the safety of patient charts?"

"Yes. I do remember most things, in spite of the lightning." Thelma Lou looked hurt. "I try very hard."

"Of course. I'm sorry. Did Alicia ask anything else?"

"She wanted to know if you were good at fixing problems in marriages. She asked one really odd thing just before Perry came out to get her for her appointment: She wanted to know if you were really an expert at detecting lies in the stories you heard from patients."

How much had Alicia concealed or distorted—and why? "What did you tell her?"

"I said you were very good, and she should bring up her questions with you."

A man came up to the desk to check in for his

appointment, and I stepped aside. When Thelma Lou was free again, I asked, "Who referred Alicia to the clinic?"

Thelma Lou hunted through her card file for the index card she fills out the first time someone calls to schedule an appointment. She peered through the bottom of her bifocals. "When I asked who referred her, she told me, 'a friend.' Wouldn't give me a name."

*Naturally.*

"How long did she wait to be seen for her intake?" Normally it's one to two weeks after someone calls.

"She called on August nineteenth. I remember I'd just had a cancellation when she called, so I asked if she'd be free the next day."

Which meant that Alicia had called for an appointment the day after she attended my lecture. Not before, as she'd claimed: She'd said she'd asked if her name rang any bells because she thought I might have seen it on my appointment schedule.

Not before. So why had Alicia assumed I'd recognize her name? As if we'd already been connected in some important way.

When I got out of a committee meeting at ten, I went to check the Psychometric Lab's log to see how many patients were waiting to be tested. I wasn't pleased to see that business was brisk, and the waiting list was growing.

Like traditional university professors, medical school faculty are expected to teach, to conduct scholarly research, and to serve on departmental and college committees. In addition, we're expected to generate a portion of our salary through a mix of research grants and patient fees, the latter billed and collected by the department.

Some clinical service areas make the process easier than others; my research grant and my position as director of the Psychometric Laboratory give me a good way to earn my keep as well as considerable leeway in how I spend my time. I needed to make sure that I didn't give Kurt von Reichenau any additional reasons to exercise his prerogative as department chair and appoint someone else as director. That meant I needed to hire two new psychometrists quickly, shouldering part of the load myself in the interim.

When I went to check my schedule for next week, I realized I'd left my appointment book in my car. Not a big deal normally, but the Rugton parking lot was closed this week for resurfacing; staff had been given temporary passes for a parking garage three blocks away. I grumbled about my forgetfulness as I slogged the distance, my face damp from the heat and humidity before I'd gone halfway.

My car is a 1960 Corvette convertible, black with white inserts and a red leather interior. I've had the engine rebuilt once, the exterior repainted twice, and I take it in annually to get any dings or scrapes touched up. I use the drive-through car wash whenever I get gas and keep old towels in the trunk so I can dry it afterward. I try to park away from other cars to keep the scuff marks on doors to a minimum. This morning I'd parked in a corner spot on the fourth floor where less than a third of the slots were filled.

I was getting out my key when I looked over toward my car. I jumped back, banging into a car. The driver's side window had been smashed. I could see the jagged pieces around the frame.

"Damn!" I felt my face flushing. "No!"

Was the vandal still lurking? I glanced around the garage. No one on this floor. I bent down so I could see underneath the cars. Nothing.

It's not that bad, I told myself, trying to wipe my eyes. I'm overreacting. Random vandalism, someone drawn to my car because it was so different. Easy to get fixed. But I couldn't stop myself from crying.

Then I tasted bile rising in my throat as I looked inside the broken window.

In the middle of the driver's seat was a dead mouse

in a wooden trap, the front paws just visible under the
dark-gray body, the eyes staring sightlessly, its back
broken by the metal spring.

I'd seen mice in traps before, but I'd never seen one
mutilated like this: the mouse's body had been slashed,
its bloody intestines pulled out, blood and guts
smeared over the red-leather seat. I felt weak and
shaky.

I looked around, listening. No sounds. No one in
sight. No other cars around mine had been damaged,
not that I expected it. Clearly not a random event, by
any means. Easy for someone to find my Corvette if
they went looking through the parking garage—
someone who knew where Rugton staff would be
parking today, someone who knew the garage would be
deserted most of the day.

I thought about Stuart's rage when I'd accepted his
resignation. I remembered Thelma Lou's story about
her friend Nancy—how Stuart had sensed the very sort
of revenge that would hit closest to home. How well
he'd chosen for me, in turn.

I called the hospital security office to report the
incident, telling the man who came to take the report
that I thought Stuart was responsible. He didn't seem
particularly interested as he looked inside my car,
saying they'd always had plenty of problems in the
parking garages. He'd keep an eye on the garage today,
and he'd circulate a copy of Stuart's ID badge picture
to other security people in case he reappeared around
the hospital, but there wasn't much more he could do
unless someone had caught him in action. Same story
for a police report: Minor vandalism wouldn't get
much attention without witnesses.

I didn't have much on my calendar for the day,
fortunately. I called around until I found a place that
could replace the broken window right away. I took a
package of paper towels and a couple of plastic trash-
can liners to the car, cleaning up everything as well as I
could, tossing the sack with the butchered mouse into a
trash barrel beside the garage. Before I drove to the

repair shop, I put a couple of layers of paper towels on the driver's seat. It helped a little, but I still felt soiled.

As I drove, I kept thinking of the mouse in the trap, its slashed body left where I would sit—an evil allegory.

When I got back from taking care of my car, I asked Thelma Lou to pull Stuart Crego's personnel folder.

Stuart had been hired by someone else, and I'd never taken the time to examine his employment application—something else I'd neglected since Ian's death. Now I saw just enough information to make me worry about the gaps.

He had graduated from college with honors seven years ago. Since that time he'd lived in three different cities, never lasting more than two years at any job. Before he came to work at Rugton, he'd completed a year of graduate course work in psychology, but he hadn't stayed long enough to complete his master's.

Maybe just a bright man with remarkably restless feet, I told myself, trying to squash my growing sense of foreboding.

I looked for letters of recommendation, notes summarizing phone calls to check references—and getting a sick feeling in my stomach when I remembered that the psychologist who'd hired Stuart had been going through a messy divorce and had left soon after. I came up empty-handed.

I looked at the three names Stuart had listed as references on his Rugton application but was reluctant to call them now. I didn't want him to hear that someone had been making inquiries about him, have him figure out I was checking on him. More to the point: I didn't want to let him know he'd alarmed me.

Then I remembered that Rosemary Overstreet was on the faculty at the university in Houston where Stuart had spent his year in graduate school. We'd worked together on a committee for the Texas Psychological Association. Surely concrete information from someone I knew would help me stop feeling so foolishly apprehensive about the man.

I hesitated a moment before I called, trying to think of someone else who might be able to answer my questions, not pleased when I drew a blank. I'd never been comfortable with Rosemary, never known how to respond to her. She had trouble striking the right note in casual conversations, coming on too strong at times, too timid at others, a jittery uneasiness that polluted simple interactions. When talking about the child abuse cases she saw as a consultant to the prosecutor's office, she'd take on the sanctimonious air of an avenging angel.

Once Rosemary had asked me when I was planning to start a family. I'd told her that I didn't particularly like children, didn't want any of my own. She'd acted as if it was a moral failing.

I hadn't told her I wasn't able to have children, a legacy of my medical treatments for leukemia. Not an area I wanted to explore myself. I had a strong suspicion about what was lurking beneath the surface.

Now I thought that Rosemary sounded preoccupied when I got her on the line. After we'd chatted a minute I said, "I wanted to ask you about a former student, Stuart Crego."

"Just a minute while I shut my door." Her voice had chilled and turned formal.

Enough time passed for her to shut her door half a dozen times. When I was beginning to think we'd been disconnected, she said, "I don't remember him all that well. He was competent enough, I think. It's been too long since I supervised him . . . you need to talk to someone who's seen his work more recently—"

"Rosemary, what's going on?"

"I'm sorry, but I'm not able to help you. I've got to go—got an appointment waiting."

Then she hung up on me.

So much for my hope that learning the facts about Stuart Crego would defuse the bogeyman.

# Chapter 11

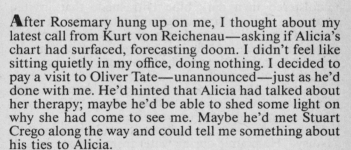

After Rosemary hung up on me, I thought about my latest call from Kurt von Reichenau—asking if Alicia's chart had surfaced, forecasting doom. I didn't feel like sitting quietly in my office, doing nothing. I decided to pay a visit to Oliver Tate—unannounced—just as he'd done with me. He'd hinted that Alicia had talked about her therapy; maybe he'd be able to shed some light on why she had come to see me. Maybe he'd met Stuart Crego along the way and could tell me something about his ties to Alicia.

His office was on the fourth floor of Pryor Hall, the newest of the hospital's four buildings. The network of tunnels that honeycombed the medical center made it possible to go from Rugton to Pryor Hall without stepping outside, but I preferred the shorter, straighter, out-of-doors paths.

When Oliver answered the door in response to my knock, he looked startled. Wary. Definitely not pleased. Then a false smile cloaked whatever I'd seen.

"I'm glad you stopped by," he said. "I've learned something about Alicia that casts a new light on her suicide." He held out his hand for me to shake.

His office seemed dim, the air conditioning chilling in contrast to the bright heat and humidity outside. I shivered as I touched his hand.

"I'll make coffee," he said, waving me toward a chair; not waiting for my answer, he turned to the black high-tech coffee maker that stood on top of a filing cabinet next to his desk. "I make great coffee."

I didn't particularly want coffee, but I didn't refuse. I wanted time to watch him.

Oliver Tate's office had the privileged air of a high-priced law firm, confident of its clout, willing to offer forceful objections whenever necessary. Positioned behind a rosewood desk at least half the size of a pool table, his desk chair was a marvel of sleek navy leather. Visitors had their choice of four overstuffed chairs upholstered in a dark blue Ultrasuede that invited stroking. Two green marble end tables sat on brass bases. One wall featured two pictures: one a photograph of molten lava flowing from a volcano, one an abstract painting. Not an office that put visitors at ease. Probably not meant to.

I watched Oliver scoop whole coffee beans into the top compartment of the coffee maker. "What were Alicia's responsibilities on your unit?"

He held up a finger to indicate it would be a minute. "Noisy." He poured spring water from a plastic jug. "I like good coffee. You have to use fresh beans each time to get the best." He pressed a switch to grind the coffee; when the low-pitched whirring ended, the smell of hazelnut-scented coffee hovered in the air. He pressed a second switch to brew it. "It doesn't take long." He sat down behind his desk.

"Let me explain how new drugs are developed, so you'll understand my operation and Alicia's part in it. Phase one is the first stage for clinical testing in humans, the earliest dose studies. We'll recruit twenty to a hundred healthy men to establish the major side effects and highest dose they'll tolerate." In contrast to his air of graciousness, his mouth and jaw looked tight, as if clamping down, holding in. "Phase one establishes a drug's safety."

He picked up a prescription pad from his desk as he spoke, writing "100," underlining the number.

*Making sure I saw how easily Alicia could have gotten hold of one?*

"Phases two and three are my bread and butter, the trials that establish efficacy and dosages. We compare results of new compounds with placebos at first; then later we contrast the new drug against a similar drug to assess efficacy."

I noticed that Oliver hadn't asked if I knew about drug development before starting his lecture. I wondered why he assumed that I'd be interested—or if it even occurred to him that I might not care. Or maybe he needed time to work on his story.

The coffeemaker sputtered as it finished. Oliver poured coffee into a blue mug. "Unadulterated, I hope?"

"Black is fine."

He handed me the mug with a flourish, as if presenting a gift for which I should be sure to express my gratitude.

"I make it strong—too strong for some people." He stood beside me, waiting for me to sample it.

I distrusted Oliver in this guise, acting as if he wanted to make sure I appreciated his personal and professional prowess. If I'd been psychoanalytically inclined, I'd have said his potency.

The coffee, hot and strong enough to peel paint, burned my tongue. "Fine. Alicia's role in the process?" I asked again.

"According to her job description, pretty straightforward; of course, I'm sure you found out for yourself that nothing was simple where Alicia was concerned. She was in charge of subject recruitment and screening when we had a new drug to test. She was supposed to oversee the records for trials, making sure results from all the different hospital labs made their way into patients' charts."

He sipped his coffee, looking at me over the rim of his mug. "She supervised data entry into the computer, ran some basic statistical analyses when we finished trials, drafted parts of some reports for drug companies and the FDA. I travel a lot, and she was supposed to make sure my unit ran smoothly in my absence. I'm on the speaker list for Eichon Pharmaceuticals, and they always want me to be part of the panels they organize for all the major pharmacology and neuroscience meetings."

"Dr. Stealth," Alicia had called him. Now Oliver wanted to be sure I recognized how much others valued his work.

Like a debutante, the quantity and quality of invitations received provided one measure of an academician's stature. Maybe Oliver always engaged in this kind of automatic preening, displaying his talents for any halfway personable woman. Perhaps he was constantly vigilant, ready for anyone who might challenge his authority. Maybe the two responses were mostly the same for him.

"How long did Alicia work for you?"

"Close to a year. Certain things about her were entirely predictable after a while. She wanted to be much more than just a research associate. She knew enough to be dangerous but not enough to realize when she needed to cry uncle and defer to me.

"On my unit, I'm the boss. No one else. Ever."

I studied the abstract painting hanging on the wall opposite my chair. Beige swirled on top, red splashed across the middle, green and beige tangled at the bottom, like troubled water. The brass plate at the bottom read A BATTLEGROUND, the scrawled artist's signature was illegible. "How did she exceed authority?"

"Any number of ways. Called me by my first name without invitation." He ran his finger around the edge of his coffee mug. "Made decisions that compromised a couple of drug trials."

"Such as?"

"She did—well, they seemed like little things, but they weren't trivial. For example, we were comparing a new drug against an established drug that was absorbed best in the lower intestine. She changed the order for the drug's protective coating when I was out of town. She claimed the drugs wouldn't have looked exactly the same otherwise, so the nursing staff and patients might have guessed which drug was which when they weren't supposed to know who was getting what. Because she made that change, the established drug got the wrong protective coating. The drug we were testing had an unfair advantage because it got absorbed at the right time; the established drug got absorbed too late.

"She claimed she made the change in the interests of scientific integrity." He rolled his eyes. "I'd been very generous to her, giving her authorship on papers from two studies. I couldn't help but think that she wanted to make sure we ended up with publishable data to make her vita look better."

"What did Alicia say about her therapy with me?"

"I don't wonder that you're interested in finding out more about Alicia—after the fact, of course."

A remark meant to sting after it settled, like poison ivy blooming a day after contact.

I looked at Oliver Tate as he sat enthroned behind his oversized desk. He had a way of sitting up straight in his chair, a military posture, tilting his head and looking you over through hooded eyes. Almost as if he was looking down on you; maybe more like you needed to prove to him that he shouldn't look down on you.

"Alicia didn't say much about her therapy, at least not directly—she just hinted that she was causing you some grief," he said.

If there was more, he wasn't going to tell me. "How was Alicia as a student?"

"Not enough persistence. She jumped at the chance to take the full-time job with me after her master's; I warned her that students who took a leave from grad school often had trouble making themselves go back, but I think that she was looking for an excuse to get out of Debra's lab."

I raised my eyebrows.

"Debra Linnell was her adviser—maybe you met her when she was still part of the faculty here, before she left to start her own company a year ago?"

I shook my head no. I thought his jaw seemed less tight, his posture less rigid.

"How did Alicia pick Debra as an adviser?"

"Not clear to me, unless it was the obvious, of course: Alicia chose the only woman faculty member, regardless—" Oliver got up from his chair. "Let me give you a tour of my unit. Bring your coffee along with you." He held the door of his office open for me, waiting until I was out before he continued.

I wondered about his "news." I'd already decided that asking directly would only delay its unveiling.

"Alicia claimed she played a major role in studies in Debra's lab that demonstrated the potential value of a new drug. Debra said Alicia performed some of the experiments under her direction, but the creativity and insights that went into designing the studies were Debra's."

"What did you think?"

"Debra undoubtedly believes she could have designed the universe better, if only she'd had the chance. When she was here on the faculty, she was insufferable—telling everyone what was wrong with their research, how they should run their labs differently. Not a popular woman."

But someone I wanted to meet, if I could figure out a discreet way to maneuver it. Debra might be able to answer some of my questions about Alicia—and provide another perspective on Oliver. "Where did she go?"

"Debra was so taken with a couple of the compounds she developed that she took a leave of absence from the university and started her own biotech company in Houston. Named it 'Linnstar,' if you can believe it. Leaving kept her from getting lynched by her departmental colleagues."

He laughed. "It hasn't turned out like she hoped. Debra had a devil of a time starting up on her own, and it hasn't gone any better since. She's gotten more and more paranoid. She has no results to show, and if she doesn't produce something soon, she'll lose her investors' backing. She wants to believe that her problems are the result of bad luck, or someone else's malice. Never her own deficiencies." He spoke with enthusiasm.

I'd followed Oliver Tate down the hallway, where he unlocked a door and reached inside for the light switch before motioning me to enter in front of him. Now I watched him position himself in the doorway, right hand on the frame behind me, left thrust too casually into the pocket of his gray trousers.

"This is our record room," he gestured at the small room that held two wooden desks with computers and a bank of filing cabinets. It smelled of new carpet.

As if reading my thoughts, Oliver said, "I persuaded hospital administration to ante up for new furnishings after the smoke damage from the fire last month—"

"Fire?"

"Surely you know all about the fire," he said, scanning my face. "We had an FDA inspection scheduled on short notice to review the records for a trial. Alicia was responsible for organizing the data, checking to make sure each file was complete. She complained she couldn't get everything together in time, then—presto, the fire took care of her problems. Half the data up in smoke. I had trouble convincing the FDA we had enough left to pass us."

*I woke up in the middle of the night, I was in my kitchen, holding a burning match . . . I must've gotten out of bed, taken a match book out of the drawer, lit one, all in my sleep.* I held my coffee cup in both hands, hoping the adrenaline surge evoked by the memory of Alicia's words hadn't been visible to him.

"You sound as if you believe Alicia was the root of all your troubles," I said.

"Alicia discovered the fire, Alicia put it out. You be the judge." He spoke slowly and deliberately, emphasizing each word. "She must have been massively out of touch—not well-connected to reality. Or it was deliberate sabotage." He looked at me, clearly waiting for me to cast my vote: Was she crazy or just angry? Either way, he had her pegged as the firesetter.

I tried not to move, or even blink.

Eventually he continued: "I'd decided to let Alicia go after the fire. I'd prepared the official letter to her, then decided to sit on it until the personnel office approved the paperwork for her replacement; it'd be rough without someone to pick up things. I left the folder on my desk when I went to Austin. Our departmental secretary just told me Alicia asked for the key to my office when I was away so she could borrow one of my journals. I think Alicia might've found the letter."

I let his remarks go without comment, judging he'd say more if I didn't indicate the depth of my interest.

"It would've hit Alicia hard—where else would she get a job if I let her go without a good reference? She wasn't ready to go back to school.

"I had other reasons to let Alicia go, not to trust her. I have a master key that opens all the doors in my unit, probably half the doors in the hospital. She borrowed it to open her office when she supposedly left her keys at home near the end of August. Then I got a bill from the hospital lock shop. Alicia had taken the number off my master key and gotten a duplicate; told them I'd bent my key and I needed a replacement.

"I learned one more thing about Alicia in the last couple of days. She made a decent salary with me, but nothing extraordinary. She always complained she couldn't save anything. Then she bought that old Cadillac—for cash, she told the departmental secretary. Interesting to speculate where Alicia suddenly got the money to buy a car like that."

I could feel Oliver weighing my reactions, trying to answer his own questions by looking for clues in my responses. Painting a picture of Alicia as a paid saboteur, waiting to see if I'd agree.

"Now maybe you understand why I'm even more

concerned about whether Alicia did anything else to mess up our current trials."

I avoided looking at Oliver as I stepped back through the chart room and out into the hallway. He walked across the hall and opened the door directly opposite the chart room. Four younger men, all wearing plastic hospital ID bracelets, sat around a television, watching a middle-aged John Wayne in a naval captain's uniform. "Torpedo the sub and get it over with," one grumbled, barely looking up as we passed.

"This is the common room for the unit," Oliver said. He gestured toward a series of open doors that lined the corridor leading from the common room. "Patient rooms, for studies where research subjects stay overnight."

A short, white-coated man with a stethoscope around his neck walked out the open door nearest us. When he saw Oliver, he stood up straighter, as if coming to attention, and said, "I can't find that tape anywhere—"

"We'll talk about that another time," Oliver cut in, his voice harsh.

Oliver turned to me. "This is Xavier. He's responsible for overseeing the medical aspects of my unit when I'm away. He came from Argentina last month on a one-year visa as a research fellow; I'm helping him get his green card so he can stay here permanently."

Xavier was no taller than five four, and I wondered how much time he had to spend in the gym to maintain the overdeveloped, unsightly muscles that strained against the fabric of his coat. Probably late forties. His mostly bald head looked small atop his bulk, and a few wavy strands were carefully combed across the top.

"I owe much to Dr. Tate," he said in a heavily accented voice, the words sounding like a familiar litany.

"I'm Haley McAlistar." He nodded, as if he recognized my name. "What kinds of drugs are you testing now?"

Oliver patted Xavier's bulky arm as he started to answer. "We won't interrupt your work any longer. I just wanted Haley to see my unit."

As we walked back toward his office, Oliver said, "His English isn't that good yet. We're testing a new antidepressant for Eichon Pharmaceuticals. It could be *very* hot, better even than Prozac. Huge marketing potential." He rubbed the palms of his hands together.

"Debra's none too happy about it, since it's close enough to one of her compounds to be big competition, and we're ahead of her in phase two testing. She'd love to find a way to shut me down."

He opened the door to his office and motioned toward the chair where I'd been sitting earlier, inviting me to sit down again.

"Did Alicia ever mention a man named Stuart Crego?" I asked, still standing.

As Oliver shook his head no, he stared left into space, the look of someone storing information without writing it down. "You're not going to tell me who he is, right? Way too much of a one-way exchange, wouldn't you agree?"

I shrugged.

After a long pause he said, "Hard to believe Alicia caused so much havoc. She was like one of those plaster kewpie dolls you win at the fair—gaudy, maybe vaguely decorative, but hardly functional."

I went over to look more closely at his photograph of the erupting volcano. I remembered Oliver pacing around my office, leafing through my books, putting his hand on my shoulder.

I used two fingers as a lever under the bottom right corner of the frame, moving it just enough to leave the left side a half-inch lower than the right. "Your picture needed an adjustment." I turned to him. "I saw Alicia differently. Thanks for the . . . enlightening tour," I said as I walked out.

# Chapter 12

The next morning, Saturday, I went to get my hair cut at Mitch's in Montrose. I stopped to admire his latest window display; a trio of plaster-of-paris pink flamingos complete with tiny wigs. The first had a blond beehive with a side curl hanging down, the second a teased and lacquered brown flip, the third a granny wig with gray curls.

Mitch had a serious infatuation with the "midcentury" look, filling his shop with 1950s collectibles. Clients waited their turn on two half-circle couches covered in black vinyl and strewn with leopard-skin pillows. An old Philco TV in its original cabinet stood in the corner; a Krazy Kat clock, complete with rhinestones, hung above it. Eight different gold sunburst clocks formed a collage on the opposite wall.

I'd let my hair grow to shoulder length because Ian liked it long; he'd said it made me look sexier—and softer. After Ian's death, cutting it short had been a kind of retribution.

Mitch had protested when I asked him to chop off two-thirds of my hair, cutting it short enough so I could comb it in place when it was wet and let it dry on its own. Too much energy to fix it daily, I'd told him, and he'd done as I asked, albeit with a few theatrical winces for accompaniment.

103

Now I said, "The usual," as he lifted his scissors.

He paused. "Dating anyone special?"

"I . . . haven't been all that interested."

He rolled his eyes. "Today I'm only going to trim the ends, shape it in a few places so it'll look good while it grows out." He made sure to avoid my eyes in the mirror. "You don't look as good in short hair."

"I want it short. I like it short. It's a pain when it's long."

"I'll cut it so all you have to do is blow it dry in the morning. Ten minutes out of your busy schedule. You don't like it, you don't have to pay me; you can go somewhere else to get it done."

"I like shorter hair. Houston's too hot for long hair."

"This is September. Summer's over. By the time next summer's here, it'll be long enough to pull back into a twist or a pony tail." He continued paring the bare minimum.

Mitch has been cutting my hair since I came to Houston twelve years ago. Every so often we go for lunch or a drink. He came to Ian's funeral.

"You need someone." He stared meaningfully at the wedding picture that sat beside his rack of combs: himself, beaming, his third wife who worked with him in the shop, and the Elvis impersonator who'd officiated at their wedding in Las Vegas four years ago.

I've heard plenty of variations on that theme since Ian's death. Odd to hear it now, though; before my haircut this morning I'd gone upstairs to pack up Ian's clothes, planning to take them to a nearby Salvation Army collection box. I did the easy part first; cleaning out the drawers. I got halfway through the closet before I stopped short when I found a costume Ian had worn to a Halloween party shortly after we met. He had gone as a magician in a black cape and a tall pointed cap.

I'd worn a body stocking underneath a black, floor-length slip. The slip was covered with words printed in inch-high capital letters, attached by safety pins: EGO, ID, REPRESSION, ORAL, OEDIPAL.

He'd guessed it right away: "A Freudian slip," he said.

We'd had a marvelous time.

This morning I packed up everything but his cape and pointed hat, leaving the cartons at the collection box before my haircut, before I could change my mind, telling myself I'd spent too long carrying around the past like a couple of heavy suitcases.

Now I said, "Long hair doesn't suit a woman of my . . . mature age"—knowing I was going to give in, in the end.

"Don't flatter yourself. You're far from midcentury yet."

After my haircut I headed to my office, not enthusiastic about the work I needed to get done. When the stack of grants had been delivered by Airborne Express yesterday, I was sorry I'd agreed to be a reviewer. I needed to write six critiques before I flew to Washington on Thursday.

Driving in, I kept wondering how Alicia could have been murdered. I'd seen no marks on her body, no signs of a struggle. I couldn't imagine how someone could have just happened to find out that Alicia had gotten a bottle of sleeping pills that very day and then had somehow forced her to take them. Maybe the medical examiner would find another cause of death besides the pills and booze—but I wasn't holding my breath. Someone had been clever.

Rugton had been an ideal place to leave her body. Who knew Alicia had been a patient? Stuart Crego, of course. But she could have told anyone: Oliver Tate claimed that Alicia had been asking questions about me, making no secret of the fact that she was seeing me.

Alicia and I were connected in some cryptic way. She'd expected me to know something about her when she sought me out. Try as I might, I couldn't see any logical link between us. But I still felt the attachment to her—felt it forcefully. From the very beginning, from the time I'd met her at my lecture, Alicia had managed to evoke strong emotions in me, to push past the protective barriers I'd erected after Ian's death.

Traffic slowed to a crawl as cars merged into the right lane to get around an accident on Kirby. A uniformed policeman was directing traffic, a white straw Stetson shading his face from the hot sun.

I felt like I was operating with both hands tied behind me. The information from Alicia's therapy sessions was confidential; I couldn't track down people she'd mentioned and ask for more details about her or the stories she'd told.

If I went around saying that Alicia's death wasn't a suicide, most people would find it ludicrous; they'd probably assume I was trying to shift the blame from myself—particularly since her body had been found at Rugton.

I'd told one person about my suspicions. "It's not suicide," I had said to Glee yesterday, when I stopped by her office after seeing Oliver. "Doesn't fit."

My strongest "evidence" against suicide—the fact that Alicia hadn't dressed for her death—sounded remarkably flimsy when I talked about it. Glee hadn't said much.

I had two candidates who might have had some semblance of a motive: Oliver Tate, who'd been away at a meeting in Austin, and Stuart Crego, who wasn't likely to volunteer any information to me. I didn't know if Oliver or Stuart were key players in Alicia's life or not. I had enormous gaps in my picture of her because she'd deliberately concealed information I needed to make sense of her.

I remembered a bookstore near the medical center and decided to make a quick detour. I looked up prices for Alicia's '59 Cadillac in a couple of used-car guides. For a car in good condition like hers, maybe ten to fifteen thousand. Where had Alicia gotten the money?

I parked in the newly resurfaced Rugton parking lot, now mostly empty. On my way into Rugton, I saw light coming from underneath Perry Urbay's office door. I stopped and knocked. He looked down at his worn jeans sheepishly as he answered. "I didn't expect to see anyone around. I have a big paper due for my psychopathology class next week," he said, gesturing at the stack of books on his desk. He rummaged around and handed me some pages. "I rewrote my note yesterday."

I'd reconstructed Alicia's intake summary as best I could and asked Perry to do the same, independently, and give the original to Thelma Lou. Not a substitute for the original dated note, but I'd almost given up hope that Alicia's chart would resurface.

"Thanks," I said. "One other thing. I wanted to ask about the last few minutes of your interview with Alicia Erle, the part I missed when I left to see my patient."

Perry motioned to the chair next to his desk, and I sat down. He hadn't shaved this morning, and he looked as if he hadn't been sleeping well.

"I've felt terrible since you told me about her suicide," he said. "I really blew that interview."

I would have conducted the interview differently, but I didn't blame Perry. I remembered my first year of graduate school, eighteen years earlier, when I'd been about to see my first patient. I'd half feared, half hoped that the patient, a forty-year-old man, would walk into the room, take one look at me, and walk out. It wasn't until midway through the interview that I'd realized he looked so oddly feminine because his eyebrows had been carefully tweezed into thin lines. During the interview I'd been unable to bring myself to ask him about his appearance.

I told Perry the story and he gave me a forced smile.

"Do you remember what Alicia said during the last few minutes of the interview?" I asked.

"I verified her address, and she gave me her insurance form." He sat slumped in his chair, considering my question. "That's about it."

"She didn't say anything else about friends or relatives?" I asked.

"Nothing else during the interview . . . but I was kind of startled when I spotted her and Stuart Crego sitting in the cafeteria after she'd been in group—"

"Alicia and Stuart, together?"

"Yeah. Stuart was leaning forward with this anxious smile glued on his face, talking fast. Alicia kept glancing around like she was bored. She turned and started to wave at someone, when Stuart reached over and pinched her hand. Alicia jerked her arm away. She gave him this disgusted look and got up. He called something to her as she was walking away; she turned and said, 'Don't be a jerk,' loudly enough so that people close by turned around to look. After she'd gone, Stuart sat there, scowling, shredding his napkin into tiny pieces."

I found myself scratching my arm, then my leg. When I'd gotten home last night I sprayed the interior of my car with Lysol, wiping it dry with paper towels, then repeated the process twice more, trying to erase all traces of Stuart's ugliness. I still felt far too conscious of normal minor itches, as if something might have crawled or jumped from the dead mouse to the car to me. Talking about him now made it worse.

"I don't think Stuart saw me," Perry said. "I was hunched over, reading a book, and the cafeteria was packed. Later that afternoon he stopped by my office and acted like he was trying to be helpful, wanting to know how I was getting along so far. It seemed odd because he'd barely spoken to me since I started my practicum here."

Perry paused, an uneasy look on his face, then he went on, "Stuart started by asking how many patients I was seeing, and I told him. Then he asked about the kinds of patients I was seeing and why they'd come here for therapy. He didn't like it when I gave him real general answers. Finally he said, 'I think I've met one of the patients in your group—Alicia Erle.' I told him patient names were confidential. Stuart looked offended and said names were certainly confidential for people who worked *outside* Rugton. Then he leaned toward me and spoke in this low voice: 'You know the story about the secret to absolution? Confess sexual sins to a Scandinavian priest, drinking problems to a Russian priest, tardiness to a South American.' He laughed like he thought it was such a hot joke; then he asked, 'So why in hell did someone like Alicia Erle chose McAlistar as a therapist?'"

*Why indeed?* "Did he say anything else about her?"

"When I told Stuart that I couldn't discuss my patients with him, he got pretty angry. Told me I should watch out for Alicia; she had a real reputation as a liar—he'd been hoping someone would take her down a peg."

Stuart might have called Alicia a liar to discredit anything she might say about him in therapy. Or he could have known something I didn't.

"What day did you see them together in the cafeteria?"

Perry thought for a minute. "The Friday just before the Memorial Day weekend. Stuart was angry because you didn't tell the lab to leave early like he said most supervisors would do."

Friday, five days before her death, Alicia had given Stuart a public brush-off. And then Stuart had tried to pump Perry for information about Alicia.

"Did Stuart say anything else?"

"He said he'd known her for almost a year; he met her at some kind of new employee orientation meeting." Perry shrugged apologetically. "Nothing else that I remember."

As I walked to my office, I thought about who might have spied on the group the night Alicia attended. The choices were limited: Only someone who knew his way around Rugton would know about the observation room adjoining the group room. Stuart was the obvious candidate.

I needed to learn more about Stuart Crego.

# Chapter 13

I worked in my office until four, and then I packed up work to take home. I left two phone messages for Rosemary Overstreet after she'd hung up on me on yesterday afternoon but got no response—hardly a surprise after the way she'd acted when I tried to ask her about Stuart Crego. Now I needed to know what she wasn't saying—and why. I decided to show up unannounced on her doorstep, hoping she'd be home on a Saturday afternoon—hoping that seeing me in person might make her more willing to talk.

It took me half an hour to get to Rosemary's house in the Bellaire section of Houston; I'd been there before for Texas Psychological Association committee meetings. I rang her doorbell, remembering when the committee had met in her sunny living room. Today the curtains were closed.

As I waited for her to answer the door, I looked around. Clearly a house-proud neighborhood, the homes were older but well-maintained; their pervasive white trim had an unsullied, fresh-paint look—an accomplishment in Houston's heat and humidity. Large oaks shaded the street; the flower beds were bright with color. I got a whiff of someone's barbecue, and my mouth watered. The house to the right of Rosemary's had a plastic wading pool on the front lawn, the one to the left had two tricycles. Rosemary's grass had been clipped as severely as an army recruit's first haircut; her empty lawn looked bare.

I looked back and saw her living room curtain twitch. I waved and smiled madly so she'd know I'd seen the movement, hoping to force her to answer the door.

I'd almost given up when she finally opened the door.

"Hello, Rosemary. I need to talk to you."

"I'm sorry, this isn't a good time." She spoke in the blasé, dismissive tone of someone trying to get rid of a pesky salesperson, but the look she gave me mixed aversion and fear. "I'll call you and we'll set up something." She made a movement to shut the door.

"Rosemary, I need your help." I reached out, putting my hand on her arm. "Please. It's very important."

Her body sagged against the doorframe when I touched her, as if I'd added a crushing weight.

When I last saw Rosemary, she'd been wearing overalls with fist-size orange-and-purple flowers over an orange T-shirt and purple socks with black high-top sneakers. She'd wiped her sweaty face on her sleeve as she gave a blow-by-blow replay of a recent skeet shooting match she'd won, talking about different models of rifles with an intimate affection I found off-putting. Now her faded denim jumpsuit hung loose on her thin frame. Wisps of short hair framed a face that looked older than her thirty-five years. Something had gone very wrong for Rosemary.

"Haley . . . I don't want to be rude to you, but I really can't help you. I've supervised too many students to remember each of them in detail."

I'd deliberately avoided any mention of the reason for my visit. "You haven't even asked why I want to know. Please hear me out." I spoke gently, wondering what had drained the life from her.

Rosemary stood staring down, her mouth open, looking as if she was trying to compose another brush-off. I pushed past her and stepped inside; she made a noise in her throat, but she didn't seem to have the energy to try to stop me. She looked up and down the street before she closed the door.

I took the chair where I'd sat on my last visit, hoping to evoke the echo of her prior hospitality. I started speaking as soon as I sat down, trying to pretend this was a normal social call, trying to get her to ignore the fact I'd forced my way inside. I began by telling her about the butchered mouse I'd found in my car. I heard my voice quiver as I spoke. Now that the adrenaline rush that propelled me inside had ebbed, I was feeling tremulous, wondering if the decent thing to do would be to leave her alone—wanting to ask what had gone wrong for her but guessing she'd show me the door if I tried.

Rosemary sat on the edge of the chair opposite me. While I talked, she played with the seam on the chair's upholstered arm, running her thumbnail along it, back and forth, staring down at it, avoiding my eyes. Twice she glanced at her watch, as if she was counting the seconds before she evicted me.

When I finished telling her about the butchered mouse, she shrugged, ever so slightly, and glanced at her watch a third time.

I plunged into the story of Alicia and Stuart, all too aware of how tenuous the link to Alicia's death sounded. "I question whether it was really suicide," I said.

"What do the police think?" Rosemary asked.

I told her how they responded to my statement that she wasn't suicidal, to my claim that Alicia wasn't in her own car. I thought her shoulders stiffened; she raised her head slightly, as if I'd finally gotten her attention. I ended by saying, "I need to know if I'm way off base—or if there's some reason for concern."

In the extended silence that followed I glanced around. Her living room looked different. The same yellow and red pillows were scattered over the beige couch and chairs; the same handsome rolltop desk sat in the corner. Rosemary's husband collected historical items related to firefighting, and I recognized parts of his collection: a red-and-black turn-of-the-century hat, a fire trumpet, antique toy fire trucks, a yellow fire-fighter's coat. Then I realized she'd taken down the framed family photographs on the wall to the right of the front windows.

Finally she spoke: "Stuart's a vindictive swine. Unfortunately he's an intelligent man, very cunning, very resourceful. He's convinced he's not a major success in his life because of stupid people who've put up unreasonable obstacles. That translates into anyone who doesn't agree that he's brilliant and highly talented and deserves a steady diet of praise."

When we had committee meetings, Rosemary always sat upright, her back straight. Now she leaned on the arm of her chair, hands clenched in her lap, her left shoulder higher than her right. "The psychology faculty decided to terminate Stuart's graduate appointment in the department. Not because of grades—that would've been easy—but because of 'personality' problems. Stuart learned the material well, but he had a lot of trouble getting along from the very first."

"'Trouble getting along'?"

"Zero tolerance for anyone who didn't feed his ego and tell him he was wonderful—including patients. He wasn't able to form friendships with other students; he said it was because they envied his abilities. I was his adviser, so I talked with him, tried to be gentle when I suggested he get into therapy.

"Maybe a week later I found a big white cake box beside my office door, a red rose taped to the lid, a typed note stuck under it that said, 'A rose by any other name.' No signature." Rosemary's pinched face had gone white.

"Inside the box . . ." Her voice faltered, and she closed her eyes tightly. "Inside the box, there was a dead mouse . . . its belly slit open, guts spilling out. Bloody. But that wasn't the worst part." She looked in my direction, looking through me, swallowing, biting her lip. "Two dead mouse pups . . . beside her.

"I screamed when I saw the dead pups, got

hysterical—such an evil, dirty, filthy thing. . . . It took a long time to pull myself together."

I tensed as I remembered the butchered mouse in my car. Then I remembered someone telling me that Rosemary had finally gotten pregnant a year ago, something she'd craved for years. I scanned the living room. No baby toys. No baby pictures.

"I thought Stuart had left the box—but I didn't have any proof, just my instincts. After the faculty gave him a written warning about his problems with patients, he got better for a month or so; just as I was starting to wonder if maybe I'd been wrong, he reverted to his old style. That's when I met with him to tell him the faculty had decided to terminate his graduate appointment. He just sat there, looking at me, an ugly, angry look." She stood up and started pacing.

"The dead mouse pups were so monstrous because I'd finally gotten pregnant. In vitro fertilization, the third time we tried. I had an ultrasound early on and found out I was carrying twins. I told everyone, I was so happy—so thrilled. I even went around showing off the ultrasound picture and got it framed. . . ." She stared at the empty wall where the pictures had hung.

"I lost the twins at the end of my first trimester. I'd been doing fine except for a little morning sickness. Then I lost them."

It hurt to listen to her pain, raw and ragged. My throat tightened in response.

"I tried so hard to do everything right to make healthy babies—everything I could possibly do, nothing to hurt my babies. I was a fanatic about diet, about vitamins, reading everything I could find on pregnancy. . . ." She walked over to the rolltop desk in the corner, took something out of a drawer, and stood holding it clenched in her hand.

"A month after I lost my twins, I finally went back to work. I hadn't been able to drag myself out of bed for most of the month, I was so depressed. I was back two days when I got a white envelope, my name typed on it, left outside my door just like the box with the mice. Inside, this—"

She thrust it at me, grim faced. An amber glass bottle, no bigger than my thumb, empty now.

A section of the label was missing. The remainder said MIFERPRISTONE, with an address in Paris. Below the address, a warning: TOXIC BY INHALATION, IN CONTACT WITH SKIN, AND IF SWALLOWED. WEAR SUITABLE PROTECTIVE CLOTHING, GLOVES AND EYE/FACE PROTECTION. In the left-hand corner, printed in orange for emphasis, a skull and crossbones. As if emphasis was needed.

"What is it?"

"It was empty when I got it. Before that, RU-486."

It took a moment for her words to register, and then they didn't make sense. "The French abortion pill?"

"I know, not an approved drug in this country. Look at the back of the bottle."

I turned the bottle around. A small label on the back said: RESERVE A L'USAGE SCIENTIFIQUE. NOT FOR HUMAN USE.

"The compound is used in research, animal studies mostly, where they want to block the action of some natural hormones." She pointed at the bottle in my hand. "That's the way the company packages it for biological labs—it's shipped in a powdered form. Concentrated.

"It doesn't have to be taken orally—you can breath it, or absorb it through the skin—that's the reason for all the warning labels on the bottle. A single dose is very 'effective' early in pregnancy. It probably only took a pinch."

My mouth had gone dry. "You really think that . . . ?" I wanted her to tell me that she didn't believe what she was suggesting, not really—that Stuart wasn't truly so cruel, so vicious.

"I think Stuart managed to get enough in me to make me lose the twins. I'd been complaining how food tasted different once I got pregnant, so I wouldn't have noticed anything. He could have sprinkled it in my coffee when I had my back turned. Or dusted my doorknob a few times.

"It took me a while to put it together. When I figured it out, I couldn't see how I could do anything about it. No evidence remained that I'd been given the drug, more than a month later. The lot number had been scraped off the label, so there's no way to trace the lab that ordered it. No way to prove any crime had been committed, let alone link it to Stuart Crego.

"That's why I didn't want to talk to you—I'm terrified of having him come after me again."

# Chapter 14

Nightmares visit during times of stress, times when you feel helpless and out of control, when the barriers that protect you from the world get too thin. When the walls are too flimsy to keep out the things that go bump in the shadows of the night and chase you down the darkest corridors of your mind. Frequent nightmare sufferers tend to be more open and more sensitive, more likely to have artistic talents—one of the trade-offs for the kind of feeling for others that lets you step into their skin, however briefly. A pity it isn't a matter of free will, something you could give back if you have trouble living with it once you've tried it on for size.

I didn't imagine that Iris Natalucci, the reporter sitting opposite me in my office on Monday morning, was troubled by frequent nightmares.

"I study nonverbal communication," I said to her. Hardly an enthralling way to describe my research. Stilted. Pedantic. If I could manage to maintain the same tone, she might be bored enough to keep the interview brief.

After talking to Rosemary Overstreet, I had vivid nightmares Saturday and Sunday night, the recurring nightmares that had begun when I was hospitalized as an adolescent: In them I was paralyzed, unable to scream for help, defenseless against a stranger hovering over me, overwhelmed by a feeling of impending doom. When I came to the office this morning, I'd asked Thelma Lou for Stuart's personnel file again. He'd worked as a technician in an endocrinology lab before starting graduate school in psychology, making Rosemary's horror story all too plausible.

Now, my fears confirmed, I didn't have any desire to sit and talk calmly about my research. Unfortunately, I didn't have much choice.

I guessed Iris was a few years short of thirty. Lovely chestnut hair, pretty face, professional makeup, and the kind of smile that displayed too many teeth. She'd tried to schedule an interview with me on Friday, saying she'd read about my work in the medical school's public relations blurb on faculty research. I'd put her off, making it clear I wasn't interested; two hours later I got a call from Kurt von Reichenau, asking me to specify the time I'd be available for an interview either that afternoon or Monday, emphasizing the importance of maintaining good press relationships, reminding me of the financial problems generated by Rugton's low inpatient census, and telling me he didn't want to get another call from the hospital director because I hadn't been cooperative. Publicity about research on deception didn't seem the most direct or promising way to fill Rugton's empty inpatient beds, but I didn't think arguing about it would help.

"How do you study deception?" Iris asked.

"We need samples of ordinary behavior, so we ask people to lie while we videotape them. My research team codes nonverbal behavior from the videotapes."

The first couple of times local newspaper articles were written about studies I'd conducted, the publicity had been a pleasant novelty. Then five years ago a convention press release featured our symposium at the American Psychological Association. Journalists made up half the audience. My phone rang incessantly for two weeks. Radio stations and smaller newspapers wanted interviews. Calls came from people across the country who wanted to know how to tell if their spouse was lying about cheating, or if an employee with shifty eyes was stealing, or if the President was lying when he talked about cutting taxes. I wasn't anxious to repeat the experience.

"You ask people to lie?"

Iris asked the question in a straightforward way, but something about her tone made me pause—an edge of something like slyness.

"To try to intentionally mislead someone, yes. We ask research subjects to smell something that's pleasant and convince others that it stinks. Or talk about someone they despise and pretend they like the person."

She reminded me of someone, but I couldn't make the connection.

"What made you pursue this line of research?"

I remembered when I was thirteen, my first time in the hospital: "This won't hurt," they'd said. Then searing pain. Sometimes they'd add, like an after-thought, "Too much. I hope." I could have steeled myself, I wanted to believe, if only I'd known. If I could divine truth.

Hardly the kind of thing I'd tell Iris, not with her sly smile, her cunning air. "Part of my broader interests in how people communicate," I said, as blandly as possible.

At the end of the interview her self-satisfied air seemed at odds with the dry material.

I spent most of the rest of the day testing a patient in the Psychometric Laboratory. When I finally finished at three, I needed a break. I headed toward the cafeteria for a soda.

I scanned the newest art therapy series beneath the Plexiglas covers as I walked past. This week's theme must have been trees. The first showed full, bushy trees set in green lawns surrounded by flowers. In the second a single tree was just leafing out. The third showed fall colors. The next only a leafless skeleton, alone by itself in the snow.

The art therapist, LisaLyn, squatted in front of the next frame, sorting through a pile of pictures on the floor, setting aside those for display. Her purple caftan billowed around her as she transferred the top picture to the discard pile after a cursory glance.

On the floor beside LisaLyn, at the top of her discard pile, I saw it: black and gray, firm lines painted with energy, the scene set at night. Unmistakably the Rugton parking lot as it would appear to someone looking down from the inpatient units on the third or fourth floors. Gray-green beams radiated from the evenly spaced mercury lights that marched across the parking lot. And near the front of the parking lot, a yellow 1959 Cadillac parked across two parking places, upstaging the trees sketched around the edge of the lot, like an afterthought. Not signed this time, but unmistakably the same artist whose chameleon I'd admired before: Vermilion.

At first I thought the dark lines a short distance from the car were shadows. When I picked it up for a closer look, I saw the shape of a person. I couldn't be sure, but it looked as though the figure, dressed in dark clothes, might be walking away from the car.

I pictured Alicia in her faded pink T-shirt and shorts. "I'd like to talk with the artist about her painting," I said.

The story of Alicia's dramatic suicide had reached everyone in Rugton within hours—trying to keep it quiet would have been as futile as trying to disguise a solar eclipse. Now LisaLyn directed me to the 3-East inpatient unit; she didn't ask why I wanted to talk with Vermilion about a picture of my patient's suicide scene, but she provided the information with the air of a teetotaler reluctantly pointing to the nearest bar. I headed upstairs with Vermilion's painting.

I was pleased to discover that Quinton Gibbs was Vermilion's attending physician on 3-East; the senior person in the department, he'd survived three decades and five changes in administration. He greeted me warmly. I told him what I wanted to do.

"Vermilion is the name she's used this week and last. But it may or may not be the name she'll use next week." He rolled his eyes upward. "As you'll discover in record time, she's acutely manic. She won't sit and talk for more than five minutes at a time, and she's refused all medications so far—says they'd interfere with her art."

Quinton gave me permission to ask Vermilion about her painting. "I don't think it'll do any harm; nothing we've tried so far has touched her, so I'm in favor of almost anything that might get through to her. She may refuse to talk to you; von Reichenau interviewed her in front of the unit staff as part of his professor's rounds last week. He kept trying to convince her to take medicine. Vermilion responded by talking about everything else under the sun. When he finished the interview, he asked Vermilion if she had any questions for him. She looked him up and down and said, 'I've been interviewed by five different people counting you since I got here, and you're one of the worst. If I were grading you, I'd give you a C, barely, because you're out to sea.'"

We shared smiles. "How did Kurt take all this?" I asked.

"When she left the room and we were discussing treatment options, he made a big point of saying how unreliable she was, how her illness polluted her judgment."

I thanked Quinton and went looking for Vermilion. I found her alone in the day room, a plump nineteen-year-old, her eyes rimmed in heavy black liner, her round, angelic face framed by short black hair gelled into stiff spikes.

After I introduced myself, she spoke in a rush, the words tumbling out. "Hello, nice day, lovely hair you have, red is the color of fire and passion. You're here to interview me, you're number six, what do you want to talk about?"

Vermilion looked suspiciously at me; before I could answer, she said, "Go away if you're here to talk about pills. I'm tired of people wanting me to take pills. I like staying up at night, I don't need much sleep." She closed her eyes and swayed in time to the rap music that blasted from the stereo beside her.

"I'm not here to talk about medication. I saw your watercolor downstairs, the one of the old yellow Cadillac in the parking lot at night—"

"You can have it, everyone likes my art, I'm going to have a big exhibit when I leave here, I paint or draw all the time, especially at night. Not much else to do when everyone's sleeping, so I sketch, then I pace, then I paint. I have trouble sitting still, so they want me to take a pill, but I know it'll make me ill. I'm just full of rhymes—"

"You saw the yellow Cadillac when you were awake Tuesday night?"

"More like Wednesday morning. Maybe two o'clock. I saw him park and walk away, I looked at my watch, I crossed my fingers and wished for company, I was going to show him his picture when he got here, I worked on it for an hour, but no one came to ask my name, no one came to make my fame—"

"A man walked away from the Caddy? You didn't see a woman in pink get out?"

She looked offended. "A *man,* not a *woman.* Dressed in something dark, wearing a baseball cap. You'd know that if you'd looked at my picture."

She stood up, turned the volume on the stereo as high as it would go, and headed for the door. "I'm tired of you, all you do is interrupt me," she shouted over the music. She slammed the day-room door behind her.

I stood still in the middle of the room, wondering about a man in a baseball cap. Dressed in something dark, hurrying away from Alicia's body. *Evidence that Alicia hadn't killed herself at Rugton.*

After I left Vermilion, I went to see Kurt von Reichenau. He remained seated, his desk and all it said about his authority firmly between us while I stood and told him Vermilion's story and showed him her picture. He watched me while I talked, his hands folded across his stomach, a faint smile on his face when I finished.

"Don't you feel that you're being a little . . . paranoid? After all, imagining that she committed suicide somewhere else, or, even more of a stretch, that someone killed her and drove her car with her body to the Rugton parking lot . . . well, that does seem unlikely, doesn't it?"

He spoke slowly and patiently, as if explaining things to a not-too-bright child. "Having a patient who kills herself is very upsetting for you, and you wish there was some way you could change what happened, but that's not possible. Now we all have to live with the consequences of your actions."

His eyes darted down to my hands, and I realized they were balled into fists. I didn't make an effort to unclench them.

"What about Vermilion's story?" I asked.

"I'm familiar with the details of Vermilion's case from my rounds on that unit; I certainly wouldn't be inclined to put much faith in her powers of observation."

The response I should have expected. I glanced around Kurt's office, trying to choke back the angry rejoinders that were running through my mind. Diplomas and certificates covered one wall. On the opposing wall, he'd mounted a display of fossils: a dragonfly, a lizard, and a scallop were the only easily recognizable shapes among them.

Maybe Kurt felt that safer than having to declare his preference for some sort of art, or perhaps he really preferred the frozen brown shapes to colors or scenes. I tended to think they reflected a key aspect of Kurt's personality: a predilection for the inanimate, creatures etched into stone eons ago, now wholly controllable and biddable.

I wanted to bellow, but I made the effort to speak mildly. As mildly as I could. "And Vermilion's painting?"

"She may have seen your patient getting out of the driver's seat and getting into the back seat. More likely, she heard the story, knew your patient was found dead in the back seat of her car, and made up the rest of it. I know you'd like it to be different, but there's nothing else to conclude."

I walked toward my office, remembering the policemen and the way they'd dismissed Rugton: *More flakes than Kellogg's*. I could just imagine how credible they'd find a witness like Vermilion. Probably as trustworthy as they'd obviously found me when I'd told them she wasn't suicidal and she didn't own her Cadillac.

Quinton Gibbs had told me that Kurt was Vermilion's fifth interviewer, and she'd kept the same count. Her picture showed the Cadillac parked across two parking spaces, just as I remembered it. Slim evidence for Vermilion's reliability, but I believed her.

That night I went back to Rugton after it got dark. I parked my car in the spot where I'd found Alicia in her car. I went to the women's restroom a couple of doors down from Vermilion's room. I turned out the light and looked down at the parking lot. The mercury lights lit the parking lot well; I could see my car clearly. If a man had gotten out of it, I could have seen him. I wouldn't have mistaken Alicia's pink T-shirt for dark clothing.

I'd been right. Alicia hadn't committed suicide in the Rugton parking lot. Someone had left her body on my doorstep. *But why?*

# Chapter 15

I walked into the funeral chapel for Alicia Erle's memorial service at noon on Tuesday. The heavy scents of roses and lilies clotted the air. I scanned the signatures in the funeral register before I added my own, not recognizing more than a handful. Stuart Crego's name wasn't on the list.

As I sat down, I watched a black-haired woman who'd come in the side door just after me. She paused near the door, holding herself as if she were an object of envy, her head held high as she surveyed the room; she looked as though she was taking the measure of the other mourners and would likely find them wanting. She wore a black raincoat, buttoned closed in spite of the heat, and she was very tall; if she didn't hit six feet, she didn't miss it by much. Perspiration glistened on her face.

She walked to the funeral register with the long strides of a man. She picked up the pen, looked down to where I'd signed, then turned to glance at me. The *Houston Chronicle* had printed a terse article describing Alicia's death, naming me as Alicia's psychologist and the person who discovered her body, information probably drawn from police reports. I might as well have worn a scarlet P on my chest.

Lightning flashed through the window, followed

closely by a low rumble of thunder. The sky had been darkening when I drove to the funeral home, but I'd been so preoccupied that I left my umbrella in my car.

More than half the pews stood empty in the small chapel. In the family pew I saw a couple who had to be Alicia's parents. Her mother sat hunched over, chewing on a corner of a wadded-up handkerchief. Alicia's father patted his wife's arm every so often without turning to look at her.

A dozen older people who had the look of relatives and family friends occupied the second and third rows. Oliver Tate and Xavier sat together two rows farther back. The sight of Gerald Yablonski in the next row surprised me when I remembered how little he'd talked with Alicia during her single group session. Perry Urbay sat alone in the next pew. A young woman sitting behind Perry took off oversized red glasses and pressed her eyes with her fingertips, obviously squeezing back tears. She looked familiar, maybe someone I'd seen around the medical center.

I wondered how many of the other mourners felt the same fallout from Alicia's suicide: a gritty coating of guilt and shame and anger rubbing against the delicate wound of grief.

As the somber piped-in music ended, a man slipped into the other end of my pew. Someone else I hadn't expected: Carlyle Stocklin, immaculate in his well-cut gray suit. Another group member, touched by Alicia? But Carlyle had been absent the night Alicia had come to group.

I hadn't spoken to Carlyle since his joint session with Bethany; he hadn't returned my call last week after he'd missed group again. I wondered what explanation he had given Bethany for his absence from group that night, what he'd say to me.

The young Southern Baptist pastor stood up and begin to speak, stumbling over his words in a way that suggested he hadn't known Alicia Erle personally, and he wasn't sure how to talk about a suicide. "Cut short in the prime of her life," he said, staring hard at his notes.

Who had Vermilion seen? Was he here today?

I turned to look at the neighboring pews, and the woman across the aisle—the woman I'd seen look me over when she saw my name in the book—looked away too quickly, the way people do when they've been caught staring. At first glance she'd looked like a twenty-some woman trying to appear older and more sophisticated than her age, the illusion heightened by the unruly dark hair that overflowed past the oversized shoulder pads of her black raincoat. A second look suggested that late forties was closer to the mark. Now she stared straight ahead.

The service ended with a processional out, the minister leading with almost unseemly haste, Alicia's parents behind him. The few people in the back rows of the chapel stayed in their seats until the trio had passed.

I waited for Carlyle to catch up with me at the end of the pew. "You knew Alicia?"

I kept my voice low, conscious of violating one of my rules; normally I don't greet patients when I run into them outside my office unless they speak to me first. Otherwise, they might be asked how they happened to know a psychologist.

Carlyle looked around without turning his head more than necessary, his glance taking in the people in front of him, then looking over his shoulder. Then back at me. I thought his eyes looked shiny, but it might have just been the angle. "Work. She was involved with . . . testing my compound."

*And that's all?*

Alicia's parents stood several feet away from the door, just far enough away to allow those who wanted to avoid a greeting to bypass them. Bleaching had turned Alicia's mother's hair as brittle and dry as scorched cornstalks during a drought. As if to compensate for the dullness of her hair, her lips and cheeks bloomed too bright, her eyebrows too dark, against a pasty-pale complexion.

The familiar-looking younger woman in red glasses held out her hand to Alicia's mother. "Lyle and I will finish packing up Alicia's house on Thursday, you can tell the landlord." She spoke in a distinctive voice, high-pitched, wandering randomly in a three or four-note range, everything spoken far too rapidly, gushing out.

"You've been such a help, Kate," Alicia's mother said, taking the young woman's hand and gripping it tightly.

Kate Wheelon, Alicia's friend. Her voice jogged my memory: We'd been stuck side by side in a slow-moving line, waiting to have our pictures snapped for our plastic hospital ID badges, an annual rite. "I've got work piled up to here waiting for me," she'd complained about the delay, using her forefinger to draw a line midway between aggressive eyebrows and wispy bangs. A research associate working on a project in the Physiology Department, she'd told me.

Now Kate Wheelon's eyes were red and swollen. "I left the key you gave me under the flowerpot by the hose," she told Alicia's mother. "Just in case you want to go back before it's all packed."

*Maybe I'll visit.* Then, before I could wonder why such an outrageous idea had come so easily to mind, Kate moved toward the door, and I found myself facing Alicia's parents. Their grief, etched in set lines across their faces, dwarfed any pain I experienced from Alicia's suicide.

"I'm Haley McAlistar," I said, holding out my hand to her father. "I'm very sorry about Alicia." Alicia's father had a heavy face, his mouth drawn down with chronic discontent.

Alicia's father ignored my hand. He raised his voice to a pitch that assured that the waiting line couldn't miss his words. "A stilson wrench in a skirt. Ms. Fix-It. Not much use, were you?" He breathed whiskey overlaid with peppermint. "Couldn't pour warm piss out of your boot if you had the instructions written on the bottom."

"It must have been a great comfort to have you as a therapist." Alicia's mother spit out the words so I couldn't miss her meaning. "Pity you didn't do better when it might've made a difference." Then, like wax dripping off a candle, her eyes filled with tears and she added, "Maybe if she'd come to me instead of you, she'd be alive today."

I stumbled as I walked away, my legs suddenly rubbery, my face on fire, all too aware of everyone behind me, all the people in line who'd seen and heard. Objectively I knew that Alicia's parents needed someone to share the blame, their shame hanging in the room like an acrid, smoky cloud. But I couldn't have felt guiltier if I'd been a hit-and-run driver forced to confront the parents of a child I'd killed.

# Chapter 16

**W**hoever decorated the Anchorage Restaurant must have wanted to make sure that no one missed the nautical motif. The sign over the cashier's desk read PURSER, the entrance to the kitchen was labeled GALLEY. The restrooms bore the legends GULLS (above a bare-breasted mermaid, seductively curling her tail) and BUOYS (no picture for guidance). A rowboat painted an unlikely shade of yield-sign yellow sat in the center of the room; plastic lobsters swarmed over the wooden lobster traps jumbled inside it. Blue, yellow, and red glass floats were tangled among the fishing nets that swathed the windows in lieu of curtains. The speakers mounted high on the walls broadcast a raucous version of "Blow the Man Down." The smell of beer and fried food coated the air. After the somber memorial service the effect was jarring, like a garish billboard in the middle of a secluded forest.

I'd paused by the door of the funeral home after speaking to Alicia's parents. Outside, the rain poured down in sheets. I cursed myself for leaving my umbrella in the car. I'd glanced around to see if there was any newspaper nearby, anything large enough to hold over my head as I made a dash for my car.

As I'd hesitated, the black-haired woman joined me, an umbrella in her hand. "Alicia's shrink, right?"

I'd nodded curtly.

"I'm Debra Linnell, Alicia's adviser when she was a grad student." She'd paused then, looking at me. Waiting to see how I'd react.

I hadn't felt like talking to anyone, but I couldn't let an opportunity pass to learn about Alicia. "I don't know about you, but I could sure use a drink. Join me?"

She'd shared her umbrella as we walked to our cars, suggesting we meet here since it was so close. I'd sat in my car less than five minutes, just long enough to gather my composure and think about what to ask Debra.

Now she was already more than halfway through her drink.

"I'd just about given up on you." Debra spoke accusingly, her voice loud enough to make the gray-haired woman at the next table lift her head from her newspaper and peer at us over the top of her reading glasses.

Debra had shed the black raincoat she'd worn to Alicia's memorial service, as if casting off old skin that didn't fit any more. Scarlet poppies the size of dinner plates vibrated against the yellow background of her dress, the short sleeves tight around her muscular arms.

Our waitress, a young woman in well-worn sneakers, drifted over to the table. "Wanna order?" she mumbled as she tried to rub a mustard-colored spot off the shoulder of her blue sailor suit, her captain's cap inching down her forehead as she twisted her neck to appraise her success.

I looked at my watch: after one o'clock. I glanced at the menu and ordered a Lone Star beer and peel-and-eat shrimp cooked in Cajun seasoning, hush puppies on the side. Debra studied the plastic-coated menu long enough to memorize it; finally she ordered another scotch and soda, onion rings, and a dozen oysters. I listened to her recite her order too soft and too fast, then, when the waitress asked her to repeat it, excruciatingly slow and loud, her tone patronizing.

We put off talking about Alicia by playing who-do-you-know with colleagues at the university.

After we established that we knew a few of the same people, I asked if she'd run across Stuart Crego.

"Not someone I've met. You know Oliver Tate?" Debra's tone seemed too deliberately nonchalant when she asked about Oliver.

"Met him last week." I thought about stopping there, then continued; I wanted to gauge her reaction to Oliver's story. "He came to see me after the police visited him to ask about his name on Alicia's prescription. He said she'd set him up, forging the prescription."

Debra leaned forward and smiled. "Really. Too bad for him. Just too bad."

I raised my eyebrows in inquiry.

"I've known Oliver since we were biology majors at Rice. Did he tell you all about how he was a football star in college?"

"No."

"I'm surprised. He usually works his athletic history into any conversation with a pretty woman as early as possible." She downed the remainder of her drink in one gulp; her tongue sidled up the side of her glass after she swallowed, mopping up stray drops.

"Quarterback at Rice University—the Rice Owls. He wasn't big enough for a major college team, but made up for it with bravado and a knack for intimidating the opposition. He still does the same thing." She looked closely at me, as if making sure I was paying attention.

"Big time, locally—led Rice to one of their rare winning seasons. A couple of years ago there was a fund-raising weekend for Rice alumni. In the evening, our old premed crowd got together at a sports bar near campus. They announced Oliver's name over the speaker when he sat down; people clapped, he waved, like a king greeting subjects. He spotted a woman two tables away, a pretty brunette, hair down to her waist, midtwenties, almost falling out of her low-cut dress. He just sat and stared at her—predatory, raping her with his eyes, ignoring everyone else—not even pretending to look anywhere else.

"Her boyfriend tried to stare him down, but Oliver ignored him; finally, her boyfriend stood up, and started walking toward our table. Everyone tensed up, waiting for a fight."

Our waitress scurried over, overloaded with plates for our table and the next, almost dropping my plate in my lap as she set them down.

"Clumsy." Debra spoke loudly enough so that the waitress couldn't miss it. A red flush traveled down the young woman's throat.

"It's fine," I said. "No harm done."

"Her boyfriend was bigger and younger than Oliver, but Oliver stared him down, watching every step he took." Debra bit into one of her onion rings, talking before she'd finished chewing her first mouthful. "Halfway there, he tripped. Almost fell. When he got to the table, he stood there, not saying anything, looking at Oliver—then he asked Oliver what he thought of Rice's current football team."

Debra snorted derisively. "That's vintage Oliver. Compulsively seductive. He still acts like his ancient athletic glories shield him from the mundane, everyday rules of behavior."

I remembered Oliver in my office, putting his hand on my shoulder, making sure I knew he'd seen me in my bathing suit.

"Oliver married Beth, a friend of mine, five years ago. Pursued her like crazy. They dated six months; she was all starry-eyed. The day before their wedding, a hysterical woman called Beth and told her she'd been Oliver's mistress for a couple of years; he'd just told her he needed to break it off before his marriage. Beth married him anyway. She left him six months later." Debra gave me a "so there" look, as if she'd told me everything I needed to know.

I took a bite of my shrimp. It had a rubbery, granular texture. Good hush puppies, fresh and hot, could have made me forget any other food on the table. The lukewarm greasy lumps on my plate didn't qualify.

"I got one of Oliver's papers to review after I left the university," Debra said. "Terrible science. Read like an ad for the drug he'd been testing, not a scientific paper. I returned it with a note to the journal editor saying I couldn't comment because of conflict of interest. I wrote the note on one of those white air sickness bags."

As I laughed, I noticed the woman at the next table smile appreciatively. I deliberately pitched my voice low, hoping Debra would take the hint and follow suit: "Why did you decide to leave the university?"

"Once I knew I had something really promising, I had to choose. The university offered safety, but the long-term payoffs, financially and professionally— much, much bigger outside."

She picked up an oyster shell, pried the raw oyster loose with the miniature fork, dunked it in seafood sauce, and swallowed it in one gulp. "I've never been big on safe choices."

Two plaques made of lacquered pine decorated the wall near our table. I read the words painted on them in gold: TITANIC and LUSITANIA. Not an omen, I hoped.

"Drug development is a horse race." Debra's face had a sheen of dampness. "With competitors for the same kind of new drug, the first one with FDA approval gets the lion's share of the business—even when they're introduced within months of each other."

She plunged her fork into another oyster like a hawk diving on a rabbit. "Take the two hydrocortisone creams introduced in 1982: The first one got a fifty percent market share, the second settled for ten percent."

"Risky."

"Risky doesn't begin to describe it. Only one out of every seven to ten drugs tested in humans ever reaches the market. But my company will make it, and make it big." She harpooned her last oyster and swallowed it.

A variant of the John Wayne school of life: No guts, no glory. And not much sympathy for those who couldn't prosper under adversity. I asked, "When was the last time you spoke with Alicia?"

"Miss," Debra addressed our waitress in a commanding voice as she passed us with her hands full of plates. "Another drink for me." She turned back to me. "Hard to say, exactly; I'm pretty busy. I'm a member of the psychobiology study section at NIH, so I'm out of town at least every other month for panel meetings and site visits. I was in Washington at a study section meeting the night Alicia died."

*Almost smooth enough to make her alibi seem like a natural part of our conversation.* But not an answer to the question I'd asked.

Debra took off her right earring, one of a pair of clip-on miniature porcelain watermelon slices. "Oliver Tate is a malignant man. I'd bet he had a poisonous influence on Alicia, like he did on a lot of women."

"Did Oliver go after Alicia?"

"I doubt it. Not his type. When Alicia came to the department, he said she looked like a midget barmaid." She looked me over. "You're the kind he chases."

"How long did Alicia work with you?"

"Two years. She worked *for* me for two years." Debra tossed her earring back and forth between her hands. "Alicia got decent enough grades, but she wasn't creative in the laboratory. Would've been a good plodder, nothing more. She didn't grasp the difference. She could run complex experiments when someone else designed them, and she thought that was all she needed. Ideas are the main currency, something Alicia never understood." Her lips twisted in an expression of disgust. "I bet Alicia told you all kinds of stories about me, about how difficult she found working for me."

I looked at her, not answering. The expression that flashed across her face could have been fear. Or simple indigestion, after she'd devoured her odd meal so quickly.

"Alicia was too sensitive. I'd review problems in the drafts of her master's thesis with her, and she'd show up with red eyes after disappearing for two hours."

Debra picked up her earring again and kept snapping the clip open and closed. The veins stood out in relief on her large, clawlike hands. "Alicia betrayed you, just like she betrayed me. In the end." When she said Alicia's name, she tugged on the clip, breaking it off. She gave it a hurt, angry look, as if it had broken itself.

"Alicia betrayed you?"

"You're not supposed to speak badly of the dead, are you?" Debra's voice grew louder, her gestures more expansive. "Alicia needed men's approval and admiration to bolster her, needed it badly. She wasn't comfortable taking the lead on her own, putting forth her own ideas; she needed a man to tell her she was a worthwhile person. She was a sitting duck when Oliver Tate needed someone to run his unit full time; he sold her on the advantages of taking a break from grad school."

The speaker on the wall near our table began to trumpet "Anchors Away." Over the noise Debra said, "Oliver put a lot of pressure on her, giving her too much responsibility for his unit, then treating her badly. The drug company that bankrolled his biggest study pulled out, so now he's down to one project. He's got to fill the beds on his unit at least fifty percent of the time to break even with the hospital's charges for his space. If he doesn't, they'll force him out and move another program in."

"And then?"

"And then he'll lose his autonomy—his empire will collapse. He'll be just another faculty member with no special pull." She gulped her drink enthusiastically. "'Big hat, no cattle,' as my grandfather used to say."

Her speech was slightly slurred. "When I got back from Washington, I had three hang-up calls on my answering machine. Later, when I heard about her death, I wondered if it could have been Alicia. Maybe trying to reach me, after . . . But it didn't make sense—did the medical examiner decide it was definitely suicide?"

"What makes you question it?" I asked, speaking

insistently, too eager to hear that someone else had doubts.

Debra looked at her watch, then scanned the room. She looked everywhere but at me. "Just a stupid question, I guess. Under the circumstances it's pretty clear, but the timing . . . who would've expected that Alicia . . ."

Then, after I asked a second time what she'd meant, she gave me a blank look.

"Where's our pathetic excuse for a waitress?" Debra's voice rose, louder than before, belligerent, warning me off. "You'd think she'd at least have the sense to bring the check so she'd get her tip."

# Chapter 17

Funerals pour gasoline on the glowing embers of old losses. Pushing myself through the rest of the day after my lunch with Debra, I kept thinking of Ian. When I left work at six, I didn't want to face my empty house. I thought of going out to dinner, but I was too wired to feel hungry.

I got in my car and headed for the freeway. I've spent a lot of time driving the endless Texas highways since Ian died. I like empty rural roads where I'm the only car in sight.

I turned on the radio, punching buttons until I found a country station. As I picked up Highway 45 and headed north out of Houston, Randy Travis was singing about exhuming things better left alone.

I thought about what Debra had said. Was it only the booze talking, or did she have some special reason that made her wonder if Alicia had really killed herself? Or—could Debra have been probing, trying to see how I'd react?

A couple minutes after I'd exited off the highway onto a rural two-lane road, I looked into my rearview mirror and saw a brown pickup truck behind me, following too closely. The pickup had been behind me for some time, turning off the freeway when I did. The windows were tinted; I couldn't see the driver.

I slowed down and pulled close to the shoulder, giving the driver ample room to pass, no traffic coming the other way. The pickup truck slowed as well.

I passed one of those yellow rectangular Texas highway signs that remind motorists to DRIVE FRIENDLY. Someone had peppered it with bullet holes.

I didn't want to play games. My 'Vette's block V-8 engine gives it power and speed, a lot more than most people expect for a car made in 1960. I hit the gas, taking it up to ninety.

After a brief hesitation the truck put on speed, coming closer again, looking as if it could continue matching my pace.

A truck like that shouldn't have been able to marshal that kind of speed. Not an ordinary pickup truck.

Maybe a cowboy who'd had one too many beers. Maybe a couple of teenage boys out for a good time, looking to harass a woman alone. *Maybe Stuart Crego.*

We had the road to ourselves, no other cars in sight. Only farm land on either side. My mirror showed the pickup coming closer, pulling over as if he might be getting ready to pass—or force me off the road.

I floored the gas pedal, willing my car to give me everything it had. Top speed for the original engine was 132, but I had a rebuilt engine, and I'd never pushed it this hard. I didn't know its limits.

Not a quiet car normally, the 'Vette now roared back at me. I was going too fast, far too fast. I watched the needle climb past 100, past 110. If I hit something in the road, if I had to swerve, I'd spin out. My damp hands were slippery on the steering wheel.

Alicia had told me she'd felt hunted at least three times: In her intake, *problems with a whole gang of piranhas, sharks, and buzzards;* at the end of group, when she likened herself to the fox in the hunting scene on the curtains; and a skeleton had stalked her in her dreams. Had I come too close to her murderer?

I looked back and forth between the road and rearview mirror. The pickup was still behind me, not as close but still not giving up the chase, waiting for me to back off my speed—waiting for me to make a mistake that would bring me within his reach.

I looked down and saw the temperature gauge had jumped from the bottom of the normal zone to the top, the needle heading steadily toward the red. I hadn't put the convertible top down because the weather had stayed so hot; now I switched off the air conditioner and opened my window halfway.

My knees were weak, my right leg starting to tremble as I struggled to keep the pedal pressed to the floor. Sweat dripped down my face.

Since Ian's death I've had a nightmare every couple of weeks where I'm driving and find I have no brakes— no way to stop. Out of control, speeding toward disaster. I wanted to wake up and find this wasn't real.

I watched the pickup recede in the mirror, the distance between us growing too slowly for my taste.

I looked down at the temperature gauge, now at the bottom of the red and still going up. I had to drop my speed to 100. I couldn't risk stalling out or blowing up.

I could still see him behind me, barely. I hoped he couldn't tell that I'd slowed, hoped he wouldn't pour out more.

The road had gotten worse here, and I hit a hole, jarring myself. It was hard to spot problems in time to avoid them at that speed, hard to navigate with the sweat that kept dripping down my forehead. Battling the truck, the road—and my growing sense of dread.

I pictured the butchered mouse in the trap that Stuart had left in my car: Was it a warning, a prelude, to what was happening now? Was my bloody body supposed to end up splattered across the driver's seat?

I tried to remember how long the road was, how far I'd come, how long until I got to the highway up ahead. Maybe I'd missed the signs back to the highway. I looked around for some clue, some way to tell where I was. There was only farmland to the horizon on either side, as flat and featureless as the ocean.

After what seemed like an eon I saw the turnoff to

Highway 59, a safe road back to Houston. Safer, at least. I couldn't see the pickup in my rearview mirror; I didn't know if he could still see me, could see which way I turned.

Maybe he didn't need to keep me in sight. Maybe he already knew which way I'd be heading if I went home.

I kept to the fast lane when I hit the freeway, dropping my speed just enough so I wouldn't be a danger—hoping I'd be stopped by police so I could tell my story. I'd gladly trade a speeding ticket for safe passage back home.

No police in sight.

A millennium later, back in the city limits, I pulled off without signaling into the parking lot of a busy McDonald's. I hadn't seen any sign of the pickup, but he could have been holding back, keeping me in sight in the growing darkness. The muscles in my right leg still quivered as if I was still trying to hold down the gas pedal. I sat trembling, trying to slow my breathing, watching traffic for fifteen minutes.

Twice brown pickups passed, making me gasp. Neither had tinted windows.

I could report the incident to the police, but I didn't know what they could do without a license plate number for identification, without a crime other than speeding on a deserted road.

I didn't want to go home alone, not now. Acting on impulse last weekend, I'd stopped at an abandoned gas station where a man had propped his stock of black velvet paintings in front of his rusting van: Elvis, Mickey Mouse, and the Virgin Mary were the featured stars, backed by assorted matadors, ballerinas, and nude women in cowboy boots. I'd bought an idealized younger Elvis as a gift for Glee. She'd always loathed Elvis.

Now I drove to Glee's house. I got the painting out of my trunk and rang her doorbell, holding it so she'd see Elvis when she looked out the peephole. I heard the sound of the television in the background as her footsteps approached the door, then a strangled laugh.

"Elvis lives," I announced loudly, my voice breaking on the last word.

"What's wrong?" Scanning my face as I walked inside, she motioned me toward the tomato-red couch, the most comfortable place to sit in her ultramodern living room. She turned off the television and sat beside me.

As I told Glee about being chased, I got teary, then embarrassed.

"I'd have been terrified," she said when I'd finished. She reached over and squeezed my hand before going into the kitchen. She returned with a bottle of wine and two glasses. "Start on this while I fix something to eat," she said. "And no, you can't help," she added, when I started to get up.

Glee made sandwiches: avocado, turkey, and mozzarella piled high on rye bread coated with mayonnaise. We ate without talking, the comfortable silence of good friends. After we finished the brownies and milk she insisted were purely medicinal, we watched an old Pink Panther movie and drank the rest of the wine.

I took her up on her offer of her spare room for the night. She insisted that Elvis share the room with me.

# Chapter 18

The next morning Perry Urbay was waiting for me when I got to my office at nine. He looked tired, his Ivy League handsomeness ill-suited to his worried expression. He told me he needed to terminate his practicum at Rugton.

"What's this about?" I gestured for him to sit down.

"I was supposed to get a stipend for doing assessments at juvenile court, but I just got word yesterday that the state cut the funding for the position. I need to get another job as fast as possible." He cleared his throat. "It's for the best, anyway."

"What do you mean, 'for the best'?"

"Alicia killed herself because of my incompetence. I know we talked before and you tried to say I wasn't responsible"—he held up his hand before I could protest—"but there's no other reason for her to have killed herself at Rugton. She wanted her message heard, loud and clear."

I had Vermilion's picture on my desk. I handed it to Perry and told him what she'd said and how I'd gone back to Rugton after dark on Monday to check out her story myself.

Perry sat unmoving when I finished, his gaze fixed on my carpet.

Finally he looked back at me. "Thanks. That picture means a lot. But I'm still stuck without a job—no way to support myself and pay tuition. I probably wasn't meant to be a psychologist; my father's a big-time lawyer, and he never liked the idea of psychology as a profession. I've already decided to work this year and go to law school next year."

"Tell me about your assessment experience," I said.

He told me. He had more than most graduate students at his level.

"Here's the WAIS-R manual." I handed him the manual for the Wechsler Adult Intelligence Scale, the most common adult intelligence test, and I pulled my test kit off the bookshelf and set it in front of him. "Administer Block Design to me."

He smiled—a wide, self-satisfied grin. He didn't bother to open the manual. He picked up one of the blocks, holding it between his thumb and forefinger in the approved fashion. "You see these blocks? They are all alike. . . ." He'd memorized the instructions, the way I'd been trained. A rarity these days.

I deliberately made an error on the first trial, an uncommon event in real life. Perry saw it immediately, and gave me the exact instructions for correction. We walked through four other WAIS-R subtests that he got letter-perfect, and then I started with tests that required more specialized experience.

Perry didn't miss a beat.

A half hour later I said, "Would you be willing to consider a position as a psychometrist while you decide if you want to be a psychologist?"

He beamed. "I'd be delighted." Then he hesitated. "This isn't charity, is it?"

We shook hands after agreeing on the terms of his appointment, effective immediately.

After Perry left my office, Thelma Lou buzzed me and asked if I'd read Iris Natalucci's newspaper article; she had a copy if I wanted to see it. Iris was Stuart Crego's second cousin, Thelma Lou informed me.

Stuart had called Thelma Lou to tell her, and to make sure I didn't miss the article.

The piece filtered so much of what I'd said about my research on deception that it was almost a parody, but that wasn't the point Iris wanted to make: She emphasized how the supposed expert on deception had told the police that one of her patients, found dead after ingesting sleeping pills and alcohol in front of Rugton, "wasn't suicidal." Which wasn't something I'd ever discussed with her. Stuart must have heard the story from someone in Rugton and used it for another phase in his get-even campaign.

I found it hard to breath for a minute as I imagined Alicia's parents reading the article, fueling their anger toward me.

"You remember what kind of car Stuart drove?" I tried to keep my voice casual as I handed the paper back to Thelma Lou.

She gave me a worried look. "No . . . but I can ask Nancy." I thanked her but didn't explain.

Kurt von Reichenau called me down to his office and chastised me for not being more careful in my contacts with the media. Then he added, "I called the medical examiner's office. He's brought in a verdict of death by suicide for your patient. I expect her parents have a lawyer who'll be wanting your patient's records, now that it's official. Doesn't look at all promising, especially in light of your recent publicity. Especially since you don't have the chart."

I looked at Kurt and knew what he was planning as clearly as if his thoughts had been displayed on a TelePrompTer. Once the lawsuit was filed, he'd put another psychologist in charge of the Psychometric Lab. I'd headed the lab for ten years and had done a good job. But a lawsuit—especially one without a chart, where I had no way to show I hadn't been negligent—he'd be able to replace me, no questions asked.

"You've caused problems on another front, as well,"

Kurt said. "I'd certainly have difficulty defending your judgment if I were put under oath right now."

"Another front?" I felt exposed and vulnerable, as if I were walking around in sandals while everyone else wore steel-toed work boots.

"That patient who calls herself Vermilion, the one you harassed about her art therapy project? She left the hospital AMA yesterday. Undoubtedly a direct result of your interference in her treatment the previous day."

AMA: against medical advice.

Kurt continued, "Surely you could see that Vermilion was a very disturbed woman. You could have shown better judgment than to bother her with nonsense."

He made it clear that he wasn't interested in hearing my side of the story. When he was finished chastising me, I called Quinton Gibbs, Vermilion's attending physician, telling him that I'd heard from Kurt that she'd left AMA. I told him how sorry I felt about Vermilion.

Quinton laughed. "Vermilion started threatening to leave and go paint in Mexico her first day on the unit, during her admission interview. She saw a magazine article on Acapulco yesterday, took that for an omen, and signed herself out. She wasn't a danger to herself or others, so we couldn't stop her. It was not a result of your conversation with her."

I felt better about Vermilion's quick exit after I'd spoken to Quinton. But I couldn't help thinking that while Vermilion hadn't been the most reliable witness, she was the only one I'd had. Now my only witness had left the country.

I would have gone to see Glee next, but she'd flown to New York this morning. Last night I'd watched her expression get grimmer as I told her what I'd been doing since Alicia's death. She'd suggested, gently, that I avoid anything that might antagonize Alicia's parents further.

Now I thought how well Stuart had chosen his latest revenge, how cleverly he'd upped the ante. The newspaper story was certain to inflame Alicia's parents.

I have a million-dollar professional liability policy; if Alicia's parents were to win a judgment for more than a million, I am personally liable for the balance. If I were to lose the lawsuit, I doubt that I'd find anyone who'd sell me malpractice coverage in the future. Practicing without insurance would mean putting everything I own at risk, or making dramatic changes in the kind of work I do.

Alicia's death could end my professional life.

I felt my stomach knot up. I felt as if I'd been wading in the ocean, taken a step, and suddenly lost touch with the bottom.

When I got back to my office I found a note that Thelma Lou had slipped under my door, signed with a webbed foot: "Honda Civic. Light blue."

Maybe Stuart last night, maybe not. He might have borrowed the brown truck, knowing his own car wouldn't have the speed or power—or the tinted windows. Or it could have been someone else. Perhaps publication of his cousin's inflammatory article had satisfied his revenge quota—or perhaps he still had some other grand finale in reserve for me.

I tried to reach Rosemary Overstreet to see if she could tell me anything more about Stuart. I hoped she might give me names of other people I could contact who might give me information without alerting him. Rosemary wasn't available, but the department secretary took a message. I'd already asked the psychometrists who had worked with Stuart; they'd taken pains to avoid him.

At noon I walked over to the hospital cafeteria in the main house, not hungry but wanting to be distracted. The cafeteria had been in an upgrade mode for six months, ever since the hospital board had allowed two fast-food restaurants to establish beachheads in the basement. A table by the entrance displayed the specials for the day, wilted and congealed beneath protective plastic domes. Inside, the newly added soup-and-salad bar featured a crock of lima bean soup that resembled sludge, encircled by bowls of shriveling greens. On the rare days when the self-serve yogurt machine didn't have an out-of-order notice taped to it, patrons could choose between flavors like mint (the color of split-pea soup), or butterscotch in a sickly shade of yellow-brown. Two carousels rotated the hot food selections past customers at a speed that managed to cool their contents to room temperature within two circuits.

I stopped by the counter optimistically called the deli and looked over stacks of bologna, well-done roast beef, pressed chicken, and turkey. I got cheddar cheese on pita bread with lettuce and a pickle, hoping it represented the least of the possible evils.

I spotted Xavier, the physician from Oliver Tate's unit, sitting at a table by himself. He was hunched over a newspaper, his muscular shoulders and arms looking as if they belonged to someone at least a head taller. I asked if I could join him. Standing up and holding out his hand to me, he looked too pleased, as if unaccustomed to company in Houston.

"I saw you at Alicia's funeral," I said.

"Very sad." He had a fruit salad, a hamburger and fries, and a bowl of lima bean soup on his tray. He took a sip of soup and looked as if he would have spit it out if I'd not been sitting across from him. "Alicia kept telling me to try this soup in the cafeteria. She was too fond of playing tricks." He pushed the bowl away and took a bite of fruit salad.

"Did you know Alicia well?"

"Not so very well. I come—came last month. She helped me learn my job."

"What do you do?"

"Physical examinations on patients who come for studies, ratings of drug effects. One reason Dr. Tate hired me was my language; we advertise in Spanish to recruit patients for the studies; I talk with them when they call."

Hardly the scarce skills that might be expected as the basis for a coveted green card, the document that gave a foreigner permanent residency; without it, Xavier would have to leave when his year as a fellow ended. Theoretically, Oliver would need to prove that Xavier was indispensable for his job, to demonstrate that no one else could perform the same duties—a lengthy, time-consuming process that involved advertising in professional journals and local papers, justifying the rejection of every other applicant. But a man like Xavier, beholden to Oliver, wouldn't make waves like Alicia. I could see why he might be just the kind of employee Oliver would prefer: compliant to a fault.

"Did Alicia talk about anything in particular in the last few weeks?"

He smoothed the sparse strands of wavy hair stretched across the top of his balding head while he considered the question. "Only her new car. She was very excited about it."

"Did Alicia ever mention a man named Stuart Crego?"

"It is not a name I remember."

"Oliver told me about the fire in his lab," I said. "Lucky it wasn't worse."

"Yes. I was sorry not to be there, to help. I was home, sleeping. After being at the hospital for night studies."

"Do you work on the graphiting studies?"

"Graphiting—I don't know that word."

I didn't understand it either, so I changed the subject; I'd been puzzled by it when Alicia described her job.

As we were walking out of the cafeteria, we ran into Oliver Tate talking with Dean Verbrugge. Oliver stood smack in the middle of the busy corridor, his arms folded across his chest, forcing passersby to detour around him, while the dean leaned against the wall, out of the way of the traffic. Oliver was laughing at something the dean was saying. Then Oliver caught sight of us, his eyes traveling back and forth between us. His expression went from warm to cold.

I felt my lunch sitting as heavily in my stomach as if I'd choked down a paperweight.

# Chapter 19

When I stopped to check messages after lunch, Thelma Lou said, "There's someone wanting to talk with you. She doesn't have an appointment." She dropped her voice. "Says Alicia Erle was a friend of hers."

I saw my visitor pacing back and forth in the clinic waiting area. Red cowboy boots peeped out beneath her denim prairie-style skirt. A red-and-blue bandanna wrapped her hair, tied in a rakish knot by her left ear. Gold hoop earrings emphasized her gypsy look. Kate Wheelon, Alicia's ex-roommate.

Her high-pitched voice erupted as soon as I was within range. "Look, I don't mean to pester you, but I need to talk about Alicia. I'll come back another time if this isn't good."

She phrased it as a request, but the truculence in her voice and the stiffness in her back didn't suggest she was prepared to yield easily.

I told her now was fine and gestured toward my office.

She jerked her head at the door. "Let's go outside—if the heat's not too much for you."

Outside Rugton the September sun was high and hot, glaring down, unprepared to show any mercy. The fierce midday heat trapped smells, holding them captive, and the stagnant air reeked of asphalt and dust, baked too long in the harsh sunlight.

Kate stuck her hands in her pockets and started down the street, walking as fast as she talked, addressing her comments to the pavement. "This guy from the medical examiner's office came to see me, investigating Alicia's suicide. Her parents gave him my name when he asked about her friends. He asked a lot of questions about Alicia—how she'd seemed recently, if she'd ever said anything about suicide, or seemed depressed. He wanted to know if she'd experienced any recent losses like a death of someone close or a boyfriend breaking up with her, or if she had financial problems. He asked particularly about any health problems, any recent medical treatment; I told him she was in one of our studies, and our subjects had to have physical exams. She'd been clean. He asked about the protocol, when I'd last seen her. . . ."

She tugged at the knot in her scarf. "He said it was mostly routine, but he had to check since you said she wasn't suicidal the last time you'd seen her." She stopped short, her sudden stillness a challenge. "When was the last time?"

I couldn't see the harm in telling her. "I spoke with her on Tuesday. First day of September."

"Not since?" she asked, her tone belligerent.

"No."

I tensed up, waiting for her to echo the tune of blame I'd gotten from Alicia's parents.

Kate pulled a pack of Virginia Slims from her skirt pocket. She extracted a matchbook tucked between the box and the cellophane wrapper, then put a cigarette in her mouth and lit it.

Yesterday at the funeral she'd worn an out-of-fashion navy-blue dress with a too-full skirt and a white collar starting to yellow at the edges. It had the look of a dress sewn for her high-school chorus, pulled from the back of her closet when she realized at the last moment she needed something sedate and dark. Yesterday she'd seemed so young and vulnerable.

"When was the last time you talked to Alicia?" I asked, more to break the thick silence than for any other reason.

Kate started walking again, fast. She waited so long to say anything that I'd started to believe she wasn't going to answer.

"Mostly on Thursday, the week before she died. We got together for a drink Thursday night. She had her usual weekly research appointment in my lab the next Tuesday, but we didn't talk much."

"How'd she seem?"

"Thursday, she was excited. Real pleased with herself. She called me at work and suggested we go for a drink; told me she'd pick me up. I looked out when I heard this fierce honking; there was Alicia, sitting like a queen on her throne in that yellow Caddy—she'd just bought it, traded in her old gray Escort. She talked about seeing you in your 'Vette, decided it'd be cool to drive around in an old car like you. Kinda wanted to outdo you, if you know what I mean; she figured the Caddy, big as it was, would draw more attention than your 'Vette. She'd taken a full day to fix it up—waxed and polished it by hand, including all that monster chrome, found gold-fringed pillows at Pier 1 that were a shade darker than the seat covers, even bought whitewall cleaner and scrubbed the tires. I asked her straight out where she got the money for it, because she always complained about not having enough; she said she'd finally gotten the first installment. Wouldn't say more."

" 'First installment?' "

"Typical Alicia." Kate shrugged. "She liked being mysterious. Then she hinted about a married man she was seeing. Got real coy when I asked her who he was."

*Married man?* "What did she say?" I tried to keep my voice casual.

"That he'd cooked chili for her after she told him she liked it, and he'd asked for a key to her house, so she was convinced he'd leave his wife for her. For her, that was, like, major proof of his devotion. Big deal. He fixes one meal, and he wants to make sure he can get inside quickly, so he's not spotted by the neighbors when he visits."

"Any guesses who he was?"

She gave me an irritated look that said she expected me to know these things already.

"No idea. I told her she was cruisin' for a bruisin', making a huge mistake getting so excited about a man who'd already been taken; she didn't want to hear it. Changed the subject, announced she'd be quitting her job, maybe even going back to finish her Ph.D. 'Big metamorphosis coming,' she told me, but wouldn't say anything else after I ragged on her about the married man."

Alicia had planned to quit her job with Oliver? Or had she seen the termination letter and made other plans already?

I would have liked to linger in the pockets of shade we passed along the way, away from the predatory sun, but Kate maintained her pace. "Did Alicia say anything else about leaving her job and going back to school?"

"Not really. It didn't seem like she'd thought it through much further."

"Did she ever talk about a man named Stuart Crego?"

"Not that I remember."

A car drove by, fanning the smoke from Kate's cigarette into my face. I had to stop myself from waving it away. "How did she seem on Tuesday?"

"Quiet, but that's not surprising. She had an NG tube down her throat most of the time."

"What kind of research is it?"

"We're looking at relationships between obesity and a person's ability to monitor stomach fullness. All our subjects are women, either normal weight or overweight." Kate ground out her cigarette under her heel, picked up the butt, and tossed it in a trash can. "We feed them through an NG tube to get past the issue of taste and their usual ideas about how much or how little they've eaten. They're given different solutions—different ratios of fiber, fat, carbohydrates, and protein—and they have to rate how full they feel at set intervals."

"Why'd Alicia do it?"

"Because we pay well. We need subjects for the full series: sixteen sessions, once a week, so we pay a hundred bucks each time. Plus a free lunch, as we always remind them.

"I remember Alicia got a little freaked at first, but not what you'd expect. She didn't mind the idea of the NG tube; once she got used to it, she didn't even have any throat irritation afterward. The thing that really bugged her was the mask we put over subjects' eyes; we've got to blindfold them so they won't see how much solution they're getting each time. She hated that mask, kept trying to talk me into leaving it off. She huffed and puffed and told me that if roles were reversed, she'd help a friend. . . ."

Kate's voice broke on the last word. She took her oversized red glasses off and polished the lenses on her skirt before putting them back on. "She must've been totally desperate, and she didn't even try to call me; I have a beeper with me at night because subjects in one of our studies stay overnight in the hospital and I have to be available for questions or problems. . . ."

Kate held her chin too high and clenched her jaw, blinking hard to restrain the tears that filled her eyes, threatening to overflow. "She knew how to dial my beeper if she needed me." She shook her head, her gold hoop earrings jiggling in response.

"Anyone else she might have tried to reach?"

"Besides *you*—or her married lover?" She pulled out her pack of cigarettes and lit another as she stared into space. "Alicia had a bad reputation as a gossip. She'd ask half a dozen people about someone, bringing up their name in conversations oh-so casually; she had a way of putting together things, finding touchy spots, guessing secrets. Didn't exactly make her popular." She shrugged and shook her head.

"I called Alicia's folks when I heard the news. They're pretty torn up. A couple of months ago she'd argued with them about something, and she'd avoided them since; they didn't think much about it—they've been through it before—but now . . .

"Her folks walked through her house after she died to see if maybe she'd left a note there. Real rough for them. Her landlord wants the place cleared out so he can show it, or another month's rent within a week. They asked if I'd pack up Alicia's things for them and offered to pay me for it." She rubbed the bridge of her nose.

"Alicia and I shared her little one-bedroom house for a year when we were both grad students—all we could both afford back then; she got the bedroom, and I had a sofa bed in the living room. She kept it for herself after I moved in with my boyfriend and she went to work for Dr. Tate.

"I didn't realize how much being back in that house would affect me. Stupid things made me cry buckets. When I walked in Thursday night, the place had been closed up tight since she died, and her kitchen smelled of chili. I remembered how Alicia always ordered it in restaurants. I packed up all her pots and pans from the kitchen; then I left." She took off her glasses and wiped her eyes with the back of her hand, one pass by each eye. "I understood her parents' reaction, in spades. Too many memories."

She blinked a few times, her eyes coming back into focus in the here and now. She gave me a quick sideways glance. "Did you *really* tell the police and medical examiner you didn't think she was suicidal?"

Her tone suggested that I'd done something as credible as proclaiming my belief in elves and fairies, and she was kindly giving me one final opportunity to deny that I'd spoken so foolishly.

"Yes."

Kate stopped short and pulled out her cigarette pack. She took her time lighting another and smoked half of it before she spoke again.

"That's really great to hear. Wow, I sound pretty weird. I mean, I kept feeling like I should've noticed something. I couldn't believe it when I heard she'd killed herself—not Alicia, not when she did."

I heard the pain in her voice—the only person outside Alicia's family who seemed to grieve for her. And, so far at least, the only person who seemed to be telling me a straight story. "Yes," I said, "hard to believe."

She looked at the cigarette between her fingers. "I cut way back on my smoking over the summer, got close to quitting, but I've been smoking like a fiend since I found out about Alicia. I've been feeling so guilty, thinking I must've been oblivious. Like I should've guessed something was wrong."

Another casualty of Alicia's death. "I know the feeling," I said, touching her arm. "Whatever happened, I don't think it had anything to do with you. Or that you could have done anything to stop it."

I saw tears welling up in Kate's eyes. She put her cigarette to her lips and inhaled deeply. She blew a smoke ring, watching it until it dissolved. "Thanks," she said, her voice husky. "Alicia thought a lot of you. She told me you cured her nightmares."

"She *what?*"

Kate's startled look made me regret the strength of my response. "She told me her nightmare about the skeleton coming in her bedroom and said you told her she'd overlooked something about the skeleton. She thought about the way it walked, and she knew who it was—she said once she knew, she laughed when it started to touch her in her dream. It fell apart when she laughed, just a harmless pile of bones beside her bed. That was the last time she had the dream."

I struggled to keep my voice calm. "When did she tell you this?"

"Thursday, when we went out. She'd told me about her nightmares before and asked if I knew a doc who'd prescribe sleeping pills; her own doc claimed he never prescribed sleeping pills for anyone. I finally got a name for her, but she said she didn't need pills anymore."

*No more nightmares. No need for sleeping pills.* Alicia had turned down her chance to get a prescription after she'd pressed me for help.

"Do you have any idea if anything unusual or different happened to Alicia in the last few months?"

"She comes to see a shrink and you don't ask her what's unusual or different—some reason she's looking for help all of a sudden?" Kate rolled her eyes upward, but the bite had gone out of her bark.

"I'm trying to make sense of what happened to Alicia," I said. "I'd appreciate anything you could tell me that might help. Anything at all."

"Well . . . I remember she said one thing that bothered me and made me worry if she might be getting a little . . . funny. Back in August she said, 'I've found out about dry labeling studies. Or something close enough to get someone in big trouble.' The way she said it, I figured that meant she'd gotten herself in trouble, one way or another."

"What does that mean, 'dry labeling studies?'" Alicia's nightmares about the skeleton had started in August.

"No idea. I tried to ask her about it, and she brushed me off—told me she was just too sensitive for her own good and made a joke of it. So I figured she was doing her exaggeration number again." Kate opened her mouth as if to say something more, then stopped and looked away. The tip of her cigarette glowed brightly as she inhaled deeply. She shook her head and pursed her lips.

"Something else?" I asked.

"It's too weird, and I feel, like, a major paranoid even saying it, especially to a shrink." She gave a nervous laugh as she shifted her weight from one foot to the other. "Maybe I'm wrong, but . . . well, it looked like her house had been searched."

# Chapter 20

With only three members present, my Wednesday evening therapy group was subdued. Carlyle Stocklin had left word that he wouldn't make group for the fourth week in a row because he had to attend a professional meeting in New York; he'd apologized profusely, but he timed his apologies for late Tuesday evening, when he knew he'd get the clinic's answering machine. Carlyle's absence meant we wouldn't have a quorum, but the group still needed to meet to handle the fallout from Alicia's death.

The only unexpected note occurred when Gerald Yablonski turned to me and asked, "Any possibility it wasn't suicide?" When I asked him why he raised the question, he gave me a vague answer about Alicia not seeming the type.

I could've blamed it on Gerald's question, but I'd been toying with the idea of visiting Alicia's house since her memorial service, half planning it since I'd talked with her old roommate. I told myself all the reasons it would be a foolish, dangerous thing to do, but I kept thinking of something else: Alicia had gone to some lengths to seek me out, to learn about me, and I still didn't didn't have a clue why she'd chosen me as a therapist. I hoped I'd find something in her house that would help me understand, maybe something that would lead me to her murderer.

I didn't know where else to go for answers.

After group I got my gym bag out of my car and changed into shorts and a T-shirt. I'd worn a blue cotton scarf around my neck today; now I tied it around my head, checking the result in the restroom mirror. Not particularly flattering, but at least my red hair wouldn't stand out like a flag.

I saw a mound of empty office supply boxes as I was heading out of Rugton, and grabbed three on impulse. Surely no neighbor would suspect someone who came armed with boxes and walked in the front door. I headed toward Alicia's house, driving in circles twice along the way to make sure I wasn't being followed.

Alicia had lived close to the medical center, on Sunset Boulevard. In an older part of Houston near Rice University, behind a larger house, the house looked as if it might have been the maid's quarters or a mother-in-law house.

I carried my armload of boxes up Alicia's driveway like a shield, trying to hide behind them. A privet hedge surrounded her house, screening it from the main house. Preoccupied with balancing the boxes, I wasn't looking down; I felt a stone roll under my foot as I took a step; then I went down in a heap, landing with a thump on my backside, the scarf popping off my head. At that moment I spotted a thin-faced white-haired woman coming out of the house to the right of Alicia's, looking in my direction. I grabbed my scarf and the boxes and hustled down the driveway, past a turn that would hide me from her view.

I hoped the neighbor wasn't already on speaking terms with Kate or Alicia's parents.

Dumping the boxes at the edge of Alicia's carport, I shoved the scarf back down over my hair. I found the key where Kate had told Alicia's parents it would be, underneath the flowerpot by the coiled hose. The main door from her carport into the kitchen, warped by at least thirty years of Houston's formidable rain and humidity, resisted when I tugged, groaning when it finally yielded.

This was the second time in my life I'd broken into someone's house. I wasn't convinced it got easier with practice.

I didn't like being alone in Alicia's house with its air of seclusion and secrets. I felt watched, followed, stared at, evaluated—as if Alicia were there, sitting on her sofa as I walked through the living room, her eyes following me around.

Her house was stifling, the windows closed, the air conditioning long off. I thought about turning on her air conditioner and rejected the idea. I hoped to be out long before it would have cooled the rooms; more important, less rational, it felt like an intrusion, as if she had deliberately left the hot stillness behind her, and if I disturbed it, I might call attention to my presence, leave traces of myself behind. So I opened the windows in her bedroom, and the inner door from her kitchen to her carport to create a breeze. I latched the screen door, wondering if Kate was right and someone else really had searched Alicia's house.

I started with her kitchen, as if the least personal place might be the least presumptuous. Switching on the light dispelled the growing shadows but not my uneasiness. On one wall she'd hung blue earthenware dishes, the kind they sell in Mexican border towns. On another she had a wall-mounted rack of razor-sharp knives displayed in ascending size from a paring knife to a cleaver. Beside the knives she'd hung four painted tiles, each featuring a mythical creature: a unicorn, a winged horse, a griffin, a centaur. All the gaudily painted creatures wore the same fierce expression, as if daring anyone to believe they could ever be docile or obedient. So like Alicia.

As she was leaving, Kate had said one more thing: *Alicia told me she was seeing you and she made a joke about it. Said she was matching wits with you—going to prove she was better than you at detecting lies.*

Better at detecting lies, indeed. Alicia hadn't left me any room for argument.

I opened each of the kitchen cabinets. Alicia had been partial to white tuna packed in water, chicken bouillon, reduced-fat microwave popcorn, Weight Watcher's chocolate mousse, and sugarless hard candy. Her mother's influence, she would have shrugged and said, sitting at the kitchen table with her legs crossed, her eyes following my every move.

A dog started barking next door, the yip-yip of a small breed. I turned out the kitchen light and pushed the red-and-white checked curtains aside to look out. I didn't see anything for a minute as my eyes adapted to the dimness outside, the only light in Alicia's yard provided by the spillover from a neighbor's patio light; then I saw a cat running across Alicia's yard, a chihuahua straining to get through the fence to go after it.

I'd thought of bringing a flashlight but decided against it; like carrying in the boxes, I needed to act as if I had a right to be there if I didn't want to make the neighbors suspicious. A flashlight would have sent the wrong message.

I turned on the light again and opened the rest of the cabinets. In the last, Alicia had two complete place settings of good china and crystal that looked new, like the beginnings of a hope chest she'd never complete.

The chihuahua stopped yipping and I froze, listening to the small sounds: the drip-drip of the kitchen faucet, the hum of a plane overhead. Nothing out of the ordinary, I told myself. No one coming to catch me.

An alcove next to the kitchen smelled of mildew. I opened the folding closet doors and saw an old washer and dryer. I lifted two gold-fringed pillows and a bottle of spot remover off the lid of the washer and peeked inside, banging it shut when the mildewy smell of a forgotten load of wash rose up to slap me in the face.

When I'd asked Kate about someone searching Alicia's house, she said, "I could be wrong, but things had been moved around, just ever so slightly. Alicia was terribly . . . precise. Everything in its place."

Kate said the searcher, if there had been one, had been careful, but she'd lived with Alicia long enough to know when things weren't right: a spoon in the wrong slot in the silverware drawer, a vase with silk daisies off-center on the kitchen table, the fishing tackle box she'd used for storing her jewelry left open. But maybe a despondent Alicia wouldn't have been so compulsively tidy, she'd said.

I glanced around her living room: a couch that did double duty as a futon bed when rearranged, a couple of wicker chairs, a half-dozen oversized pillows in bright colors. Not much space for hiding something; besides, I didn't expect something intensely personal or important in her living room. Beneath her stereo she had a collection of tapes, heavily country along with a sprinkling of folk music.

I went into Alicia's bedroom next. Greenery was everywhere: dripping from hanging baskets, sprouting tall from brass buckets on the floor, creeping along the top of bookshelves fashioned from boards and cinder blocks.

Alicia had replaced the cover for her bedroom ceiling light with a beige Chinese umbrella, cutting the bamboo handle short; the dragon printed in red on the shiny waxed paper cast its shadow across the walls and floor, its claws reaching toward the windows.

I switched on the bedside table lamp to dispel the shadow and saw that she'd replaced the standard bulb with a pink one. What man had she wanted to lie beside her and admire the rosy glow on her face? Did she have him in mind when she bought her crystal and china? Was she killed by him?

Alicia had a two-drawer file cabinet in the corner; on top of it sat the fishing tackle box she'd used for her jewelry box, the lid left open as Kate had described. I scanned her collection of costume jewelry. Nothing looked valuable except a string of pearls and her silver charm bracelet, each settled on its own strip of black velvet.

A tray beside her jewelry box held makeup. I recognized her distinctive pink lipstick along with matching nail polish. Mascara, eye liner, foundation, and eight colors of eye shadow filled the rest of the acrylic tray.

The typed labels on the files in the top drawer of her filing cabinet walked me through the last five years of tax returns, filed in ascending order. Her most recent showed that her job with Oliver Tate provided her only source of reported income; after living expenses, it would've fallen far short of what she'd paid for the Caddy.

The files in the bottom drawer seemed related to her graduate work, labeled by topic. I opened a few at random and leafed through the Xeroxed articles. One set of articles had been heavily highlighted in yellow: a series on tardive dyskinesia, a central nervous system disorder and a side effect of long-term use of antipsychotic drugs. Patients with tardive dyskinesia can't control some facial movements like lip smacking, cheek puffing, or lip pursing. It was an odd topic to arouse Alicia's interest.

The chihuahua started yipping again. I turned off the ceiling light and the bedside table lamp and looked outside. Nothing.

I went back to the darkened kitchen and looked out that window but didn't see anything moving. Probably the cat had dashed past the yip-yap, winding him up again.

Back in her bedroom I tried to close her curtains, but a small gap still remained. I opened the door to her clothes closet, then stepped back, rapidly, feeling my heart accelerate. I had trouble breathing for a minute.

The cloud of gardenia perfume that enveloped me evoked her presence so strongly that I almost expected her to step out in front of me. Or walk in behind me.

Alicia had sorted her clothes by season, then color, then by long or short sleeves within each season. Four vinyl shoe bags hung from the closet rods; shoes were ordered within each bag by color and heel height, companion purses heading up each colored column, all the easier to grab the purse to complement her shoes each day. An ordered, methodical streak, now laid bare.

I'd been putting off opening drawers, feeling more than ever like an interloper, wanting to be out of there, feeling soiled and sneaky. The first drawer held lingerie, silky and lacy and piled high, vivid reds and blues and lots of black, all slithering with life in front of me. Shorts and T-shirts were stacked in the second drawer. The third held well-worn jeans. I went back to the top drawer. Women hide things at the bottom of lingerie, I remembered reading, a place where burglars always search. I felt along the bottom of the drawer and pulled out an envelope that had been pushed down in the back.

I opened it: Alicia's birth certificate. Her given name was plain Alice, her birthday a year earlier than she'd listed on clinic forms. More embroidery in her personal history.

I felt around the bottom of the drawer again and came up with another sheet of paper. Dated September 2, Wednesday, a week before her death: the title for her Caddy. Odd that she'd put the title here, rather than filing it. I put the envelope and title back where I'd found them.

Alicia's bed was queen sized. Red and purple diamonds danced on the comforter that covered it, and a red dust ruffle wound around the bottom. It was made up with a hospital neatness. I got down on my hands and knees and lifted the dust ruffle. Nothing underneath.

Sticking my arm between the mattress and box springs, I felt a stiff edge of cardboard. I pulled out a blue folder. A dark-blue color, just like the patient charts in Rugton. Working my way around the bed, I found another, pushed almost to the center. I reached in again and pulled out a videotape in a cardboard jacket. I went all around the bed once more, lifting up the mattress this time. Nothing else. I smoothed the bedspread back into place.

I picked up the tape I'd found. TD plus a nine-digit

number written on the white cardboard jacket stained with brown—like paper scorched by smoke or fire. Then I turned over the two blue charts. The names on them were those I'd somehow expected as soon as I saw the distinctive blue color: Alicia Erle and Carlyle Stocklin.

My missing patient charts. Hidden in Alicia's house.

I remembered Alicia coming back into the group therapy after she'd been gone for ten minutes, looking upset; she could have stolen the charts when no one was around, hiding them somewhere, retrieving them after group. Oliver had mentioned Alicia's efforts to get a master key. She'd managed to find one that opened the Rugton record room.

I could understand why she wanted to see her own chart, why she'd want to find out what we'd written about her, but I wondered about Carlyle's chart—and about his presence at her funeral. Was this chart only her usual insatiable curiosity about the people around her? Or was it something much more personal: her married lover's psychiatric chart, prime bait for a woman who took such pleasure in ferreting out people's secrets.

I stopped moving when I heard sounds that seemed to be coming from the direction of the open door by the carport. First a scraping sound. Then silence. Then a bump. I called out: "Kate?" No answer.

I went to look, feeling apprehensive.

As I passed through the living room I smelled smoke and heard the sound of a fire crackling. In the kitchen smoke was curling in through the screen door, the glow of flames outside near the edge of the carport, fire licking up one side of the pile of boxes.

I thought of the garden hose coiled by the side of the house. There was enough time to put the fire out before it spread—safer than taking time to call 911. I unlatched the screen door and stepped forward. I heard a noise behind me, then felt a terrific blow across the back of my head, as if part of the roof had fallen on me. I think I moaned as the force of the blow pushed me forward and down. The concrete floor of the carport came up to meet me, lights like stars in front of my eyes, the smell of smoke all around me as I blacked out.

When I came to, I found myself lying on my back, my arms down by my sides, my check against cold concrete that smelled of grease and dirt and smoke. My clothes were wet and clammy. My head throbbed. My eyes couldn't seem to focus.

I blinked, trying to clear my vision. On the concrete in front of my face lay a knife, the edge of the blade red and wet.

I felt myself starting to lose consciousness again and struggled against the blackness clouding close around me. I tried to fix my gaze on the knife, holding the image. My stomach churned; I took a deep breath to try to keep from throwing up, regretting it when I inhaled smoke and grease.

The smell of smoke brought back the fire; the jolt of adrenaline at the thought of flames around me gave me the strength to force myself to sit up. I was still in Alicia's carport, sitting in a pool of water, trying hard not to give in to the waves of darkness, to stay conscious. I saw a sodden mound of charred cardboard, the hose still trickling water beside the remains of the boxes.

I looked down and saw my T-shirt bunched up above my breasts, my bra hanging loose, dark red stains on the elastic waistband of my shorts—red smeared below my breasts. It took a moment to register. Blood—mine. I touched the bottom of my breast and felt the sting of a fresh wound. A line carved across the bottom of my bare breasts. I pulled my T-shirt down, feeling frightened—and ashamed. And angry.

My head throbbed again, and I saw the wall wavering in front of me. I closed my eyes, then touched the back of my head gently, wincing at the soreness. Opening my eyes, I looked at my hand, now wet with blood. Even the thought of trying to stand made me dizzy. *Sit up for a while,* I told myself; *lean against the wall for a couple of minutes; then use it for support when I make myself stand up.* I started to scoot over to the wall, still sitting. I felt my ankles stinging against the wet concrete, the same behind my knees. Twisting my right leg, I saw more lines of blood.

The cuts had been made with an artist's fine touch, the lines straight and true—like the hard-scored marks of tailor's chalk, a map to show the planned alterations: two parallel lines bisected my hamstring, two parallel lines crossed my Achilles tendons. I checked my left leg; the same two sets of parallel lines.

I'd been drawn a thoughtful, detailed guide to what I could anticipate if I continued following the trail of Alicia's death, the knife left in front of my face so it would be the first thing I'd see when I opened my eyes. Next time, the cuts would be deep enough to cripple and disfigure me.

# Chapter 21

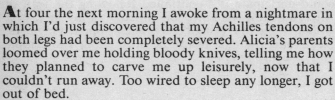

At four the next morning I awoke from a nightmare in which I'd just discovered that my Achilles tendons on both legs had been completely severed. Alicia's parents loomed over me holding bloody knives, telling me how they planned to carve me up leisurely, now that I couldn't run away. Too wired to sleep any longer, I got out of bed.

Last night I'd thought of driving to the emergency room and having a doctor take a look at my head. But I felt horribly ashamed, terribly embarrassed—as if I'd done something wrong and been punished. This was not rational, I kept telling myself—but I couldn't imagine trying to make up a reasonable story to satisfy nurses and doctors. I cringed at the thought of allowing strangers to touch me. So I'd forced myself to stay awake for a few hours once I finally made it home, making sure I didn't develop any new, worrisome symptoms that would compel me to seek treatment.

Today I'd planned to fly to Washington on an early afternoon flight; getting there in the evening would have been fine, since the grant review panel wouldn't meet until Friday morning at eight. I'd intended to clean up some paperwork in my office this morning.

My head hurt, the cuts on my breasts and legs throbbed with an intensity that had little to do with their severity. Outside, rain played against my window like a dirge. I felt weak and afraid.

I called to change my afternoon reservation to the next flight out.

I requested my usual aisle seat; only center seats were left. I don't like being boxed in, I don't like it a lot, but I wanted to get out of Houston as fast as possible.

Once on board I wedged myself into the seat between a woman already busy with her laptop computer and a teenage girl immersed in an article titled "Take Control of Your Life With Tarot!" Thankful that they looked like the nonchatty sort, I closed my eyes and listened to the roar of the engines as we took off. As I started to doze, loud screams from an infant across the aisle jerked me awake, driving sleep firmly away.

I looked around for a place to move to, but I couldn't see any open seats. Then a man with frizzy blond hair in the seat in front of me reclined his seat, imprisoning me. The frizzy-haired man's companion adjusted her vent, blowing most of the air back onto me.

A nonstop flight had seemed like such a good idea when I booked it.

I tried to scan an article in *Psychological Bulletin* that had looked interesting when I'd stuck the journal in my briefcase, but I couldn't concentrate. As I replayed my assault and its aftermath at Alicia's house, I kept thinking of Ian, wishing he were here, wanting to tell him everything that had happened. Ian would have supported me, told me I'd been right to investigate. I wished I had someone to reassure me, to tell me what I'd done was OK.

Yesterday, after regaining consciousness for the second time, I looked at my watch; I'd been out for at least twenty minutes, maybe more. I remembered blacking out when I'd tried to stand, using the wall as support, thinking of trying to find a neighbor to call an ambulance, but forcing myself to stand on my own again, trying to ignore how much the effort cost me.

When I'd stood, I could see what had happened: The

intruder had set my boxes on fire on the driveway just outside the carport to lure me out of the house.

I'd felt humiliated. I'd felt exposed, weak, small, puny—powerless. Wanting to get even—*needing* to get even.

I'd gone back inside Alicia's house. I hadn't heard any noise during the interval I'd been conscious but I'd been half-hoping that whoever had knocked me out was still around. Holding the knife in front of me, I'd hobbled into the kitchen, my hand gripping the handle tightly. One of the middle knife slots stood empty in the wall-mounted rack, a slot just big enough for the one left in front of my face.

I'd wanted the chance to even the score.

I'd looked in the open door of the empty bedroom. No patient charts where I'd dropped them, no videotape. The fishing-tackle box still stood open, displaying Alicia's jewelry as before, her pearls and charm bracelet still gleaming against black velvet—not a robbery in the usual sense. Nothing else had been disturbed.

As I splashed cold water on my face, I'd tried to make up a story in case I couldn't get out before a helpful neighbor arrived on the scene; perhaps I could suggest that one of the neighborhood kids must have been playing with matches near the cardboard boxes, and I'd come out when I smelled smoke, slipping on the wet cement in the carport after I put the fire out, banging my head. An asinine cover story, but I hadn't been thinking well enough to do any better.

I'd considered calling the police, but only for an instant; how could I have told them I'd been searching Alicia's house without her family's permission or knowledge, found her missing psychiatric chart under her mattress, and then a mysterious intruder had knocked me out, stolen her chart and a videotape (but nothing else of value), and carved me with a knife?

They would've found the kid-playing-with-matches story significantly more credible than the truth. Especially after talking with Alicia's parents as part of their investigation.

I hoped that the white-haired neighbor who'd seen me carrying boxes would be away at work when Kate came to pack up Alicia's house.

I'd somehow managed to clean up the remains of the burned boxes, put the key back under the flowerpot, and stagger back to my car—without once letting go of the knife. I didn't remember much of my drive home from Alicia's house, only that I'd been on automatic pilot, driving slowly, avoiding main roads.

I thought about the fire setter's timing. At the funeral, Kate had told Alicia's parents that she'd pack everything up on Thursday; she'd told them where she'd hidden the key so they could get inside if they wanted. Someone could have overheard and come to make their own search. Someone who wasn't pleased to find I'd gotten there before them when they looked through the window and saw me searching.

Oliver Tate and Carlyle Stocklin were the likely candidates—but Debra Linnell had been at the funeral, as well.

I shivered when I pictured the fire setter, standing outside in the dark, looking at me through the lit windows, watching me search, waiting to see what I'd found, then knocking me out and taking it from me.

My attacker couldn't have stayed long after setting the fire. The sight and smell of smoke curling above the thick shrubbery would have been too likely to attract the neighbors. Maybe this time I'd been "lucky."

My stomach rumbled, interrupting my ruminations; I hadn't eaten anything for dinner, and I'd only been able to choke down a glass of milk for breakfast. The endless bags of peanuts served with drinks had left their smell permanently etched into the seats. The aroma actually made my mouth water.

I was more than ready when the flight attendants finally maneuvered the serving cart through the narrow aisle. Steam from the entree burned my hand as I removed the foil. The smell evoked my grade-school cafeteria: overdone baked chicken that had kept company too long with canned pineapple. The remainder wasn't any better: a white roll with the staleness of day-old bread, a quarter cup of wilted lettuce, limp and rubbery green beans laced with red pimento, and a tasteless sliver of chocolate cake.

"Food that would make a jackal nauseous," the svelte woman with the laptop computer muttered after she declined lunch.

I ate everything on my tray.

The grant review meeting started at eight the next morning in one of the hotel's conference rooms. I sat at the table, one of the dozen reviewers who would evaluate fifty grants on interpersonal relationships and health. Four National Institutes of Health program representatives sat in chairs that lined the walls. My friend Esther Fernandez, the Scientific Review Administrator for the panel, shared the head of the table with the chairperson. Dressed all in black—a black turtleneck topping pleated black gabardine pants—Esther looked as aloof and detached as a high priestess, ready to oversee arcane rites.

During the midmorning coffee break, I walked down to the end of the room where a table held coffee and a plate of soggy chocolate doughnuts. Esther joined me as I was pouring coffee. I offered her the first cup and poured a second for myself. "Hope this isn't an omen of things to come today," she said, jerking her head toward two reviewers who'd disagreed ferociously about the merits of a grant; now they stood glaring at the chairperson positioned strategically between them. "For dinner tonight, how about we—"

"You have it easy, Esther," a man interrupted, his voice patronizing. He clapped her on the shoulder, jarring her hard enough to slosh her coffee over the side of her cup. She grimaced and reached for a napkin.

"You should have seen the blowup when the Psycho-biology review panel met last week." He wore a faded-blue work shirt over baggy chinos, dark socks under well-worn leather sandals.

I'd leafed through my closet four times before I finally settled on packing a green silk jacket, a green-and-cream striped shirt, and cream silk pants. I would have worn a skirt and heels, but I wanted to cover up the cuts on my legs.

"Vernon Brundige." He held out his hand to me.

I reluctantly shook his clammy hand, murmuring my name.

While Esther blotted coffee from her pants, Vernon told me about his position as a member of the program staff in the neuroscience branch, as if I'd expressed interest. I was about to excuse myself when he said, "I saw on the roster that you're from Houston, Debra Linnell's territory. Know her?"

"Not well. I met her once."

"I wish I'd never met her. I could cheerfully wring her neck for the trouble she caused."

"How's that?"

"Debra's a terror as reviewer. She always finds multiple faults in other people's research: They didn't know relevant literature; they didn't have clear enough hypotheses; they didn't have enough subjects; they didn't use the right measures; they didn't analyze data correctly; they misinterpreted their results; their work adds nothing new to the literature."

An echo of Debra's approach to our waitress. I wondered again how she'd treated Alicia—and how Alicia, with her eye-for-an-eye philosophy, had responded.

"At the Psychobiology meeting last week, Debra behaved true to form when she was the primary reviewer on one grant; she trashed it, making the point several times along the way that her lab found another technique more productive. The second reviewer liked the grant and went to bat for it. Debra took it personally and started arguing with the second reviewer. Then the chairperson made the mistake of saying that perhaps Debra needed to reconsider the grant's merits. That's when Debra went nuclear: She stormed out, yelling that she wasn't coming back."

He picked up one of the oversized chocolate doughnuts from the table beside him, demolishing a third of it with one bite, talking as he chewed.

"Debra's response seemed way out of line, so the chair assumed that once she'd had time to cool down, she'd be fine. They broke early for lunch; then the chair tried to call her hotel room, figuring he'd placate her. The front desk told him she'd already checked out and caught a taxi to the airport."

I wasn't sure I'd understood him through his mouthful of doughnut. "She never came back?"

"Never came back, leaving Psychobiology with a half-dozen grants that had to be deferred because of her missing reviews. If you see her, you can tell her that her name is mud."

So Debra had lied when she said she'd been in Washington the night Alicia died. She had gone out of her way to lie to me.

At noon two white-coated waiters wheeled carts crowned with trays of cold cuts, bread, and sodas into our conference room, and we broke for lunch.

I made myself a ham and swiss on rye. I saw Vernon Brundige slather one side of a bun with mayo, the other with ketchup, then pile it high with turkey, ham, two kinds of cheese, and tomatoes. He'd been staring at me throughout the morning; I'd tried to avoid looking in his direction.

I went to sit by Esther. Vernon had been standing at the end of the food line, holding his plate. As soon as I sat down, he joined us, pulling a chair so close to me that his knee touched mine. "I understand you're a widow," he said.

Esther looked at me and raised her eyebrows slightly; I looked away, quickly, as I saw her mouth start to curve up.

"I worked at the FDA before coming to NIH," Vernon continued, as if we'd been in the middle of a conversation. "That's where you really learn about dealing with difficult people," he added, glancing over at Esther, his tone condescending.

Vernon inhaled a mouthful of his thick sandwich. A slice of tomato oozed out, landing on his plate, splattering his shirt with juice and seeds. He dabbed at the spots ineffectually with his napkin.

It took a minute for his comment to register because I'd been thinking about how to change seats gracefully. FDA, the Federal Drug Administration. The drug-trial police. "How difficult would it be to manipulate a drug trial?" I scooted my chair away from his as I asked.

Esther gave me a disbelieving look as if I'd suddenly started speaking a foreign language, but Vernon didn't seem to register the strangeness of the question.

"Easy. To make a new drug look good, you could compare it to a drug in the same class but with more severe side effects than your new drug, making your new drug look positively benign by comparison. That's something drug companies don't mind overlooking when they're the ones funding the research—with profit at stake, they don't necessarily have the same standards as government-funded research. And lots of drug companies don't do tough reviews before they give someone money to test drugs."

He wiped his hands across the napkin in his lap without looking down, missing the napkin and leaving a ketchup stain on his chinos.

"In theory, if a study's really double blind, then the people running a trial don't know which of two drugs someone's actually getting—they'll just know it's drug one or drug two—and the patient doesn't know either. But if the people in charge figure out who's getting the new drug, they could select patients with less severe forms of an illness for that group and get a better success rate."

Vernon licked mayo and ketchup from his fingers.

I pictured myself shaking his hand this morning. I didn't remember washing my hands since then. I set my sandwich on my plate and pushed the plate away from me.

"One guy I remember ran lots of trials, testing all kinds of different drugs. This one drug was supposed to reduce the number of angina attacks. His protocol says he's going to recruit patients who have frequent attacks, and his notes show that his subjects had up to twelve attacks in the week before treatment. We do a thorough audit, we find out that half his subjects didn't even have an angina attack the week before they went on the drug—nothing like his records. So—big surprise—when these same patients don't have lots of angina attacks *after* he puts them on the drug, it looks like the drug's effective. Once we found one problem, we looked a lot closer at this guy's research. For another drug he tested, the X-ray reports from the radiologists didn't correspond to the glowing results he'd reported to his sponsor: Only one out of ten X rays actually matched his case notes.

"There are lots of shady ways to rig drug trials, many of them not so easy to detect," Vernon continued. "Then there's graphiting."

"Graphiting?" The odd word Alicia had used.

"Slang for data fabrication in drug testing. Means creation of data with a pencil, rather than actual testing."

"Same with 'dry labeling'?"

Vernon nodded regally as he patted me on the knee, his fingers lingering too long, his gesture simultaneously patronizing and lecherous. His fingers left a greasy smudge on my silk pants.

I scooted my chair farther from him, but he didn't seem to notice. Vernon was the kind of a guy who liked to hear himself talk, who'd keep lecturing as long as he had an audience in range.

Alicia had told Kate that she'd found out about dry labeling studies. Or something close enough to get someone in big trouble. "What happens to someone like your guy with the fake X rays when they get caught?"

"At a minimum, it finishes the drug-testing career of

the researcher. In some cases criminal charges are possible."

"What if a researcher wasn't personally responsible? What if someone else in their lab cooked the data?"

"Even if the physician in charge isn't the culprit, he's signed a form promising he'll be the watchdog for correct usage; the FDA uses that signature to establish liability and prosecutes."

Vernon shoved the rest of his sandwich in his mouth and kept talking as he chewed. "All of the research files for drug trials have to be available for FDA review at any time. I used to hear the wildest stories about why data weren't there. We called it the *'Andrea Doria* phenomenon': tales about how all the records went down with the ship."

Now I understood part of what Alicia had said. Finally. How her knowledge could have put her in danger.

And anyone else who came to share it.

# Chapter 22

Sunday afternoon, after I flew back to Houston from Washington, I spent three hours in the medical school library. As a rule, I like libraries a lot. I like the old-book smell, the low-voiced conversation, the rustling pages, the promise of hidden treasures in the stacks. Normally a soothing place, but today I felt ill at ease, skittish.

I'd come back on an early-morning flight, the plane full again. The man who sat beside me kept moaning about his terrible cold, punctuating his complaints with sniffles, jolting me awake when I dozed with a sneeze like a honking goose. I returned from a cool Washington morning to a sweltering day, humidity holding the heat even closer.

I'd gone home before coming to the library, my stomach tight and my jaw clenched as I drove into my driveway. The timing was about right for another surprise from Stuart Crego. Or maybe a message from the police—a command to come to the station to talk about how I'd broken into Alicia's house Wednesday evening.

I'd walked around the outside of my house before going inside, looking for problems. My house alarm was set just as I'd left it. Even so, going inside, I walked through every room. Finally, not able to put it off any longer, I'd hit the play button on my answering machine.

Once away from Houston, able to think more clearly, I'd realized that if the white-haired neighbor who spotted me dropping the boxes had spoken to Alicia's parents or Kate, I'd be in worse trouble than I was already. They'd only have to hear the most cursory description—"a woman with short red hair"—to figure out that I'd been at Alicia's house. I might as well have carried a banner.

I'd held my breath as I listened to the messages: Thelma Lou confirming that Carlyle would be coming to my office at eight o'clock on Monday; three hang ups; a recorded sales pitch for aluminum siding; a wrong number.

Nothing else—yet.

Now I passed the oil paintings of former deans in their academic robes (all men, I noticed) to get to the computer terminals. I started with an author search, using three names: Oliver Tate, Debra Linnell, and Carlyle Stocklin. Oliver had published eight first-author articles over the last five years, compared to sixteen for Debra—but Debra had only one paper to show for the last eighteen months; when she started Linnstar, she'd put the brakes on her productivity. Nothing recent showed up with Carlyle Stocklin as the first author.

While I was in Washington, I'd called Thelma Lou to check in. It was then that she told me that Carlyle wanted to see me as soon as possible, saying it was something he couldn't discuss in group. I'd told her to schedule him early Monday morning—and thought about Carlyle's Rugton chart, hidden under Alicia's mattress.

I searched for the journals where Oliver and Debra had published their research, then copied all their first-author research papers.

My last foray to the stacks took me by the glass case that held part of the library's history-of-medicine collection. From a collection of wax models used for teaching medical students in the last century they'd chosen a profile of a face, a bandage wrapping the head; a deep, angry red lesion encrusted with white pustules dominated the cheek—an ugly illustration of untreated syphilis, circa 1876.

A collection of small glass medicine bottles from 1865 rested in a canvas carrier, the two dozen bottles filled with colored powders or pills. A typed note laid across the canvas bag warned: DO NOT OPEN BOTTLES. CONTENTS MAY BE UNSTABLE AND EXTREMELY HAZARDOUS. It would have made a terrific gift for Oliver Tate.

A spring lancet used for bloodletting in 1850 still looked sharp. I thought of the way I'd been carved. The cuts on my legs had been made first, before he'd turned me over. Then he'd pulled up my T-shirt and unhooked my bra, exposing me, getting the maximum effect from the lines carved beneath my breasts.

A deliberate effort to humiliate—as well as frighten. Oliver Tate, I guessed; he'd been at Alicia's funeral, heard Kate mention the key. I felt my stomach tighten as I looked around me.

Next I went to the *Science Citation Index* and copied the pages that tallied citations for Oliver's and Debra's articles, going back four years. Citations and the accompanying bibliographic references provide one measure of a researcher's impact: Influential research gets mentioned more often.

Oliver averaged around fifteen citations a year, low for someone with his seniority. In contrast, Debra averaged over a hundred citations each year, suggesting that her arrogance about her work wasn't unfounded.

I looked up articles from other researches who had referenced Debra's or Oliver's recent work, and I copied the ones that seemed most closely related, trying to shut out the pictures that kept coming into my mind. I forced myself to turn to the work in front of me, trying not to worry about the new troubles that could be lurking down the road.

Debra had conducted plenty of experiments with

mice, a handful of studies with human subjects. I didn't find any research where she'd recruited more than twenty subjects or any clinical field trials with new drugs; no wonder she'd found it rough going when she struck out on her own.

She had focused her research on a single area, mechanisms of antidepressant drugs, and conducted a series of interwoven studies that had served as a stepping stone for others who were doing similar research. I couldn't see how she could have cooked her data without her fellow researchers noticing discrepancies between her results and their own.

One of Debra's papers had stimulated a commentary from a group of researchers at Yale who'd run a similar experiment and gotten virtually identical data, but they'd come to different conclusions about possible underlying physiological processes.

Debra's overblown rejoinder managed to convey a distinctly vituperative tone. Three of her subsequent articles included gratuitously snide comments about the Yale group's research. It was remarkable that she could sound so surly amidst the dryness of scientific writing.

I could imagine how angrily Debra would have reacted to a mere graduate student like Alicia questioning her work.

Soft footsteps sounded on the linoleum somewhere close; I looked quickly over my shoulder, but bookshelves blocked my view. I had started reading another article when a shadow fell across the work spread on the table in front of me. I jumped up, my hands balled into fists.

A young Korean student gave me a fearful look as he grabbed a book from the shelf behind me and scuttled away.

I moved to one of the vinyl couches that sat in full view of the check-out desk, hoping to feel less jittery in a public area as I looked through Oliver's papers. I opened each one to the results section, comparing his data with the results from other laboratories conducting similar studies. When I finished, I looked at the

table I'd made; Oliver reported larger differences between groups and less variability within his drug
groups in five out of six comparisons.

The net result: Oliver Tate reported larger drug
effects than other laboratories.

Three of his studies had used double-blind designs in
which neither the researchers nor the patient knew
whether the patient was receiving an active drug or an
inactive placebo. In each case Oliver reported that
fewer patients responded to the placebo medication
than colleagues who had conducted similar trials. His
data seemed too perfect: too few patients who responded to placebos, too little variation in his results.

Nothing so unusual or odd that someone who didn't
compare all his papers would notice it; the drug companies funding Oliver's studies would have been delighted by such supportive results. Because Oliver was
describing the results of disparate drugs in different
journals, I didn't think anyone else would have made
systematic comparisons.

Then I pictured Alicia's four shoe bags in her clothes
closet, sorted by color and heel height.

I looked for the footnote on each article that told
when it had been submitted to the journal.

Oliver had accused Alicia of manipulating his drug
trials.

All but one of Oliver's articles predated Alicia's
arrival in his laboratory.

# Chapter 23

**W**hen I came out of the library at four, I found rain pouring down, the gutters full to overflowing—and I'd left my umbrella in my car. Naturally. I got drenched in the two minutes it took me to sprint to my car.

I'd planned on going jogging, hoping to shake the sense of foreboding I had since my return from Washington. Jogging was out of the question now; I'd have to go to my health club if I wanted to do anything physical. I drove home to get dry clothes and my gym bag.

As I pulled into my driveway, lightning flashed across the sky. In the brief bright flash I spotted something big and boxy in the corner of my front porch, sheltered by the eaves. I wasn't expecting any deliveries, especially not on Sunday. The logical alternative—Stuart Crego's latest "message"—promised to be nasty, fully justifying my uneasiness. I parked my car in the driveway and stared at the box for a minute; I thought it jiggled once, but I couldn't tell much in the rain.

I was conscious of the unpleasant way my clammy clothes molded themselves to my body, the weight of my sodden shoes, but the chill I was feeling wasn't just the result of my recent soaking. I got out, my keys in one hand, my other hand gripping my umbrella, fighting the wind's efforts to snatch it.

As I started toward the porch, the rain came down all at once, hurtling itself at me, big raindrops hitting so hard that I felt as if I was being blitzed with lead sinkers. The onslaught whipped my flimsy umbrella, the fabric bowing under the weight; then a gust of wind grabbed it from me, flipping the ribs in the wrong direction so that it was truly useless against the assault. I kept it in my hand, thinking I could always use it as a weapon against whatever had been left on the porch.

Without the umbrella's protection the rain freely pounded my face, the torrents slapping at my eyes. I blinked hard, struggling to see through the curtain of water. I desperately wanted to race to the house and shelter myself from the storm, but I didn't want to approach too close until I knew what was waiting on the porch. I needed to get near enough to see if I should go for help.

Lightning flashed again, chasing the shadows so I got a better look at the shape I'd seen from my car: a big cardboard box, half as tall as myself. Now I could see that it was open on top, but the contents weren't visible. I walked a few steps, stopped, hesitant to come closer despite the fierceness of the storm. I still couldn't see anything to give me a clue about the contents.

I took aim and pitched my keys against the side of the box with as much force as I could muster, the impact producing a satisfactory clatter. I heard a loud wail from the box, then a sad whine. I saw the sides of the box moving, something banging around inside.

I came closer, holding the mangled umbrella in front of me like a sword. The black puppy inside spotted me at the same time I saw him; he started trying to jump out to me. A note taped to the outside of the box said: PLEASE GIVE ME A GOOD HOME, with a birth date and puppy shot dates listed underneath.

I groaned when I recognized Glee's elegant handwriting—I'd just received her answer to the black-velvet Elvis. She'd tried to convince me to get a dog after Ian died, but I hadn't felt like making the commitment. The puppy looked like a Great Dane: The black fur ball with oversized feet and ears would outweigh me in a year. If I kept him.

I went inside and called Glee. "Found something you must have left at my house by accident," I told her answering machine, trying to keep the smile out of my voice. Then I remembered that she was supposed to have gotten back from New York yesterday and then planned to leave this afternoon for another meeting—so she wouldn't be back again until Thursday. Undoubtedly part of her strategy.

I went outside and picked up the fur ball. "Pavlov," I said as he licked my chin, without having consciously thought about a name for him.

I knew I'd been hooked as soon as I spoke.

I played with him for a few minutes, then looked for something to feed him; nothing looked right for a puppy. I brought the box inside and lined the bottom with old newspapers, then lugged it upstairs and set it beside my bed, a layer of plastic underneath.

I left Pavlov in his box while I drove to Wal-Mart. I bought puppy chow, chicken wire, and wooden stakes; when the rain let up I'd build him a chicken-wire pen under the trees, where he could stay while I was away. I'd worry about more permanent arrangements later.

Three hours after I'd spotted the box on my porch, wondering the whole time if I really wanted a dog, I finally arrived at my health club.

The flower bed beside the club's main entrance followed the natural growing seasons in unnatural ways. In honor of fall, full-grown mums had suddenly appeared, the zinnias and marigolds and petunias that had represented summer weeded out, probably tossed in the trash. The newly planted mums had taken a beating from the storm.

Casey, a college student who worked part-time, was on the phone as I went by the front desk, and we waved at each other as I passed. The staff dressed in the uniform of the day, always coordinated. Today Casey wore green shorts and a tan T-shirt. I wondered if the staff received the directives in a weekly memo—and if they had a seasonal rotation, like the flower beds.

I started on the Nautilus circuit, beginning with the upper body weight machines. A woman in a leopard-spotted leotard caught my eye as she struggled with one of the Nautilus abdominal machines. As short as Alicia, it took her three tries to jump high enough to land in the seat.

"These machines aren't designed for short people," she complained as I walked to the next machine.

I suddenly stood still, staring openmouthed at the wall, picturing the gold-fringed pillows sitting on top of Alicia's washing machine, beside the bottle of stain remover. Kate Wheelon had told me that Alicia bought gold-fringed pillows a shade darker than her car's upholstery. I could visualize Alicia's short, almost stunted legs; she'd have needed both pillows for driving that enormous 1959 Cadillac—one pillow to lift her high enough to see over the mammoth hood, one behind her back to push her far enough forward to reach the pedals.

*Sitting like a queen on her throne,* Kate had said.

The pillows weren't in her car when I'd found her, or anything else that would have served as substitutes.

Vermilion had told me how she'd seen a man park Alicia's car at Rugton and hurry away. Someone who'd killed Alicia and tried to make it look like suicide. Only the one small detail he'd missed.

"Trying to decide if you should take up running?" I jumped as I looked behind me and saw one of the weight-room attendants wearing the ubiquitous green shorts and tan T-shirt. I realized I'd been standing there, staring at a sign on the wall: DID YOU KNOW THAT FOR EVERY MILE YOU RUN YOU MAY EXTEND YOUR LIFE BY 22 MINUTES AND REDUCE YOUR MEDICAL BILLS BY 24 CENTS?

I nodded vaguely and wiped the sweat from my face and arms with my damp towel. I moved to the biceps machine and thought about what I'd learned in the library.

Oliver Tate had an obvious motive; if Alicia had gone to the FDA with what she knew or guessed, she could have derailed Oliver's research career. Oliver had told me he was away at an Eichon meeting in Austin when Alicia died, but he could have driven from Austin to Houston in less than three hours, especially late at night.

Oliver wasn't the only candidate. Carlyle could have driven from Austin to Houston as easily as Oliver. I thought about Carlyle Stocklin's chart nestled next to Alicia's under her mattress, Carlyle at her funeral. Her married lover.

Tasteful light rock music mixed with oldies was piped throughout the club, nothing too extreme to offend. As I moved to the triceps machine, I heard Patsy Cline singing about her cheating man and her sleepless nights. Obviously not a woman like Bethany, who'd said she'd divorce Carlyle if she found out he was unfaithful.

A tall muscular young woman in a pink-flowered leotard and white tights stood by the wall to my right where they had the "movement of the month" posted. I watched as she followed the instructions for an upper arm exercise using hand weights.

Another scenario had been running through my mind since I'd learned about Stuart Crego's link to Alicia. Stuart had been furious with me, and Alicia had given him a public brush-off. Could he have murdered Alicia and left her body at Rugton, a two-for-one revenge special?

Who else? Debra Linnell had lied to me about being in Washington. Oliver had said that Alicia claimed she'd played a major role in Debra's studies; I could see how Alicia's claims might give Debra a good motive. Oliver had also told me that Alicia had bought her car for cash, and wondered where she'd gotten the money. No reason for him to mention it if he'd paid her off. I pictured Debra, dressed in dark pants and a sweatshirt, her hair stuffed under the baseball cap that shadowed her face, walking across the Rugton parking lot with long strides. Looking down from her window, Vermilion could have mistaken Debra for a man. But why would Debra have questioned whether it was suicide if she killed Alicia?

I had one more Nautilus machine to go to finish my circuit. I pushed myself through twelve reps on the leg abductor while a teenage boy with a buzz haircut stood watching me, his arms folded across his chest, glowering as he tapped his foot impatiently. When I finished, he set the weight at the maximum, a smirk on his face.

I thought about the way my attack at Alicia's house had been staged. The fire had served to decoy me outside; my attacker needed to get me out-of-doors where he could hit me from behind without being seen by me. Maybe he couldn't risk waiting until I headed for my car, when I'd be looking around more carefully. Or he wanted to get me before I'd had a chance to take a closer look at what I'd found. Maybe he wanted to make sure I wasn't in any shape to search further.

A man with a passion for athletics would carve my legs at the most vulnerable points, appreciating how threatening the message could be. I thought of how my breasts had been exposed and cut—getting a sick, angry feeling in my stomach at the memory. I remembered Oliver Tate in my office, his eyes traveling down my body.

Oliver had said he played racquetball twice a week. I went to the front desk. "May I see the court schedule for next week?" I asked Casey.

"Sure." Displaying a purple tongue and wafting the smell of grape bubble gum toward me, she set the scheduling book on top of the counter for me and continued to chew gum at a measured rate, as precise as a musician responding to a conductor.

Oliver had court reservations for Monday at five o'clock. I could ambush him then.

I went to the locker room, which was more crowded than usual because of the rain. I shared space on the bench in front of the lockers with eight other women who ranged in age from teens to sixties.

How could Alicia have been murdered? I'd seen her body up close. No marks, no evidence of a struggle. The medical examiner's office had brought in a verdict of death by suicide; they certainly would have checked her stomach contents and blood, undoubtedly finding pills and alcohol, more than enough to kill her. Her body would have been carefully searched for anything like bruises or needle marks as part of the autopsy, especially since I'd made a point of saying she wasn't suicidal.

I was certain Alicia had been murdered. She couldn't have driven her car without the pillows or a substitute. Someone else, someone bigger, had driven Alicia's car while she lay in the back seat, dead or dying. But I didn't have a clue how Alicia could have been killed without leaving a mark.

# Chapter 24

"**I** was having an affair with Alicia Erle. I've got to talk about it. She killed herself because of me, and now I can't think of anything except her suicide. I've been such a bloody idiot." Carlyle Stocklin sat in my office early Monday morning, scuff marks on his Italian shoes, a grease spot on his Pierre Cardin tie, and dark circles under his eyes.

He'd started speaking as soon as he sat down, as if he felt pressured to unload dangerous cargo as rapidly as possible. "Thanks for seeing me on short notice. I've got to talk about Alicia with someone who knew her, someone who'd understand. Uh, Alicia never spoke—never said anything about me, did she?" His tone was pleading.

I wondered if he was Alicia's killer—and if the real purpose of his appointment was to see how much I'd guessed. Or if he was guilty of nothing but poor judgment.

When I didn't answer immediately, he asked, "You wouldn't have put her in group if you'd known, would you?"

"No, I wouldn't have put her in group—if I'd had any idea you were having an affair with her." I'd delayed my answer, hoping the irony might register.

His shoulders dropped a little, as if one source of

strain had been relieved. He took his handkerchief out of his back pocket and blew his nose. "Allergies. Probably ragweed, this time of year. I've tried everything, including shots, but they didn't help much——"

"Tell me about you and Alicia."

He fingered his tie as he studied the floor. "I met her through Oliver Tate in May. I've developed a compound that looks very promising—great market potential. I'm virtually guaranteed a major promotion if it pans out. Eichon gave Oliver the contract for testing it. I went to meet him." His voice grew steadier, more confident as he talked about his work. "I found out Alicia would be handling the nuts and bolts and asked her out for a drink. Just to make friends so I could ask how things were going. I wanted to make sure something stupid didn't screw up the trials." He spoke intimately, frankly.

As if imitating someone telling the truth.

"We had a terrific time together, that first time. Alicia had the technical background to appreciate my work. I loved talking to her about it. But it turned sour pretty fast." He glanced down at his shoes and made a noise of disgust. He moistened one corner of his handkerchief with saliva, and tried to scrub off the scuff marks on his shoe, making a face when it didn't come clean.

"What happened?" I hoped I didn't sound as intolerant as I was feeling.

"You wouldn't believe what she was like after a while—clinging doesn't begin to describe it. One time I forgot to take a towel into the shower. I came out to get one and found Alicia looking through my appointment book. She screamed at me, 'Who the hell's this Haley McAlistar you see every Wednesday night?' I hadn't told her I was in group therapy, hadn't wanted to, but I blurted it out. Anything to make her stop shrieking at me. She wanted me to tell her what I talked about, and I wouldn't. Then she showed up in group. That's when I started to panic."

Now, finally, I understood Alicia's question: *My name doesn't ring any bells for you?* Alicia had hoped I'd betray knowledge of her in some way, by recognizing her name or by refusing to let her join the group; either way, she'd have known that Carlyle had cared enough about her to talk about her in therapy. Failing that, she wanted to see her impact on him when she appeared in group without warning: her revenge for his silence.

Alicia had asked Thelma Lou if I was any good at fixing up problems in marriages; maybe she worried that Carlyle's therapy might bring him closer to Bethany, leaving her out in the cold. Maybe she thought that materializing in group would interfere with any steps Carlyle might take in that direction.

Now Carlyle gave me a quick anxious look, biting his lip, then continued: "Another example. Alicia found out where I always stayed when I went to Austin on Eichon business, this Marriott near Eichon's headquarters. She used to call and leave suggestive messages until I told her to cut it out. That's all I needed—someone from the hotel to joke about it to another Eichon person."

"How did you know she joined the group? You weren't there when she came."

"I talked to . . ." Carlyle closed his eyes and swallowed, then shook his head back and forth. He gave me a pained look, as if waiting for me to guess the most likely name, to fill in the blank so he wouldn't really be the one who supplied the lie. Waiting for me to take care of him, follow the script he'd honed well with women.

"No," I said. *The truth, for a change.* It took an effort not to say it aloud.

Carlyle wiped his forehead with his handkerchief, leaving behind a smudge of shoe polish. He didn't look at me as he started speaking again. "I came to Rugton for group and saw Alicia walking down the corridor, away from me; she didn't see me, and I followed her to see where she was going. I couldn't believe it when she actually went into the group room and didn't come out again. I slipped into the observation room and turned on the sound system to eavesdrop, figuring she was just waiting to ambush me when I got there, and I'd wait her out. Then, when you said she was a new group member, I waited for her to tattle on me."

"You sat there watching the whole time?"

He nodded, looking chagrined. "I knew it was wrong, but once I heard her tell those stories about getting even with old boyfriends, I couldn't leave. I started worrying what she'd do to me.

"I was planning to call it all off, tell her we could only be friends; then I got scared, afraid that if I tried to drop her cold, she'd muck up the trials for my compound." He twisted his handkerchief in his hands. "Maybe even tell Bethany."

He shifted uneasily in his chair and cleared his throat. "I need to ask a favor of you. I paid the receptionist cash for this session before I came in, and I asked her to make sure it won't appear on my clinic statement. Would you double-check for me? I don't want a scene with Bethany where she wants to know what I needed to discuss privately with you."

"Bethany doesn't have a clue about Alicia?"

"Why would Bethany have any suspicions about Alicia? When they met, I wasn't sleeping with Alicia yet."

On the ledge outside my window two gulls had been fighting over a piece of bread. The loser shrieked at the winner as he flew away. Carlyle didn't seem to notice the raucous dispute.

"No chance Bethany knows?" I asked.

"No way."

"How did Bethany meet Alicia?"

"Eichon holds this big July fourth company picnic every year at Lake Houston. They invite everyone from the community who's been useful, or who might be useful in the future. Eichon does a lot of business with Oliver, so they invited him and his lab group. They put out a big spread with food and booze; we swim and play softball and volleyball. Great bash, terrific public relations.

"When we got to the lake, Bethany spotted Oliver playing softball. I'd told Bethany he wasn't coming this year. It really ticked her off when she saw him without warning. She gave me bloody hell for it."

Something of my incredulity must have shown in my face. He gave me a quick look, then started talking more rapidly.

"Well, if I'd told her, she wouldn't have gone with me, and I needed her there; it wouldn't look right to my boss and other senior staff if I came by myself—it would've looked like I had trouble in my marriage or something."

Even knowing Carlyle's penchant for changing the subject to avoid difficult issues, I couldn't let that one pass. "Oliver Tate and Bethany?"

"Her ex-husband. Their marriage only lasted six months, and they've been divorced for five years, so it's not exactly recent."

Bethany had mentioned her ex-husband, Noll. I'd forgotten it was one of the nicknames for Oliver.

"So I joined this contest to see who could tolerate the hottest food—adding chili peppers, onions, hot sauce to tacos; then they got passed around, and everyone had to take a bite followed by a chaser of tequila or drop out of the circle. I like hot food, but I'm a piker compared to Alicia; she got into it and won hands down. She really hammed it up at the end, actually finishing half of the last taco herself when no one else would take any more.

"Alicia got really funny when she got smashed. She started talking about being a subject in a feeding disorders study, how she didn't have to worry about packing a lunch on Tuesdays, all about their protocol. Made it sound absolutely hilarious.

"So, picture this: Everyone's roaring, having a great time—except Bethany; she just sits watching like it's all beneath her, arms folded over her chest. I was thinking I should try to jolly her into a better mood, but then this pretentious friend of hers came over, Debra Linnell, who always manages to make me feel small. The pair of them sat together, watching, looking like they smelled something bad. I walked over to say hello, tried to joke with Debra about how difficult it was to run drug trials; she took it the wrong way, and the two of them froze me out." His voice had a whiny quality, like a child complaining that he hadn't been allowed to play with his favorite toys long enough.

"I joined the volleyball game, figuring I'd leave them alone for a while. When the game ended, Bethany had left with Debra—she hadn't said a word to me. Put me in a bad light. I had to tell people she'd been feeling a little peaked. Then Alicia spilled some taco sauce down the front of her T-shirt. Asked me if I'd give her a ride home since she'd drunk too much to drive herself. I figured Bethany wouldn't expect me home until after dark when they'd finished the fireworks, and, well . . . that's when it started."

He smiled, a ferocious smile that made my heart accelerate; then his face was blank again.

"What makes you think that Alicia killed herself because of you?"

He folded his handkerchief like someone refolding a map, putting the creases back in exactly the same places, and put it back in his pocket, taking his time tucking it in. "We had an argument the last time I spoke with her," he announced to the floor. "I asked her to bring some data home with her, so I could see how my trial was going so far. I looked at the data, then asked Alicia to fix a minor problem with one of the groups."

"What kind of problem?"

"A few of the patients were real hypochondriacs, whining about every little thing to get sympathy. I told her she didn't need to write down each and every complaint." Carlyle had spent enough time in the States to bleach out his British accent, but it got stronger whenever he was stressed. It was strong now.

"The 'hypochondriacs' were getting your drug?"

"Right. My bad luck."

"The trial wasn't double blind?"

He gave me an appraising look, as if my question made him wonder if I'd already heard the story. From Alicia.

"It was double blind."

"Then how . . . ?"

"I knew which group was receiving my drug because I'd opened a capsule and tasted it." His voice got loud, belligerent. "Damn it, this trial is important to me. I need it to work."

And then I watched his demeanor change back to excessive civility. "I mean, it wasn't like that, really. Truthfully, I just needed to make sure that something inconsequential didn't give me misleading data."

Truthfully, indeed. Just as he'd been expelled from medical school over an honor code violation he'd described as "trivial."

I thought of a patient I'd seen once, a chiropractor accused of murdering his two stepchildren by poisoning their Halloween candy. He said they must have gotten the tainted candy when they went around the neighborhood for trick or treat.

I'd administered a Rorschach as part of the forensic evaluation. Looking at an ink blot, he'd said, "That part's a volcano. It's blown recently—you can see where lava flowed down the side." He'd traced the area with his finger. "Still molten; you can tell by the red color."

"Anything else about it?"

"There's still plenty of lava inside, heating up. It'll erupt again, no doubt."

I had suddenly felt cold.

The chiropractor had confessed when the police confronted him with the large insurance policies he'd taken out on his stepchildren. Later, they found he'd taken out one other—twice as large—on his wife.

I'd just felt that same chill as I listened to Carlyle.

Before I'd left the library yesterday, I'd copied all the articles related to Oliver's research, then tracked down

Vernon Brundige's address in an NIH directory. I'd drafted a cover note describing my concerns, asking him to pass the information to an appropriate FDA official, found a large envelope at home for the thick packet, and mailed it at a self-service post office before I went to the health club. Now I hoped that a thorough FDA investigation of Oliver's lab would also spotlight problems with Carlyle's study.

"What happened when you asked Alicia to fix things for you?" I asked.

"She took it the wrong way. First she gave me a lecture about scientific integrity, how she couldn't do what I wanted. I tried to reason with her; I told her she hadn't had as much scientific training as I, she didn't know how things worked in the real world. . . ."

"And then?"

"Alicia said maybe she should talk with Oliver Tate about the situation, since she didn't have 'much scientific training.' "

He got up and walked over to the window. He started talking again, keeping his back to me, his voice barely audible. "I tried to patch it up, apologized, told her I hadn't been thinking clearly. I tried to make love. I couldn't . . . perform. She took it personally—asked if I didn't find her desirable enough anymore. Bloody hell. I told her I'd call her; we'd set up a time to get together when we were both feeling better. She wanted me to stay, to try . . . again. I had to get out."

He sat down opposite me again and looked me in the eye. "That was Friday before the Labor Day weekend. I told her I'd be out of town in the early part of the week, and I'd call her when I got back. That was the last time I spoke with her."

Alicia had boasted that her married lover made chili for her. Alicia's house still smelled of chili after her death, Kate had said.

If I hadn't seen how well Carlyle lied to Bethany about stepping outside his marriage, I would have believed him now.

"I got this showy box of hand-dipped chocolates

delivered to me at the Marriott in Austin on the Tuesday afternoon before she died. No note, but I figured Alicia sent them, discretely for a change, an apology for our fight. Chocolate-covered raisins, one of my favorites. I ate three or four while I was dressing for the big banquet that night. I started wheezing. I broke one open to look closer: Chopped-up apricots were mixed in with the raisins. She knew about my allergy to dried apricots, she knew the banquet was important to me—she deliberately sabotaged me, getting even. I had one hell of an asthma attack. I always carry a spare inhaler in my travel bag, but the one I had with me was empty; hard to believe it was simply a coincidence. Finally I went to the emergency room at the hospital for a shot of epinephrine."

He folded his arms across his chest. "That's the whole of it. I haven't been able to sleep, my appetite's gone; I can't stop thinking about it. I'm grateful to you for seeing me today. There's no one else I could talk to."

I studied the tautness in Carlyle's posture, tighter now than when he'd sat down, like poorly tempered steel ready to snap. He was holding back something.

"I was surprised that Alicia didn't park outside my house to kill herself. At least she spared me that."

As soon as he finished speaking, he dropped his head and covered his face with his hands, like a child dodging the scary part in a movie. Or a man afraid that his face might give too much away.

I walked over to my filing cabinet and took out Vermilion's picture. "One of the inpatients in Rugton couldn't fall asleep the night Alicia died. She sketched the scene." I handed it to Carlyle.

I watched the color drain from his face.

# Chapter 25

Carlyle left hurriedly after seeing Vermilion's picture, saying he couldn't be late to work. He responded so strongly because he'd been shocked by the thought of Alicia, dying alone in her car in front of Rugton—or so he claimed.

Carlyle could have easily driven to Houston and killed Alicia, leaving her body at Rugton. He could have made up the story about the doctored chocolates, deliberately eating apricots after he returned to give himself an alibi.

Had I been set up, had Carlyle scheduled his session with me so I'd be bound by confidentiality if he was ever accused of Alicia's murder? He had a motive, he had the opportunity, and he'd avoided telling me something important. But something he'd said— The phone rang, and the edge of the thought faded before I could grab it, a memory of something important, a link I was missing.

I spent the next fifteen minutes on the phone with a woman I'd never met, explaining several times that I wasn't interested in writing a letter to her mother-in-law, telling her that she needed to seek professional help for the psychological problems the daughter-in-law felt were patently obvious—if only I'd listen more carefully.

As the caller scolded me, I reminded myself that Carlyle wasn't the only person with a motive who'd been less than truthful. Debra had made a point of lying to me about being in Washington the night Alicia died. After I hung up, I looked up Linnstar's address in the phone book. Leaving my office, I tried to ignore the fact that my desk was piled high. I would work late, something I'd done all too frequently since Ian's death.

To get to Linnstar I drove southeast, past the Astrodome, to an industrial area where half the buildings looked abandoned, weeds high around them. On the corner, a fast-food restaurant had been boarded up, the only one I'd seen in the area. It was the kind of isolated stretch where you could dump a body and no one would spot it for a good long while.

Debra's building looked in better shape than most, the aluminum siding on the outside recently painted blue, the asphalt parking area in front newly resurfaced. The blue and purple petunias in the flower bed beside the door had probably been planted the requisite distance apart back in spring; now they'd overgrown, sprawling against their neighbors like sloppy drunks unable to stand upright. The sign by the door instructed me to ring for admission, but the door wasn't locked so I opened it without ringing, shutting it loudly behind me by way of announcement.

I entered into a reception area. No one sat at the desk to greet visitors; judging from the dust on the desktop, no one had occupied it for some time. Two doors led off from either side. I heard the sound of a chair being pushed back; then a phone started ringing. I heard Debra say, "Shit!" then, politely, "Linnstar, please hold." The door on the right opened, and she appeared.

"Something you needed?" Debra didn't look any more welcoming than she sounded. She stood with her hands on her hips, wearing a red dress and red heels that emphasized her height. The dress had two silver chains that cut across her body, forming a diagonal from her left shoulder to her right hip. All she needed was a sword to look like a modern-day Valkyrie, poised for battle.

"I've learned a couple of things about Alicia in the last few days that . . . puzzle me. I hoped you might be able to help me make some sense of them."

Debra stood staring at me as if waiting for the punch line. Finally she opened the door on the left and pointed inside. "Sit in the boardroom. I have to finish a call you've interrupted." She shut the door behind me, firmly.

A round table as big as a respectable flying saucer dominated the boardroom. Made of a gleaming dark wood, it had brass bands radiating from the center like spokes on a wheel. Too large to fit through any of the doors or windows, it must have been disassembled into sections and reassembled inside. Oversized chairs made of the same dark wood sat around the table, each centered between two brass spokes. Impressive. More than that: formidable.

I waited a moment; then I opened the door, turning the knob quietly. I could hear Debra's voice on the phone in the office across the hall, her tone cordial. "Yes, we're still looking for subjects for our drug trials; let's run through some questions and see if you qualify."

As I listened to Debra ask age, height, and weight, I looked at the oil painting on the opposite wall. Set in an elaborate gilded frame, it showed a mountain lion leaping on a terrified deer.

After Debra asked the caller about current medications, her tone changed from warm to brusque. "Sorry, doesn't look like you'll fit our protocol." She hung up without saying good-bye.

I had shut the door to the boardroom and planted myself in a chair by the time Debra reappeared, a blue coffee cup in her hand.

"So what's your news about Alicia?" She perched on the arm of the chair next to me, making it clear she wasn't planning to stay long. The position she'd chosen accentuated her height; she loomed over me.

"I was in Washington on Friday. I met Vernon Brundige. Seemed a little peeved with you for your sudden departure from your study section."

"So?"

I looked down and saw her right foot tapping like a metronome set fast, broadcasting her anxiety, giving lie to her apparent composure. Debra followed my gaze and stopped the movement abruptly. Her expression hardened.

"Vernon said you left in time to catch the midday flight back home," I said. "Would've gotten you back in Houston in time for dinner."

I waited for a moment before I added, "You went out of your way to tell me you were in Washington the night Alicia died."

The sun chose that moment to come from behind clouds, and bright streaks of sunlight shot through the window, lighting up the room. The sunlight played across the surface of the mammoth table and chairs, spotlighting places where the wood had been scratched, then touched up. More than a year's worth of normal wear and tear. Expensive furniture, bought second-hand.

Debra strode to the window and yanked the curtain closed. She spoke from across the room, her back straight and stiff: "Interesting work you chose, spending your time asking personal questions. Like a pig, enthusiastically burying your snout in piles of dead and decaying things. Pretending to forage for truffles."

I could feel the heat rise in my face.

She took a swallow from her coffee cup, then turned to adjust the curtain where it had bunched up. "What's your urgent, late-breaking news about Alicia?"

I waited until she turned around before I took Vermilion's picture out of the folder I'd brought with me. "A patient in Rugton couldn't sleep the night Alicia died. She sketched the scene from her window."

Her walk seemed a little unsteady as she came over to look at the picture.

Debra sipped her coffee three times while she studied the picture. Finally she set her cup on the table beside her, staring me down as she spoke. "Shrinks are like witch doctors. Equally useful professions."

That was the second time she'd avoided a key question by belittling me—a woman used to attacking to camouflage her real emotions. A dangerous woman.

I returned her stare, waiting a heartbeat before I picked up Vermilion's picture again. "The patient who painted this said that someone got out of the driver's seat of Alicia's car and walked away. The driver didn't come back."

"Meaning that someone else left her there. That one won't fly for me. I didn't know Alicia was seeing you for therapy. I wouldn't have known to leave her car at Rugton." Debra gave me a scornful smile. "Now, if you'll excuse me, I've got work to do."

"How much money did Alicia demand from you to keep quiet about her patent claims?"

Debra's arm jerked, knocking her coffee cup to the floor. The blue porcelain shattered on the tiled floor, fragments flying like small missiles, one leaving a gash on Debra's ankle. Drops splashed on my leg and felt cool through my hosiery. The pungent smell of coffee and alcohol floated up from the dark brown puddle. Coffee laced with Kahlua liqueur? Or maybe just straight Kahlua.

Debra's hands were clenched into fists, her lips drawn back, showing teeth. I pulled back in my chair, reflexively.

She didn't look down at the mess at her feet as she spoke. "Any time in the last two years, Alicia could have requested a review of authorship and patent issues by a departmental ad hoc committee. She could have petitioned the university's Office of Research to review her claims. She could have solicited informal mediation from the university Ombudsman. If she'd done any of those things, if she'd gone through any of the usual channels, then I'd have had the opportunity for other scientists to take the necessary time to assess and weigh her contributions to my compound's discovery and development."

Her voice carried a caustic, smoldering current of bitterness.

"Instead, I got a registered letter saying that she was contemplating a civil suit—so nicely, so precisely timed—just as I was about to start the next phase of my trials."

"What did you do?"

"I called her and asked her to meet me to discuss her concerns. She set the time and place—the Spindletop at the Hyatt Regency, one of the pricier places, naturally, and far from convenient for me—knowing I wasn't going to argue minor points.

"Alicia acted so cool when I saw her, like she knew she had me. I'm sitting there, trying to talk to her, and she's playing with her makeup." She pantomimed someone putting on lipstick in a prissy, overdone way.

"She said that she'd been thinking about all the time she spent in my lab—all the *contributions* she made." Debra was speaking more rapidly now, slurring her words slightly. "If she'd said the same things a year ago, I would've laughed in her face. But I can't afford a wrong step with Linnstar. Not now. And Alicia knew it."

"What changed in a year?"

"It's hard work, lining up investors for drug development. I've spent the better part of the last two years setting up my trials, a lot longer setting up Linnstar. Phase one turned out to be twice as expensive as projected and took half again as long as my original time line. My investors started getting skittish."

"If Alicia had crowned it all with questions about the patent—?"

"No way she would have won anything in a civil suit, but I couldn't afford to let it go that far."

Debra looked at the mess at her feet and made a face. She bent down and started picking up the larger pieces of the broken cup, stacking them in her left hand.

She looked up at me. "It wasn't just her idea alone, of course."

"Who—"

"Oliver Tate, who else? Had to be. Oliver's determined to beat me, whatever it takes. He'd love to see me fall flat on my face while he shows Eichon he can carry the banner for them. I'd bet he pushed Alicia to threaten me; it sure sounded like someone had counseled her, told her just what to say."

I remembered Carlyle's tension when he left my office, the feeling that he'd left something important unsaid. Maybe he'd goaded Alicia, encouraged her to get her due. A way to harass his competition.

"I know enough about Eichon's compound to know that mine's better, with fewer side effects." Debra spoke in the tone of someone absolutely convinced of the rightness of her judgment. "Any fair race, I'd win."

She walked over to a brass wastebasket in the corner. "So Alicia did talk with you about the ideas she'd concocted on the basis of her groundless concerns, her perverted memories?"

Rather than setting the pieces of the cup gently in the bottom, she started lobbing them in. The pieces crashed against the wastebasket's metal sides.

I couldn't stop myself from wincing at her noisy barrage. I felt my heart beating faster. "No. If Alicia had told me, I wouldn't have raised the issue with you."

"Sure." Her voice was heavy with sarcasm. Another shard clanged against the basket.

I raised my voice to be heard above the noise: "Alicia told a friend she'd found out about 'dry labeling studies,' or something close enough to get someone in big trouble.'"

"That bitch! I gave her money so she wouldn't sabotage my trials. I didn't give her money to cover up research fraud." Debra flung the rest of the pieces into the basket, the cacophony echoing in the room.

In the silence after the echoes died away, Debra spoke in a quiet voice that bothered me more than her shouting: "And now we get to the real reason for your visit—blackmail. You're trying to squeeze me, just like Alicia, right? First you tell me about talking with Vernon in Washington, then you pull out your phony picture, then you try to find out just how much Alicia managed to extort—so you'll know how much to ask. So just how greedy are you?"

She'd moved beside me as she spoke, standing too close. I stood up, not liking the way she towered over me when I was seated, all too aware that Debra stood a head taller than I.

"I'm not interested in your money, just information—"

"*Of course* you aren't. You really mean that you're not sure how much to ask—yet."

"When did you last see Alicia?" I felt myself breathing too fast; I spoke slowly, hoping she couldn't hear my nervousness.

"I didn't see her again after we met at the Spindletop at the end of August. I didn't want to see her again. My attorney gave her a check. *After* she signed a release for all present and future claims."

"Why did you attend her funeral?"

"I wanted to meet Alicia's parents. See how they'd react to me—whether she'd told them anything or not. They seemed friendly enough to me—not like the way they went after you," she said with a mocking smile.

"Where were you the night Alicia died?"

Her hands clenched into fists.

The doorbell rang in the hall. She stood staring at me, breathing hard—as if deciding what to do. The doorbell rang again.

She put her face a couple of inches from mine. "Get out of here. *Now.*"

# Chapter 26

**I** stopped in a Rugton restroom after I got back from my visit to Linnstar and unbuttoned my blouse so I could sponge my underarms with a wet paper towel, trying to erase the odor of fear. I still had too many loose ends with no obvious way to weave them together, but I felt safer back on my own turf. I decided to track down Xavier and ask him more about Oliver's lab. At least *he'd* be pleased to see me if I showed up unexpectedly.

I took some paperwork over to the cafeteria. I sat in a corner where I could scan the room but not be easily spotted by someone coming out of the cafeteria line. The smell that insinuated itself even as far as my remote corner telegraphed today's featured luncheon special: fried cod. The tables were half filled, the clamor of conversation and cutlery still tolerable, when Xavier showed up after 11:30. I watched him look closely at the nearby occupied tables as if hoping for company before he finally seated himself at an empty table for four. I waited until he unfolded his newspaper and started eating before I got a cup of coffee and made my way to his table.

Xavier stood up quickly when I greeted him, just as he had the last time; this time, though, instead of smiling and shaking my hand, he picked up his tray and held it between us, as if needing a physical barrier to insulate him from any contact with me. His rapid jerky movements slopped his bowl of tomato soup onto his tray. He looked around quickly, scanning the nearby tables.

"Back to work. Much to do," he mumbled, addressing the red puddle on his tray.

I looked down at the half-eaten hamburger lying on his tray, then back up at him. "I'm sorry," I said, meaning it.

Xavier continued to avoid my eyes as he grabbed his newspaper and bustled away.

I stood with my coffee in my hand, unsure whether to stay or go, trying to act nonchalant. I found myself checking out the people around me, hoping no one I knew had seen Xavier's hasty exit. I flashed back to the time when I'd been diagnosed with leukemia. I was thirteen. Girls who'd been my friends suddenly pulled back when I came close, worried about "catching" my disease. I'd tried to pretend it didn't matter.

I took a deep breath and started walking back to my office. Outside the cafeteria I remembered when I'd walked out with Xavier and we'd passed Oliver Tate as he stood in the corridor, talking with the Dean. Oliver hadn't looked pleased when he saw us together. Xavier could have told him I'd asked about graphiting studies or the fire in Tate's lab or Xavier's mundane job duties. Any one of those topics would have provided ample reason for Oliver to suggest that Xavier avoid me in the future.

I remembered when I'd first met Xavier in Oliver's unit. Oliver had cut him off when he'd started to say something about a missing videotape.

Maybe my questions to Xavier had made Oliver decide to search Alicia's house.

I definitely needed to talk with Oliver Tate again.

I used the information I'd gotten about Oliver's racquetball schedule to ambush him. On Monday I went swimming at five o'clock; after I finished, I took the time to dry my hair and reapply my makeup, timing everything so that I was standing behind the glass wall of Oliver's court, my gym bag in hand as if just leaving, during the last ten minutes of his match. I'd dressed in a navy T-shirt and white shorts, exposing the fading scratches on the backs of my legs.

Standing in front of Oliver and his opponent, my hand on my hip in a show-me stance, I watched their game for a few minutes before his opponent, a mid-thirties man with a short ponytail, caught sight of me. I saw him signal my presence to Oliver with a couple of words and a jerk of his head. Oliver smiled broadly when he saw me, pointed at his watch, held up five fingers, his eyebrows raised in inquiry. I nodded. They played their final minutes with greater intensity, sur-reptitiously looking over after good shots to make sure they'd been noticed.

The ten- to fifteen-year gap in age favored Oliver's opponent, but Oliver played with a ferocity his oppo-nent couldn't duplicate. After slamming the ball one final time and his opponent missing the return, Oliver raised both fists in victory. They shook hands, and Oliver joined me outside the court, saying he'd meet me for a drink in the club's café that overlooked the pool as soon as he changed.

He sat down opposite me ten minutes later, show-ered, his close-cropped hair still damp, wearing a plaid shirt, chinos, and boat shoes without socks.

I'd ordered orange juice, making sure to pay for it before he arrived. After Oliver asked for a rum and Diet Pepsi, he smiled at me. "Good to see you, away from work."

I remembered a story my father once told me about a pirate who always took a pinch of gunpowder with his rum. I think it was Blackbeard, but that might have just reflected my feelings toward Oliver Tate.

Oliver rolled up his shirt sleeves twice on each side, stopping below the elbow, a deliberate slowness in his movements. "Warm in here today." Dark hair covered his arms. He didn't look down as he rolled his sleeves, but kept his glance on me.

I unzipped the side of my gym bag and pulled out a manila folder. "One of the patients in Rugton couldn't fall asleep the night Alicia died and sketched the scene from the window." I handed Vermilion's picture to him, adding, "The artist said the driver was a man."

I watched his face, his arms, his body as I gave him the news.

Oliver looked at the picture carefully, turning it toward the light. "Good artist." Then he handed it back and flashed me a genuine smile, raising his hands in front of him, palms outward.

"I did it. You caught me." His voice had a lazy, come-hither quality. "How did you guess?"

*He was telling the truth.* "Tell me about it."

"I couldn't fall asleep Tuesday night, so I decided to skip Eichon's final breakfast meeting in Austin and leave early. When I got home, I found Alicia's car parked in my driveway."

He looked down toward the end of the pool where a woman wearing a barely-there orange bikini was climbing out of one of the suntanning beds. She moved her towel aside, uncovering a sparkling pile at her feet. She fastened gold chains around her neck and wrist and ankle, adding a thick gold wristwatch last, in case the glitter wasn't obvious enough.

He knocked on the glass, sharply, three times, and she looked up. She smiled and ruffled her fingers at him. "Went out with her a couple of times," he said, as if assuming I was interested.

"Alicia's car was parked in your driveway?"

He turned back to me. "She knew I was scheduled to be back at noon. She also knew my housecleaning service was due Wednesday morning—she got snippy with me when I asked her to schedule them while I was away—so they'd find her body; I assumed she enjoyed the vision of me returning from Austin, finding my driveway full of police who wanted to ask me questions. She'd chosen her time so I'd come back without any way to counter her malice.

"It was close to two when I found her." An expression passed over his face so rapidly that I wasn't sure what I'd seen. Irritation, maybe. He cleared his throat. "I checked her pulse. Nothing. She was gone, her body already cooling."

*Dead already? Her body in Oliver's driveway?*

"I had a beer and thought about what to do. She'd made her final statement to me in a way designed to maximally embarrass me. I didn't appreciate it. No way she'd get the last word if I could help it. I knew she'd been seeing a shrink; the parking lot of a psychiatric hospital seemed like the ideal place to leave her. A final joke on her. I drove her car to Rugton."

*Surely she didn't kill herself at Oliver's house.* "Did Alicia leave a note?"

"No note. I checked her purse and her pockets, searched her car. After I left her car at Rugton, I went to my office and searched my desk and her desk on the unit. Nothing. It's out of character, obviously." He paused. "You're the psychologist, what do you make of her omission? The dog that didn't bark, and all that?"

"Did you take anything out of her car?" I pictured the pillows she needed to reach the pedals.

He sat up straighter. " 'Take anything out of her car?' What an interesting question. I've already told you that she didn't leave a note. Either you don't believe me, or—you think there was something else.

"You don't want to believe that Alicia really killed herself, do you?" A mocking smile. "There wasn't a mark on her, you know. I did look carefully; I didn't want to get caught driving a car with a murder victim and be accused of the crime."

So someone else had left Alicia's body in Oliver's driveway—if I could believe him.

I pictured him coolly drinking his beer and considering his alternatives for disposal of the body. Concentrating on how to win his final battle with Alicia. "So you abandoned her body at Rugton. . . ."

"I wasn't sure what other nasty surprises she might have left me. Particularly if she'd planted any little bombs with you. Having you implicated by association defused anything you might say."

I thought of Wayne, a man I'd dated in college. Wayne kept his high school football trophies on his bureau, his team's picture, framed in silver, on his wall, and a shoe box full of Polaroids under his bed—nude shots of women he'd dated and bedded—that were shown with pride to his male friends.

Wayne had asked me to let him take a Polaroid of me, nude; he never mentioned the rest of his collection. I refused. He never asked again. Two months after I broke up with him, I found out he'd gotten his picture, anyway: He uncovered me one morning when I'd been sleeping in the nude. I wasn't the only sleeping woman in his collection, I heard.

I never said a word to Wayne about the nude photo he'd taken of me. Instead, I broke into his house when I knew he'd be away for the weekend, climbing through a back window as he'd done once when he locked himself out. I found the shoe box with nude photos under his bed, just as I'd been told; I emptied them into his kitchen sink and set them on fire, leaving the charred bits for him to clean up. I'd brought a plastic bag of ripening roadkill with me, the remains of a raccoon, dumped the contents into the shoe box, and left it where I'd found it, under his bed. I turned up his heat as high as it would go before I left.

I thought of the stories Alicia had told about getting even. I wasn't a stranger to that impulse.

Oliver Tate, sitting in front of me, clearly enjoyed telling his story. He expected me to appreciate his cleverness, his resourcefulness.

I wanted to wipe the smugness off his face. "And if I go to the police with this information?"

He gave me a tolerant look. "I drove back to Austin after I took care of the trouble here. I never bothered to check out of the hotel; everything was billed directly to

Eichon during the time set aside for the conference. No one even knew I'd come and gone.

"As for the police—well, they weren't overly impressed with you. When they came to me with the sleeping pill bottle, they told me how you made their job more difficult by denying Alicia was suicidal. We had a good laugh when I reminded them that Chaucer said women excel at 'weeping, weaving, and lies.'" He chuckled. "By the way, do they know about your 'scholarly interests' in deception?"

I struggled to keep my voice conversational; I didn't want to give Oliver the satisfaction of seeing how angry I was. "Why did you leave the pill bottle in her car?"

"Think about it . . . logically. They'd confirm cause of death on autopsy, then they'd look for a source for the pills; if they didn't find a pill bottle, it might have looked odd. It was easier to let them have me up front. I was out of town when Alicia got the prescription filled, after all. I have dozens of witnesses in Austin."

I looked at him as he sat in front of me. Expensive grooming, styled hair, buffed nails, a cultivated air of privilege. Oliver couldn't stand taking second place in a contest: He had to be the Alpha male in the troupe— and was prepared to sandblast anything that got in his way.

"You told Xavier to keep his distance from me, I gather."

I had trouble finding a comfortable way to sit in the chair. I crossed my legs. Oliver's eyes followed my movements, lingering on my bare legs.

He could have been admiring them, or he could have been checking to see how his handiwork at Alicia's house was holding up.

"I just educated Xavier—told him how industrial spies work, pretending to be friendly while they ask leading questions."

And Xavier probably wouldn't question any explanation from Oliver, no matter how weak.

I thought about my options, none of them good. No

doubt if I asked him if he'd knocked me out at Alicia's, he'd deny everything. Worse, even if I was right, I could be handing him ammunition to use against me; he'd be able to say I'd confessed to breaking into Alicia's house, then accused him of mugging me there.

I could see why he didn't worry about what I'd say to the police.

He gave me a lazy smile that made me wonder if he'd been having similar thoughts. "In fairness to you, when Alicia's parents sue you for malpractice, I'd be willing to testify that Alicia was quite impulsive, and you might not have been able to do much, even if you'd known she was suicidal. But only if you don't try to make trouble by going to the police—or anyone else."

"How very . . . thoughtful of you," I said, my voice hard. *When* Alicia's parents sue you, he'd said. Not *if*.

I thought of the papers I'd mailed to Vernon Brundige. A double-edged sword.

"I should think you'd be grateful for any assistance I could offer you in that regard. After I visited you the day Alicia died, I stopped by to see your boss; I know Kurt from our term together on the medical staff credentials committee. Naturally, we talked about Alicia and my visit with the police; he didn't seem overly fond of you, I must say, talking about other recent problems with your judgement on a test report for a custody case."

I stood up, suddenly. I felt like driving my fist into his face.

As I turned to go, he said, "Does this mean I'm to be denied the pleasure of your company at an intimate dinner tonight? Such a disappointment."

After I left Oliver sitting in the restaurant, I borrowed a phone book from Casey at the front desk. I looked up Oliver's address and headed for Houston's expensive River Oaks section where he lived.

Who could have left Alicia's body in Oliver Tate's driveway? Debra Linnell was the obvious choice. Debra believed Oliver had goaded Alicia to harass her, to press her patent claims. Maybe Debra thought it would be a neat trick to send Alicia back to Oliver—dead.

Oliver's neighborhood had the drowsy quietness of a well-fed cat. The trees stretched up tall, like complacent giants that deigned to shade the properties. The lawns were uniformly smooth and immaculate, but no mowers intruded on the silence; lawn service elves probably came during the day to cut the grass and edge the flower beds and yank out any weeds rude enough to trespass. The houses were in the price range of most people's fourth or fifth home, for those lucky enough to make it that far; no children's voices disturbed the stillness. I saw a man practicing his golf swing in a driveway a few doors down; otherwise, the street was deserted.

Dense shrubbery lined Oliver's long and winding driveway, giving the sense of a carefully orchestrated maze that led you by the hand exactly where he wanted you to go. At the end of the driveway, I could see that his house had a gray slate roof; nothing else was visible from the road.

This wasn't a neighborhood where I could count on miraculously finding a nosy neighbor who had spotted Alicia's car parked in Oliver's driveway. If that was what had really happened.

I suspected that Oliver had admitted he'd left Alicia's body at Rugton because he wasn't sure how much Vermilion might have seen. Confessing up front was a way to undercut whatever she might have said. A preemptive strike.

If Alicia had really been dead when Oliver found her body that night.

# Chapter 27

After dropping my things at my office on Tuesday morning, I walked over to the office of the Biomedical Human Subjects Research Committee in the administration building. I wanted to see if I could get information to make sense of the videotape I'd found in Alicia's apartment.

The brass plate on her desk informed me that Lucille Rustbult was the administrative assistant for the committee. She was busy making lunch plans on the phone, simultaneously filing dagger-length nails painted a garish red. She'd outlined her lips in red, filling in the rest with a gooey, shiny pink. Neither color flattered her pale face. She glanced sharply at me when I walked into her office but made no move to end her conversation.

When she finally hung up, I asked for a list of approved protocols from the last two years. In preparation for the visit I'd worn a navy-blue suit, a white silk shirt, and heels, wanting to look my most official.

"Not available to students." She didn't break her rhythm with her nail file.

I pulled out my faculty ID card and handed it to her. She made a show of looking it over closely, comparing my face with the picture. We'd clashed before when she lost the paperwork I'd submitted for one of my studies. I didn't think she'd forgotten me.

"Not really policy to distribute those lists, you know."

My nose was getting stuffy and my throat felt scratchy, probably a legacy from my plane ride back from Washington; I wasn't inclined to be conciliatory. "Under the sunshine laws, all the committee's records are open to public scrutiny. Is there a problem?"

"Hard to get those lists together. May take a long time." Lucille Rustbult gave me a baleful look from eyes she'd carefully rimmed in black. "You can check back in a week or two."

I held up the bulging briefcase I'd brought along for this very contingency. "No problem waiting." Since her office only had room for her desk, four file cabinets, and a small visitor's chair that hugged the edge of her desk, my proximity seemed like my most lethal weapon.

"Maybe you could wait out in the hall." She gave me her best frozen smile with the suggestion.

I sat down in the spare chair. "I think I'm getting a cold. Kind of cozy in your office. Maybe we could chat about the committee while you look for the lists." I pulled out a tissue and blew my nose loudly.

In less than five minutes I had the lists I'd requested. It took me five minutes more to find what I'd expected, a protocol reviewed by the committee a year ago, "describing a new drug for the treatment of tardive dyskinesia."

I asked to see a copy of Oliver Tate's submission, giving Lucille the date and approval number.

She patted her well-lacquered hair, looking as if she was considering how she might evade my request. I pulled out another tissue and blew my nose again. Lucille searched through her file cabinet and pulled out the protocol. She banged the metal drawer shut.

Oliver Tate had proposed to test a new drug to treat the uncontrollable facial movements associated with tardive dyskinesia following long-term use of antipsychotic drugs. I knew the basics before I read the protocol, but the method section had the part I'd hoped to see: Patients' faces would be videotaped before and after treatment with the drug, the tapes rated with the Tardive Dyskinesia Videotape Rating Scale.

Changes in facial movements would demonstrate the drug's effectiveness. Maybe supposed effectiveness in this case.

TD: the abbreviation on the smoke-stained videotape I'd found hidden under the mattress in Alicia's house and the subject of the heavily marked articles in her files. When I'd visited Oliver's unit, Xavier had tried to talk to Oliver about a missing videotape; Oliver had shut him up.

"If you *don't mind*—I don't appreciate the noise," Lucille said.

"Sorry." I realized I'd been whistling "Smoke Gets in Your Eyes" under my breath.

I remembered Vernon Brundige's story about the FDA's response to the physician whose X rays didn't match the case reports submitted to the drug company. If Oliver's tapes showed behaviors that didn't jibe with the ratings, he would have had a good incentive to set the fire before the FDA visit. Maybe he'd timed it so Alicia would find the fire before it spread. Maybe he'd planned to put it out himself, and she appeared unexpectedly.

Alicia's sleep had been invaded by nightmares of walking skeletons; she'd even lit a match in her sleep. She was already stressed by her qualms about Carlyle and their clandestine relationship; a traumatic incident like putting out a fire could have triggered her flurry of nightmares—especially if she'd suspected the fire wasn't an accident.

Alicia must have found the fire too early and rescued at least one of the tapes he'd meant to destroy. After hearing the questions I asked Xavier, Oliver had wanted the missing videotape back badly enough to set another fire and knock me out.

I gave Oliver's protocol back to Lucille and thanked her for her help.

"I'll need to make sure that Dr. Tate knows you asked to see his protocol." She gave me a triumphant smile. "In case there's ever any question of whether you copied an idea from him."

Ensuring that Oliver would guess I'd sent the FDA after him; ensuring that Oliver would be as unhelpful as possible in any malpractice trial. "I understand perfectly." I tried to keep my voice composed while my mouth went dry.

I still didn't have any idea how Alicia had been killed. I'd only succeeded in undermining my malpractice defense, feeble as it was.

I called Rosemary Overstreet for the third time since I'd visited her. She wasn't in her office, I was told—again. I left another message.

I went home midafternoon when my running nose and aching head got the best of me. After I took a cold capsule and changed into shorts and a polo shirt, I fed Pavlov. I played with him for a while outside, and then I brought him in the house with me.

The combination of the cold medicine, my sleep deficit from last night, and my stuffy head made the thought of sleeping more enticing than anything else at the moment. I put Pavlov in his box and lay down on my bed, still dressed, planning to take a short nap.

I awoke after ten that night, my mouth dry, my stomach rumbling. Pavlov was sleeping quietly, so I left him in his box and went downstairs. I poured myself a tall glass of milk and slathered peanut butter and strawberry jam on two dozen Ritz crackers—comfort food, something I'd eaten often when I was younger. As I sat at the table and looked at my reflection in the darkened window, I remembered how I'd been watched from the darkness outside while I searched Alicia's house. Feeling uneasy, I pulled down the shades on the kitchen windows that I used to block the morning sun.

I tried to read the newspaper but couldn't concentrate. I felt tired, drugged. I got my appointment book out of my purse, wondering how heavily I was sched-

uled and if I could sleep a little later tomorrow. My
earliest appointment was a nine o'clock on the burn
unit, another new admission they wanted me to see.
Then the memory of talking with Roy Hilderbrand in
the burn unit hit me like the blinding dazzle of head-
lights after walking in the dark.

I suddenly knew how Alicia could have been murdered without leaving a mark, without leaving any
evidence detectable by autopsy. In a way that murder
could never be proven.

I heard Pavlov whining upstairs, and I grimaced at
the thought of carrying him outside, standing around
waiting for him. Better the work than the clean up, I
told myself. I was halfway up the stairs when I heard a
noise like a firecracker, then the sound of glass shatter-
ing in my kitchen—the sound of a window giving way.
Shot out, I realized, a second later.

As I ran upstairs to my bedroom and locked the door
behind me, I thought I heard someone yelling, then a
second shot. No breaking glass this time. I picked up
my phone with shaking hands, thankful it had a lighted
dial so I didn't have to fumble in the dark to dial 911.
The man who answered took the information and told
me they'd notify the police immediately. He told me to
stay on the line.

I looked at the panel for my security system on the
wall beside my bed, a duplicate for the ones by the
doors downstairs. I'd set the perimeter alarm earlier,
and the red light told me the doors were still secure. At
least I'd have some warning if the intruder got through
the door. The windows weren't wired, so I wouldn't
know if he came in that way; he could climb through
the broken window—but he'd have to get rid of the
jagged glass around the rim. I strained to listen, hoping
I wouldn't hear any more glass breaking.

In the silence the doorbell rang. I jumped at the
sound. It rang twice more, insistently. I thought I heard
a woman's voice calling my name. Not the police yet,
the 911 dispatcher said. Stay put.

I looked around the room for something to use as a

weapon. Nothing—unless I threw shoes. Nothing that would stop bullets.

Pavlov had started whining and trying to get out of his box as soon as I came back into the room. I leaned over the box and petted him while I held the phone, wondering who'd shot out my window. Oliver Tate was capable, but I couldn't picture him taking this kind of extreme action—not something so risky now, not when he could do other things to hurt me. Stuart Crego seemed a better bet.

But whose voice had I heard? Who rang the doorbell? The dense shrubbery that screened my house from my neighbors also served to muffle sound. Unless someone had already been in my driveway, I doubted that they could have pinpointed the source of the noise—or rung the bell so soon after the shots.

I thought about how Alicia had been killed, remembering the alcohol and pills that had been pumped out of Roy Hilderbrand's stomach through his NG tube. If I was right, everything depended on the killer having the medical training to insert an NG tube to deliver a fatal dose of pulverized sleeping pills and alcohol directly to Alicia's stomach. Oliver Tate and Debra Linnell were physicians. Carlyle Stocklin had been kicked out of medical school. Any one of the three probably had the necessary knowledge to kill Alicia and make it look like suicide.

The murderer needed to know Alicia was in the feeding disorders study, a point she'd dramatized at Eichon's July fourth picnic. Oliver, Carlyle, and Debra had all been there. Alicia's repeated NG tube feedings as a research subject meant that any abrasions left by another NG tube insertion could be easily explained if the medical examiner spotted them during the autopsy.

The killer needed to write a prescription on one of Oliver Tate's pads with Tate's DEA number. Oliver and Carlyle had the easiest access, but I couldn't rule out Debra entirely. She undoubtedly had been in Oliver's office in the past, and she still held a faculty appointment in his department.

Stuart didn't fit well anywhere. If I was right about the method, he wasn't the murderer.

I didn't hear the police when they arrived; they must have come without sirens. Finally the man on the phone told me it was safe to go downstairs. Come out the front door, he said.

At least my runny nose had dried up, courtesy of the major jolt of adrenaline I'd gotten.

At the base of my stairs I have switches that I can use to turn on all the lights in front and in back of my house. The front yard lights had shorted out during the weekend downpour, but the back ones still worked. I flipped all the switches; then I went to an upstairs window that gives me a view of my backyard. I lifted up a corner of the drape.

Off to the side, standing between two uniformed policemen, I saw a woman dressed in dark clothes—Rosemary Overstreet, I realized, after a minute. *Rosemary, here?*

Closer to the house I saw the shape of a man holding a rifle, crouched and aiming, positioned in front of the shattered kitchen window. I jerked back, then saw it was only a cutout, one of those life-sized plywood silhouettes sold as yard ornaments.

A few feet away from the silhouette I saw people in white gathered around a man lying on his back, a gun beside his hand, a gaping red hole in his chest. Stuart Crego.

# Chapter 28

The police questioned me for a long time, making me repeat my story several times. They took my fingerprints, asked if I'd fired a gun recently, sprayed something on my hands for confirmation. Finally they told me how Stuart had been killed.

Rosemary had been coming to visit me, she told them; she'd just gotten word that I'd been trying to reach her and decided to apologize in person for not answering more quickly. She'd spotted Stuart parked beside the entrance to my driveway where he was taking the silhouette out of his trunk. She'd driven on past, then doubled back and parked along the road beyond a bend. Guessing it was some kind of dirty trick for me and not sure what else to do, she'd grabbed a rifle she still had in her trunk from a recent skeet shooting contest and jogged back down the street.

Rosemary found Stuart setting up the silhouette where I'd seen it, facing my window; then he'd pulled out a gun and fired into the kitchen window—the only lighted window in the house. Once he fired, she had to stop him. She'd called out, telling him not to shoot again, warning him that she had a rifle aimed at him. He'd turned around fast, his gun pointed, and she shot him.

She'd rung my doorbell when she couldn't see me

inside, hoping I wasn't lying somewhere, wounded. Then she'd jogged over to a neighbor's house and asked them to call 911.

She'd been very forthcoming with the police, reminding them about the butchered mouse in my car, telling them about her difficulties with Stuart. Obviously such an unstable man; she'd been very concerned when she saw him skulking around my house.

Evidently it was a reasonable, convincing story as she told it, entirely consistent with the story I'd told, and apparently entirely consistent with the physical evidence at the scene. She'd shot Stuart in self-defense, maybe saving my life in the process.

But the police didn't know Rosemary, and they hadn't seen what I'd seen when I looked down at the tableau from upstairs: Rosemary had been wearing her avenging angel look.

As I drove down San Felipe to work the next morning, I wondered if Stuart could have played any role in Alicia's death. Nothing fit, if I was right about the method. But if he hadn't been involved in Alicia's death, why had he taken such an extreme step last night? And why had Rosemary "just happened" to drop by?

I'd told the police that Rosemary had never visited me at my home before, but that hadn't seemed to make any impression. I wondered if Rosemary's police connections through her child abuse work helped her credibility; I could see her playing them for all they were worth. I hadn't known what else to say or do.

I knew Rosemary was holding back something important.

Stuart's death last night had been too late to make the morning paper, but I was dreading the onslaught of media today. Listening to the radio now, I heard how a dispute over an arrest for public drunkenness had escalated into two shootings and a riot last night, with one section of downtown still blocked off. A tropical storm in the Gulf was gathering force, putting Houston in the path of a hurricane. Blood tests had confirmed that a state senator who'd been touted as a leading candidate for governor had fathered the baby of a sixteen-year-old girl. A triple murder in a River Oaks mansion included a prominent lawyer dressed in drag, a scrapbook full of pictures showing it wasn't the first time, and a report that he was much more attractive as a woman than a man. With luck, Stuart's death would continue to get short shrift.

I thought about Alicia's death and how it had been maneuvered.

The first step would have been the most difficult: Somehow sedate Alicia, probably by getting the first round of sleeping pills and alcohol into her.

The first dose of sleeping pills would taste bitter, so they couldn't be concealed in ordinary food.

But something hot and spicy might do the trick, especially if she had something alcoholic to wash it down and enhance its potency.

Hot and spicy food like the chili she loved. And Alicia's house had smelled of chili after her death.

Alicia had boasted to Kate that her married lover had made chili for her. I had trouble imagining Oliver or Debra bringing a meal to Alicia without making her suspicious.

A battered green van cut in front of me so sharply, I had to break hard to avoid rear-ending it. I honked and the driver made a rude gesture. He had a Confederate flag flying from his antenna and three bumper stickers on the back of his van: NONREHABILITABLE TEXAN; THIS PROPERTY PROTECTED BY A PIT BULL WITH AIDS; and AUSTIN CITY LIMITS.

Austin wasn't far; Carlyle could have easily driven to Houston to kill Alicia, then driven back to his meeting—just as Oliver had.

But why would Carlyle have left Alicia's body for Oliver? Maybe to divert suspicion from himself, implicating another man by association? But Carlyle wouldn't want to jeopardize things with Oliver, not when Oliver was in charge of testing his compound.

I'd see Carlyle in group tonight. I could make a better judgment in person.

At work I found a message in my mailbox that Carlyle Stocklin had left for me yesterday, after I'd gone home in the afternoon: "Just got word of an emergency Eichon meeting in Austin on Tuesday and Wednesday. So sorry I can't come to group this week as I'd promised. Next week for sure."

So convenient, an emergency meeting.

Maybe Carlyle wasn't avoiding me; maybe he wouldn't have had sufficient training as a medical student before he was expelled. I called Quinton Gibbs, hoping he'd tell me it required more advanced training to insert an NG tube.

"Not at all difficult," he said, not, thankfully, asking the reason behind my question. "Someone who's familiar with the technique can do it in a minute or two, as long as the patient's cooperative. Use a lubricant like K-Y jelly, and it slides right down. I've seen parents trained to do it so they can take care of their children."

The picture of Alicia's body flashed in my mind, the shine above her upper lip I'd assumed was sweat. Traces of the lubricant used to insert the tube.

So much for eliminating Carlyle from my roster of suspects.

I felt steadily worse as the day wore on, much like yesterday. I was about to call and leave messages for group members saying that I had to cancel tonight when Thelma Lou buzzed me: Gerald Yablonski was here and wanted to talk to me for five minutes; it was urgent; it couldn't wait until group tonight.

Gerald started speaking as soon as he sat down in my office. "I've been working up my courage to come see you. I've just got to tell someone about Alicia."

Sweat stains circled the armholes of his blue dress shirt. It was the first time I'd seen him when he wasn't wearing his navy-blue windbreaker.

"I was really turned on by Alicia when she came to group. I—I went to her house a couple of times. At night. After dark. I . . . watched her; she didn't know I was outside."

Just as he'd peeped in neighbors' windows as a teenager.

"The second time I went—it was the night she died. I parked down the street like I'd done before and snuck up to her house. Just as I was almost close enough to her window to see inside, the door from the house to her carport opened. I ran behind the bushes along the driveway."

He was perspiring heavily, drops of sweat dotting his forehead. He wiped his face with his hands, then wiped his damp hands on his gray trousers.

"It was another woman coming out, not Alicia. She opened the door to Alicia's car, then she—she went back inside, leaving the door open. She brought Alicia out next, dragging her out on a blanket or something, real slow and careful. Alicia wasn't moving. The woman went back inside and came out with a purse and a big towel. She looped the towel under Alicia's arms; then she got in the back seat and pulled Alicia up using the towel, like a sling. Took a while; she had to get out the other side and push Alicia up twice. Then she got in the front seat and drove away."

"A woman? You're absolutely sure it was a woman?" Even as small as Alicia was, most women would have been hard pressed to lift her—but it sounded like someone had thought out that problem well in advance.

"Yeah, a tall woman, dressed in a dark T-shirt and sweatpants, loose fitting, but I saw boobs—excuse me, breasts—for sure. She had a black scarf tied around her neck. Not someone I recognized."

Debra Linnell. Debra would have savored the irony of leaving Alicia's body in Oliver Tate's driveway, his name on the prescription bottle. A perfect way for her to even the score with both Alicia and Oliver at the same time.

I remembered the secondhand furnishings at Linnstar, the empty reception desk at the entrance. Debra was reaching the end of her cash reserves, needing everything left to pay for the next phase of her drug trials.

Alicia had told Kate that she'd bought the Caddy with the first installment. Maybe Alicia had been so gratified by Debra's initial payment that she'd demanded more.

*A woman in dark clothes.* I pictured Rosemary as I'd seen her last night, dressed in dark colors. Just a coincidence—had to be. She didn't fit the rest of the scenario. But Debra didn't feel quite right, either. I was missing something.

"Have you talked to the police?"

"No way. Absolutely no way. What I said has got to be kept confidential. No police. I can't afford to get into trouble for peeping again." His voice was firm, resolute. "I didn't want to talk about it in group because someone might tell on me. I can tell you because you're obligated to keep it secret."

# Chapter 29

Feeling truly rotten, I drove home. Gerald had been adamant about avoiding the police, and I didn't see any other way to convince them that Alicia had been murdered. My nose was rubbed raw from my sneeze-wipe blow-wipe routine, and my throat felt like sandpaper. The cold capsule I'd taken left me feeling drugged and lethargic, and I had a throbbing headache.

At home I walked around the house, somehow expecting it to look different in the daylight. It looked the same; Stuart's death still didn't seem real to me. I had two messages from reporters on my recorder; I erased them and set the machine to answer the phone on the first ring, not wanting to talk to anyone tonight. I changed into cut-offs and an old white T-shirt, dressing for the cleaning I needed to do. I'd left a key for a handyman who does odd jobs for me and he had replaced the broken window, but I needed to clean up the debris.

After I fed Pavlov, I tried to clean up the kitchen, but he wanted to play, staying so close to my feet that I tripped over him and fell hard, skinning my knee and elbow. I brought Pavlov up to his box in the bedroom and put him inside, then flopped across the bed, planning to doze an hour or two, hoping I'd wake up feeling better.

I was exhausted—so, naturally, sleep danced ahead of me, just out of reach. Lying in bed, drugged by my cold and the pill I'd taken, my mental wires crossing, I made the connection I'd been missing. I knew who killed Alicia—and why. And at least part of how. Like the medical adage about alternative diagnoses: *When you hear hoofbeats, think of horses first—but don't forget that zebras make the same sound.*

Because Vermilion had seen a man get out of Alicia's car, I'd overlooked the obvious. A woman had murdered Alicia—but it wasn't Debra Linnell. I got out of bed and started pacing back and forth, seeing things in a new light. I thought about how people hang things on their walls that reflect their personality. I remembered the chill I'd felt, listening to a story. I remembered her wrathful expression when I'd last seen her.

But what to do about it? Lay it out for the police and pray they'd listen to me? I didn't have high hopes, not when they'd already closed the books on Alicia's "suicide."

Confronting her seemed like the best alternative. I'd tell her what I'd guessed, give her a chance to tell her story, hope she'd let something slip.

But could I really be right? Was my cold clouding my thinking, making me stretch the story to fit the facts? Did I truly have the answers to Alicia's death?

I looked up a phone number, dialed, and listened to the phone ring twice. "Hello?" A half-second pause. *"Hello?"* The voice was sharp edged the second time, openly hostile. The timbre of her angry voice fit my newly revised picture of her perfectly: a woman over the edge, a woman who'd lost faith in her plans for her future, a woman who couldn't stand to lose. I hung up without saying anything.

I needed to plan carefully. I thought of how much cunning had gone into Alicia's murder. I couldn't afford to make a mistake.

I'd call her and insist we meet in a public place, then tell her the story of Alicia's murder as I understood it, carefully watching her every reaction. I'd protect myself by writing down in advance everything I knew or had guessed; I'd tell Glee everything beforehand, give her a copy of my letter, ask her to keep watch at a distance.

My head throbbed like a drumroll of doom as my rush of adrenaline ebbed. I'd think through my plans more carefully when I was feeling better. I lay down again. It wasn't the time to act, not quite yet. . . .

A muffled noise brought me wide awake, out of a bad dream. My heart raced and my breathing came fast until I realized I was lying on my bed, safe. What had I heard?

I listened now, hearing the usual creaks of the house, the night sounds of crickets and frogs. An owl hooted. Then Pavlov whined in his box beside me, and I knew what must have awakened me. I looked at the illuminated dial on my alarm clock: almost eleven.

I picked up Pavlov and carried him downstairs to the front door; even if the police hadn't asked me to stay away from my backyard and the yellow tape around it, I wouldn't have gone out there now. I entered the code on my security system to deactivate it. As I hit the porch light switch, I remembered I still needed to call an electrician to fix the short.

Pavlov wiggled in my arms and complained, so I opened the front door and set him outside before I got a pocket flashlight from the kitchen and the poker from the fireplace. I felt anxious, apprehensive, as if Stuart's malevolence still floated around the yard, seeking a target.

The night had turned dark early when heavy clouds moved in, and they made the starless, moonless night even darker, the weak beam of my pocket flashlight barely adequate to pick out Pavlov's dark shape where he'd wandered down the driveway. He promptly watered the grass as soon as I spotlighted him, and I praised him and started toward him.

I didn't hear anything until it was too late, my mind

still fogged by bad dreams and my cold. Suddenly I found myself staring into a much brighter light—a high-powered flashlight, held so I could see that the person's other hand held a gun.

"Don't make a sound. Drop the poker and the flashlight, then raise your hands over your head, slowly. Any fast moves, any noise—you're dead." The voice was calm and soft, and for a minute I thought I was still dreaming.

A woman's voice.

The woman I had called.

"Keep your hands over your head. Very slowly, go back inside."

I did as she ordered, my knees so weak that they threatened to buckle under me. She kept her light on me, pinning me in its glare.

I walked through my front door, and I heard Pavlov running on the stone walk behind us, trying to catch up. I heard her slam the front door, Pavlov whining outside.

"Walk over to the couch, slowly, and switch on the lamp. Don't turn around."

I switched on the lamp. Something whizzed by my ear, and I jumped and gasped.

She laughed—a harsh, metallic laugh, like thick aluminum foil bending grudgingly.

I thought she'd fired a bullet at my head. When I caught my breath, I realized it was only a June bug that had flown in the open door. She turned off the ceiling light, leaving only the pool of light from the lamp around me, like someone in a movie preparing a suspect for interrogation.

"Turn around and sit down, slowly."

I moved as slowly as possible. I could hear the tension in her voice.

"Lean all the way back against the sofa. Put your hands inside the waistband of your shorts."

I leaned my back against the cushion and eased the tips of my fingers inside the top of my shorts.

"Not just your knuckles." Her voice was sharper now. "Put your hands farther down, so the waistband covers your wrists."

I wriggled my hands in farther.

Bethany Stocklin then seated herself on an ottoman across the room. Carlyle's wife.

The flashlight, now switched off, lay against her left leg. Bethany was using both hands to hold the gun she was resting on right knee, her finger on the trigger—too far away to try to jump her, too far from any place I could run and hide. Nothing was close enough at hand to use as a weapon. Just like last night, a bad dream that kept repeating itself: nothing at hand for defense, nothing solid enough to stop bullets.

The closest thing I had to a weapon in my living room was my teapot collection. Bethany was sitting with her back against the wall where they sat on wooden blocks. She wasn't going to let me get up, pick up a teapot or two, and toss them at her.

The only other bright idea I had about getting out of here alive was so bizarre I might have laughed out loud under other circumstances.

"If you try to move from the sofa, I'll shoot you."

She'd seen me looking around, judging distance. "Bethany, what's this about?" I tried to sound calm and reasonable, but my voice came out hoarse and pinched.

"I trusted you when Carlyle and I came to see you together. I figured he'd kept quiet about Alicia with you, just like he lied to me. Then I read the newspaper story that said Alicia was one of your patients. I knew she'd have told you about her affair with Carlyle, even if he hadn't; I felt like such a fool. You colluded with Carlyle to trick me. To lie to me. Just the way Alicia did."

Impeccable logic, wrong conclusion—but a good way to justify my murder to herself. I got a rush of adrenaline, my breathing so loud and fast that I thought she must hear it across the room.

"I saw the second newspaper story, the one about your work where you said that Alicia wasn't suicidal. Debra told me you'd been out to see her, asking questions about Alicia. You talked with Carlyle on Monday. Tell me what you found." Now her voice was soft, almost cajoling, as if talking to a young child or a pet.

"Bethany, you've got the wrong idea—"

"You tried to call Carlyle earlier today. I saw your phone number on the caller ID box when you hung up on me."

I remembered the chill I'd felt with Carlyle, a delayed response, a crossing signal flashing red after the train had already passed—after Carlyle had told me that Bethany had been married to Oliver, after he'd assured me Bethany didn't have a clue about his affair with Alicia.

So comforting to know I'd guessed right.

"You're going to die tonight. The longer we talk, the longer you live. If you don't talk, if you want to play the innocent, you'll die sooner."

So I needed to stretch it out as long as possible. Back to the beginning, to what I'd overlooked. "You fed your father through an NG tube after his accident."

"I kept expecting that if I took good enough care of him, he'd recover. Miraculously. Then I found the letter he'd written to his mistress before his accident, with his plans for leaving me—leaving us, me and my mother—and starting over. I gave him a few extra pills."

"And no one questioned his death," I said, "since he'd been so badly injured."

Bethany wore a black long-sleeved turtleneck, black stirrup pants, and black sneakers. She had black gloves on her hands and a black scarf wound around her hair. Dressed for hiding in shadows. Dressed for killing, just like before.

I could feel droplets of sweat running down my side. I could smell the odor of my fear around me.

"You heard Alicia talking about the feeding disorders study at the Eichon picnic. That's what gave you the idea for using the NG tube with her."

"Alicia made an exhibition of herself at that picnic. She wore this T-shirt that said, 'It's not how deep you fish, it's how you wiggle the worm.' She used so much perfume, she almost knocked me out when she walked by. I smelled that same perfume on Carlyle, twice, after the picnic. I was sure." Bethany's voice broke, and she swallowed.

"The second time, Carlyle thought he was being so subtle when he told me a 'friend at work' had nightmares and wanted a prescription for sleeping pills. Asked if I knew a doc who'd write one without making a fuss about it. That's what gave me the idea."

"How did you forge the prescription?"

"Going through some old papers, I found a sleeping pill prescription Noll had written for me just before we were married; I never had it filled. I blocked out my name and the date, wrote in Alicia's, and ran it through the copy machine. Easy."

I'd missed the obvious links.

"I knew Noll would laugh at me if he found out about Carlyle and Alicia; he cheated on me when we were married, now Carlyle was sleeping around. Imagining Noll laughing at me again, seeing me humiliated—again—by another man cheating on me, that drove me as much as trying to keep Carlyle. I decided it was payback time. I left Alicia's body in Noll's driveway, with Noll's name on the sleeping pill bottle."

Of course. Bethany had known that Oliver would be in Austin at the same Eichon meeting as Carlyle. A macabre touch of revenge. I prompted her, wanting to keep her talking: "You left Alicia's body in Oliver's driveway?"

Bethany nodded. "I saw the newspaper story that said you'd found her body at Rugton, so I knew that Noll must have gotten back early and discovered the surprise I'd left for him. At least I caused him some trouble along the way."

I could understand her anger at Oliver all too well. For a moment I felt a flicker of sympathy.

"What made you decide to kill Alicia?"

"I'd been out of town on business for a few days in early August. When Carlyle picked me up at the airport one Saturday night, I could tell by his breath that he'd made his special chili, loaded with hot sauce and garlic and onions. His way of showing how much of a Texan he's become. It took me back to when we were dating; he'd made a pot of chili on Saturday, and we'd spend the day drinking margaritas, eating chili, making love. I was happy—touched that he'd made it to celebrate my return. I didn't want to ruin his surprise, so I didn't say anything.

"We got home—no chili, anywhere. I remembered Carlyle and Alicia at the Eichon picnic, competing to see who could tolerate the hottest food. I realized what he'd done. He'd made it for her."

Inside my waistband my hands were damp and clammy, my nails digging into my stomach so hard that I wasn't sure if the dampness was sweat or blood. I took a deep breath. "How did you sedate Alicia so you could get the NG tube down her?"

"I looked through Carlyle's pockets one night after he'd gone to sleep, found a key, and figured it must be for her house. I took it to a store down the road and had them cut me a duplicate.

"I used my key to get inside Alicia's house after I phoned to make sure she'd still be at her office. I left a bottle of tequila, a bottle of margarita mix, and a crockpot with really hot chili spiked with pills. I wrote a note, imitating Carlyle's printing: 'Got back early to make you a surprise. Call and let the phone ring once when you've eaten it—if it's not too hot for you!' I figured Alicia wouldn't be able to resist the challenge, any more than she had at the picnic. I waited an hour after I got a one-ring hang up; then I called and let the phone ring twenty times."

"Then you went to her house with the rest of the pills

and the NG tube." I wished I could see her better. The light beside me was bright, and the black outlines of her clothing seemed to blend in with the shadows behind her, giving her an air of invisibility. Invincibility.

"Sure. It's not difficult to insert an NG tube when someone's as sedated as she was, not when you've had a lot of practice. I crushed the pills so they'd slide down easily, then washed them down with some of the tequila I'd left for her."

I watched the June bug crawling on the lamp shade beside me; the odds that it would outlive me looked pretty overwhelming. I heard Pavlov outside, protesting. What would happen to him?

"You risked a lot, killing Alicia." I hoped she might think again about the risks involved in killing me.

"Not really. Worst case, Alicia wakes up and stops me—but I'd given her enough pills in the chili to put her out. If someone else had come to her house and found me there? I'd have said that I found out about her affair with Carlyle and came to confront her, found her door open with Alicia passed out in her kitchen, a bottle of tequila on the table. If I'd been stopped driving her car—well, she parked in our driveway, killed herself, and I found her car and body there. I moved her body to foil her attempt to get back at Carlyle." She gave me a self-assured smile. "I even found a way to make sure that Carlyle wouldn't come home early and catch me."

The apricot-laced chocolates that brought on Carlyle's asthmatic attack—just another part of Bethany's careful strategy. I felt cold when I thought of the meticulous planning she'd put into Alicia's murder.

She'd undoubtedly put the same carefulness into planning for my death. *Go for the jugular*—the motto she'd hung in her office.

"Did you go back to Alicia's house after her funeral?" I asked.

Bethany sat up straighter, shifting her grip on the gun. "Go back to Alicia's house? Why? I'd already looked through her things and found a picture of Carlyle hidden in her underwear drawer. I made sure she didn't have anything else to connect them, just in case. Something I missed?"

I'd wanted to keep her talking and confirm my suspicion that Oliver had knocked me out, but Bethany's vigilant response made it clear I should have kept quiet.

"What did you mean?" Bethany asked. "What did you tell Carlyle?"

"Tell Carlyle?"

"You tried to call Carlyle after Alicia's death—I found your message on the answering machine—then I found your cash receipt in Carlyle's shirt pocket when I was washing clothes Monday night. When I asked him about it, he stammered around and finally told me you asked him to come in for an individual appointment, since he'd missed so many group sessions. He wouldn't tell me what you talked about."

Carlyle's lie had brought Bethany here tonight. "You were afraid I'd tell Carlyle what I suspected."

"Of course. You already colluded with him once. The way he acted Monday, I didn't think you'd told him, not yet, but I need to know exactly what you talked about. I can make it easy or hard on you, depending on how you cooperate. If you don't want to talk, I can shoot you once, not a fatal wound, and let you lie in pain until I'm satisfied you've told me everything."

"Bethany, how can you possibly hope to get away with this?"

She smiled as she looked at me—a chilling smile. "You kept me waiting tonight. I thought you'd come out earlier with your puppy."

She'd been watching me, watching my routine. She'd planned something for me, just as she had Alicia. Was I supposed to be another suicide?

I didn't have any illusions about Bethany's willingness to kill me. She'd put the NG tube down Alicia's throat, filled her with pills and tequila, then searched her house while Alicia lay dying. She probably planned to search through my things after she killed me. I had one card left to play, a joker.

"Until tonight, I hadn't guessed that you killed Alicia." I deliberately spoke too quickly in a way that made it sound patently false, and I shot an obviously furtive glance down at the box on the floor beside the couch before I looked back at Bethany.

"Sure. That's why you knew everything already," she said, her voice heavy with sarcasm. "What's in the box?"

"Nothing. Nothing important. Not to you, anyway."

"Pick it up and open it."

"It's nothing, really. Nothing at all."

"Show me."

I made a show of slowly withdrawing my hands from inside the waistband of my shorts and reluctantly leaning down to pick up the box. I set it on my lap and looked at her.

"Open it. Now."

I used my fingernails to rip the paper tape that held the cover firmly in place on both sides.

She kept the gun trained on me while she fumbled for the flashlight she'd set beside her on the ottoman. She picked it up and switched it back on.

"Lift the lid off, very slowly, and tilt the box so I can see inside."

The June bug took off from the lampshade, flying toward the newest bright light as I lifted the lid. I watched it bounce into Bethany's face, and she dropped her flashlight and waved the gun as she swatted at it.

I hoisted the box to shoulder level and heaved Ian's ashes straight at Bethany, putting all the strength I could muster into the motion. She fired once before the ashes cascaded over her.

I felt my left arm near my shoulder blaze, as if I was holding it in a fire, and screamed with the pain. I heard her choking and coughing as I turned and ran.

I opened the front door wide, then turned to punch the panic button on my security system panel before I ran out of the house. It should've set off a klaxon of alarms, waking the neighbors, signaling the security company to call the police.

Nothing happened. I must have hit the wrong button.

I was fumbling with the panel when a second bullet whizzed closed to my ear and smacked into the wall beside the alarm panel, loud enough to make my ears ring. No mistaking it for a June bug this time.

I took off, running.

I didn't bother wasting my breath yelling for help. No one would be close enough to hear me unless a random jogger just happened to have gone for a late-night run. If a neighbor heard the sound of a gunshot filtered through the dense shrubbery, they'd be hard pressed to pinpoint the origin—if they didn't assume it was just a car on the road, backfiring. Getting all the way down the driveway to the street and flagging down a car was my best chance. My only chance.

The clouds still hid the stars and the moon, the light I needed to see my way. After sitting inside with the light in my eyes seemingly forever, I had trouble seeing. Where was Pavlov?

I wasn't far down my long driveway when I heard Bethany's running footsteps on the concrete behind me. I'd gotten out of the house, but I hadn't slowed her much. She fired again, missing me, not by much.

I headed for the dense bushes on the side of my yard; if I stayed in my driveway, the only clear place to run, she'd have a straight shot at me. My white T-shirt must stand out like a beacon in the night.

I heard Pavlov's excited barking behind me; then I heard a thud, as if Bethany had tripped on the concrete, and Pavlov whimpering. I thought of Pavlov underfoot in the kitchen. Maybe a second chance to get away.

I thought I heard a car coming down the street, but my thick shrubbery screened everything from sight. If I could just make it as far as the street, get to where I could be seen, maybe I'd be safe.

In the darkness I didn't see the clump of low bushes in front of me. I tripped over them, wrenching my left ankle, pitching face forward. I put my arms in front of me as I fell, crying out as the impact traveled up my left arm. I smelled the dirt and the pine branch that pushed up against my face. I smelled the blood from my arm.

I tried to get up, and my ankle jolted me with pain. I tried again and fell, then started crawling toward the street. I tasted the salty tears streaming down my face, tears of pain and fear and desperation.

I heard noises out by the road—maybe somebody close enough to hear me. I yelled, my breath ragged: "Help me!" I heard Bethany moving again behind me. I'd lost my last chance.

In a second she stood over me in a shooter's stance, her gun held in both hands, her face and black clothes streaked with Ian's ashes. She was breathing heavily, her expression grim. She'd torn out the right knee in her pants, and blood oozed from the spot.

Pavlov ran over, close to her feet. She kicked him once, hard. He ran away, yelping.

I couldn't get enough air and my heart threatened to burst from my chest. My nightmare brought to life: wounded and paralyzed, unable to scream for help, defenseless against the woman hovering over me, overwhelmed by a feeling of impending doom. I looked up at Bethany, waiting for her to pull the trigger.

I heard running footsteps down the driveway, then "Police! Freeze!"

The moon came from behind the clouds. Two men in uniform were running toward us, pistols in hand. I heard more sounds near the street and saw bright lights.

Bethany turned and saw them coming toward her. She looked as despairing as I'd ever seen anyone look. For what seemed an eternity she stood, unmoving, holding her gun trained on me. She held the pose—the same perfect stillness I remembered when she'd come to my office with Carlyle.

She nodded, once, as she looked at me. Then she put the gun barrel in her mouth and pulled the trigger.

# Chapter 30

Unbidden during the day or night, I'll see Bethany's face in front of me and feel my heart accelerate. I'll take deep breaths and wait for my panic to subside. I learned the police had come in response to the alarm I never knew I'd sent; in fumbling for the panic button I'd simultaneously hit a second button, turning the signal into a silent "duress" alarm.

Alicia's cause of death was changed to murder, following my testimony and Gerald Yablonski's, once he'd thought more about it.

When I'd spoken with Alicia about her nightmares, I counseled her on ways to deal with the fantasy variants, like her walking skeleton that never existed. Real-life terrors etch memories like acid, and those bad dreams don't fade easily or quickly. I'm sure I'll relive my ordeal many times. I'm reminded all too often now, whenever my wounded arm aches, or my broken ankle gets hot and itchy beneath my walking cast. I can only hope the images and thoughts will fade as I heal.

Vernon Brundige called me after he got my package. I imagined him rubbing his palms together as he promised to deliver them personally to a former FDA colleague who would take a keen interest. Vernon assured me that Oliver's current trials, as well as his past work, would be very closely scrutinized, with meticulous attention to any data "lost" in the fire. The case would be particularly timely, he thought—recent publicity had made the FDA eager to apply all pertinent sanctions for any wrongdoing.

I saw Carlyle one last time before he returned home to England to look for work there. Too many memories here, he said. He planned to return here only long enough to settle Bethany's estate.

Two weeks after Stuart's death the grand jury decided that Rosemary Overstreet had killed him in self-defense, exonerating her. After I heard the news, I drove to Rosemary's house in the evening, unannounced. She hadn't returned any of my half-dozen phone messages, and she either hadn't been home or wasn't answering her door whenever I'd tried to visit her. But with the grand jury behind her, maybe she'd talk to me now.

Rosemary was on her knees at the edge of her flower bed when I drove up. She looked up once as I got out of my car, then returned her attention to weeding.

"I want to hear the rest of the story," I said, sitting on the grass beside her.

"I thought you'd corner me, sooner or later." Rosemary was wearing black cotton gardening gloves, jeans, and a T-shirt; her face was fuller, not as pinched, as if she'd gained a few pounds. I watched as she dug out a dandelion, gouging deeply around it, exposing the taproot, taking her time. She didn't look at me as she spoke: "When you came here and told me what Stuart had done to you, I kept thinking about everything he'd taken from me. First I lost the twins, then things started to fall apart with my husband. We didn't have the money to try in vitro fertilization again. I wanted to take out a loan; my husband wanted to forget about having a baby, get on with our lives—as if that were possible." She pulled out the dandelion with its long root intact, setting it in a pile with other weeds.

"Fall quarter at the university didn't start until late September, so I had free time. Instead of going to the office, I started parking down the street from Stuart's duplex, following him at a distance when he went out. It wasn't difficult—he didn't go many places. For the first time in a very long time, I felt powerful. I thought he spotted me once—I lost him when he went out— then he came home in a brown pickup with tinted windows. I didn't try to follow him until his blue Honda Civic was back in his driveway a couple of days later."

*The brown pickup that had chased me.* In spite of the heat, I felt a chill at the memory.

"At first just following Stuart gave me a feeling of power—I shadowed him, and he didn't know I was there. After a while, stalking him wasn't enough. I started thinking about hurting him. I wanted to know the best time, the best place to get him.

"I wanted Stuart to feel hunted. I went to a garden supply place on Westheimer where they sell those life-size black plywood silhouettes as yard ornaments. I bought two: the hunter with the rifle, and one that looked like a man in a hat standing and smoking a cigarette."

She looked down where a mosquito was circling her left arm. She watched it, waiting until it landed, then slapped it once, hard, with her black-gloved hand. It left a bloody smear on her arm.

"Late on a Saturday night when my husband was out of town, I left the man smoking the cigarette for Stuart; I set it up so it looked like the guy had been looking in his window, placed it where it'd be the first thing Stuart saw when he opened his front door. Two nights later I left the hunter with the rifle in his front yard— positioned so it looked like it was aiming at the door. You know the rest." She looked away, evasively.

I realized she'd left something out. Something important. I watched her as she weeded, thinking what it could have been. "Rosemary . . ."

She looked over at me.

"You left a bloody mouse in a trap each time, didn't you?"

Her eyes widened. Then she smiled, ever so faintly. A smile tinged with malice.

"You wanted him to think I was getting back at him," I said. "You set it up so he'd think I was after him."

She started excavating another dandelion, not speaking until she'd added it to her pile of weeds. "You or someone else—that was up to him."

I felt cold. She'd left her taunting messages for Stuart, pushing him hard so he'd strike back with maximum force. Making sure he'd feel invaded, diminished. "Deliberately fanning the flames—sending Stuart after me—that wasn't something you controlled?"

"I did it for my dead children—probably not something *you* could understand."

Blood vengeance.

"I wanted to hurt Stuart," Rosemary said. "I wanted him to see me there with a gun, waiting for him. Have him realize there was no way out, no way to save himself. I wanted to look him in the eye when I shot him. I wanted him to see me watching as he suffered, to know I was responsible.

"He needed to know there were consequences for hurting people," Rosemary said, standing up and taking off her gloves. "If he hadn't gone after you, it would've been someone else. You got off easy with him, in the end."

Rosemary had wound Stuart up like a top, knowing he'd have to do something to get even. She could guess that he'd probably end up at my house, so she didn't have to shadow him too closely. She had set me up as part of her plan, well aware that she might not be able to control whatever happened. If Stuart had gotten in trouble for injuring or killing me and she hadn't hurt him herself, it would still have been a partial victory, in her eyes.

I thought of a story my father had told me. I was thirteen at the time, hospitalized: *Sigura the Mighty, King of Denmark in the first century, was fighting the Scots. After killing the Scottish leader, he cut off his head and hung it from his saddle—a gesture to the Scottish troops he'd conquered. The head banged against his saddle while he rode. One of the teeth cut his leg. He died of blood poisoning.*

An odd story to entertain a child too weak and too sick to read or watch television, when other girls heard about Snow White or Sleeping Beauty—stories where the prince rescues the maiden. My father had told the story with relish, a moral fable about the toughness and perseverance of the Scots.

Looking at Rosemary now, I thought about its other moral; the corrosive effects of vengeance. I took a deep breath and let it out slowly, not saying anything as I turned my back on her and walked to my car.

I'd painstakingly cleaned up Ian's ashes from my living room. Three weeks after Bethany's death I went away to the coolness of Maine for four days, leaving Pavlov with Glee. I went to places along the coast that Ian and I had visited together, remembering the good times. On my last day in Maine, exactly a year after his death, I scattered Ian's ashes in the Camden harbor at dawn.

# Acknowledgments

I am grateful to a number of people. George Solomon, Suzanne Felten, Robert Bornstein, and Phil Johnson provided perceptive suggestions that shaped key story events. Phrases lifted from David Felten's colorful conversations appear throughout. Detailed comments from Jill Kiecolt and Barbara Haggard were much appreciated. Susan Solomon contributed ample doses of real-world wisdom. The scholarly writing of Bella DePaolo and Paul Ekman on deception and Phil Brown on the intake as a mystery story provided helpful background. My thanks to Nancy Love, my agent, who was willing to take a chance on a new fiction writer. Ann McKay Thoroman's insightful editorial comments helped polish and focus the manuscript. Most importantly, Ronald Glaser's support and encouragement helped me stay the course when the road to the end seemed interminable: This book is for him.

JANICE KIECOLT-GLASER is Professor and Director of the Division of Health Psychology (Department of Psychiatry) in the Ohio State University College of Medicine. A clinical psychologist, she has published over a hundred scholarly articles and chapters on stress and health as well as editing the *Handbook of Human Stress and Immunity* (Academic Press, 1994) in collaboration with her husband. She is currently writing her second mystery featuring Haley McAlistar.